ADRIANNE
STRICKLAND

LIFELESS

Woodbury, Minnesota

First Edition
First Printing, 2015

Book design by Bob Gaul
Cover design by Lisa Novak
Cover image: iStockphoto.com/40086126/©Nastyaaroma
Word Family Trees: Llewellyn Art Department

Flux, an imprint of Llewellyn Worldwide Ltd.

Library of Congress Cataloging-in-Publication Data
Strickland, AdriAnne.
 Lifeless/AdriAnne Strickland.—First edition.
  pages cm
 Sequel to: Wordless.
 Summary: Now a prisoner in Eden City, Tavin Barnes is cursed with being the next Word of Death and can kill with a touch, but Ryse, the Godspeaker charged with Tavin's training, is pushing him to be an elite assassin and he must rally his fellow Words in order to subvert the Godspeakers' master plan of dominating an illiterate wordless class.
 ISBN 978-0-7387-4222-9
 [1. Prisoners—Fiction. 2. Assassins—Fiction. 3. Blessing and cursing—Fiction. 4. Literacy—Fiction. 5. Fantasy.] I. Title.
 PZ7.S91658Li 2015
 [Fic]—dc23
                                                    2015010324

Flux
Llewellyn Worldwide Ltd.
2143 Wooddale Drive
Woodbury, MN 55125-2989
www.fluxnow.com

Printed in the United States of America

To Deanna: my mother, my number one proofreader, and the only person who will still love me after dedicating a book called *Lifeless* to her.

WORD FAMILY TREES

Words: b. 2000–	Words: b. 1965–d. 2005	Words: b. 1930–d. 1970

Word of Life: Khaya
- Father: Hayat, Word of Life
  - Father: Word of Life
  - Mother: Donor (Saudi)
- Mother: Donor (Israeli)

Tavin
Word of Death: ~~Herio~~
- Mother: Morte [Em], Word of Death
  - Father: Word of Death
  - Mother: Donor (Italian)
- Dr. Eli Swanson
  Father: ~~Donor (French Basque)~~

Word of Light: Brehan
- Mother: Prakāśa, Word of Light
  - Mother: Word of Light
  - Father: Donor (Indian)
- Father: Donor (Ethiopian)

Word of Darkness: Mørke
- Father: Mörker, Word of Darkness
  - Mother: Word of Darkness
  - Father: Donor (Swedish)
- Mother: Donor (Norwegian)

Word of Water: Pavati
- Father: Water, Word of Water
  - Father: Word of Water
  - Mother: Donor (African Amer.)
- Mother: Donor (Native Amer.)

Word of Earth: Tu
- Mother: Tsuchi, Word of Earth
  - Mother: Word of Earth
  - Father: Donor (Japanese)
- Father: Donor (Chinese)

Word of Air: Luft
- Father: Luft, Word of Air
  - Father: Word of Air
  - Mother: Donor (Swiss)
- Mother: Donor (German)

Word of Fire: Agonya
- Mother: Agonya, Word of Fire
  - Father: Word of Fire
  - Mother: Donor (Soviet)
- Father: Donor (Russian)

Word of Shaping: Cruithear
- Father: Shaper, Word of Shaping
  - Mother: Word of Shaping
  - Father: Donor (British)
- Mother: Donor (Scottish)

Missing Words:
   Word of Time: d. 1919, suicide
   Word of Naming: d. mid-19th century, assassination
   Word of Movement: vanished centuries ago

one

I wanted to kill the woman next to me. I could have, with only my bare hands and a simple command. My fingers twitched, and my eyes wandered to the slender stretch of throat exposed above the white collar of her lab coat. One brush of my fingertip, one whisper, and she would be dead.

She could have a heart attack, simplest of all, or her blood could boil, her flesh could melt off, her head could roll from her neck... the Words in my head told me how I could do all of those things and more, each Word like a piece in a puzzle, building to the eventuality of her end. There was only one Word of Death, of course, but I heard the sinister whisperings as many Words in one, all bending toward the same result.

It would be so easy. And part of me would be happy to see her die.

It was a day like any other in my new life that revolved around death.

The woman, Ryse, knew what I was thinking and smiled from where she stood next to me in front of the sterile steel table. The smile reached her near-black eyes, only to make them crueler. Her straight, shoulder-length hair was also black, in stark contrast with her ghostly pale skin. Ryse was stunning, but in the way of a graceful predator as it stalked and toyed with its prey.

"Do it," she said.

She knew I wouldn't. While a part of me *yearned* to kill her, muttering in a dark corner of my mind like a crackhead with a craving, a stronger part of me told the first one to shut the hell up.

"Death," Ryse crooned, addressing the crackhead in me. "You know who you are. Do it."

I took a deep breath, resisting the urge. The lab smelled like antiseptic, as sharp and unforgiving as the fluorescent lighting and metallic furnishings. My hands tightened on the edge of the table as if holding themselves down, my fingers white-knuckled against the cold steel.

"That's not my name," I said, the words coming out strangled, my throat fighting not to let anything else escape—like Words.

The City Council had let me keep my name. They'd made the decision after they began my rudimentary reading and writing lessons, placing an electronic stylus and tablet in my hands and a bigger screen in front of my face, which flashed individual letters and announced their sounds for me to copy. I couldn't emulate the sounds, of course, since my mouth was strapped closed at the time, but I tried to write. They'd lengthened the leather belts running from my bedrails to the padded cuffs around my wrists so I could reach the tablet with the stylus. I was only given these traceable electronic tools, not pens or paper or anything I could hide and try to use to get a message to the outside world—not that I could have written anything even if I'd been coherent enough to want to.

After all, the City Council didn't want me to remain wordless as the newest addition to the Words Made Flesh: their elite team of super-powered individuals who carried the Words of the Gods within their bodies. But also, they were hoping the lessons would distract me from the Word ravaging my brain and dominating my every action. I couldn't become their trained killer if I was insane and constantly trying to kill *them*.

The Word came to me late in life—too late, according to the experts, for me to be able to control it. The others received their Words at the preordained age: five. I was seventeen, and my becoming a Word was one big catastrophe in the City Council's eyes. And mine. Until they handed me that tablet, all I could do was shout ways for everyone to die—when my jaw wasn't strapped shut—or fade in and out of reality in a drugged stupor, cuffed to a hospital bed in my locked white room. Eventually I just lay there for about two weeks, with a tube stuffed down my nose to feed me.

That was one of the best things about being up and around, able to walk and talk like a relatively normal person again: eating a meal that didn't come in liquid form, squeezed directly into my stomach. And my name was what had done it.

Once I learned T-A-V-I-N, the letters of my first name, it was all I wrote for days on end, covering my tablet from the top of the screen to the bottom with my sloppy scrawl, electronic page after page. I could have filled books with only my name.

And in turn, over the next couple of weeks, my thoughts became something like: *TAVIN-die-TAVIN-kill-TAVIN-destroy-TAVIN...* until my name finally drowned out the Words raging through my mind. I held on to my name like a life preserver in the midst of a tsunami, because it was the only thing that kept me from killing anyone and everything within arm's reach.

Like Ryse, the Godspeaker in charge of me, standing only two feet away, taunting that barely suppressed side of me with a smile. She didn't actually want me to kill her, of course, but to give in to the killer instinct. Aside from making my life a living hell, this had been her sole purpose in the month since she'd been assigned to me. She made the time I'd spent tied down in the hospital seem like a dream vacation.

On the table, there was an open glass cage that held a small white rabbit. It was fluffy and fat and cute as hell.

"Don't," I said to her, gritting my teeth. "Don't make me. Please."

The last word came out sounding a bit pathetic. I would have rather spit in her eye than begged, but spitting wouldn't inspire any mercy in her. Not that begging would, either.

She took a half-step closer to me.

"Roaches, okay," I continued, babbling as if I could distract her—or distract myself. "I would have stomped on them anyway. Mice ... less okay, but I can understand the argument that they're pests." Mice had come during the second week and required twice as much godspeaking as the roaches. "Rats, yeah, they're bigger pests, but what did they do to anyone? You know, aside from the bubonic plague?" I'd been assigned that topic in my history lessons the third week, as if it would encourage me to exterminate them. It hadn't. I'd been a shivering, ranting wreck for hours after killing a single rat. "But a bunny? Gods, come on!"

"Shh." Ryse shushed me and spoke in a soothing tone that I didn't find soothing at all. "Rabbits are far easier to kill than some . . . *things* . . . and practice makes perfect."

I knew she was forcing me to work up to "something" much bigger than a rabbit. More human-sized. But I couldn't let myself think about that now or I would be raving in no time. Already I was trying not to look into the rabbit's eyes and chanting to myself: *I'm Tavin, I'm Tavin, I'm Tavin . . .*

It wasn't just that the rabbit was cute. There was another component to my inner defense against the Word of Death. Not only did I drill it into my skull that I was still Tavin, but I couldn't view the beings I touched as nameless victims, or it would be too easy for the Word to strike. So, anyone I wanted to kill—basically anyone near me—I pictured wearing a certain face with long dark hair and dark eyes. Or at least I made myself see some aspect of this girl in everyone, and then the thought of touching her with Death made the Word recoil within me as if her beautiful face had burned it.

The further from human a creature was, the easier it was to kill. But even in the rabbit's deep brown eyes, I could see a flicker of life that reminded me of Khaya. She was the Word of Life, after all.

But it was getting harder and harder to see anything I wanted to save in Ryse.

"Death," Ryse crooned at me again, as if countering the name I was repeating in my head. She lifted a finger to run it along my bare shoulder, over the Words that streaked down my back like black ink.

Like the morbid whisperings inside of me, the markings on my skin made up the Word of Death. Khaya had explained it to me—a Word was like a concept, a seed, involving so many components, so much potential. She'd been talking about herself and the Word of Life, but now I was getting to experience it firsthand in my own twisted way. The multiple, shifting Words on my back, constantly changing to new ones, all spelled the same thing in the end: Death.

I was shirtless, of course. I spent most of my time shirtless these days. And not because I liked showing off. I shuddered, my skin twitching. Ryse's fingertip was cold; she'd taken off her black glove. The glove was made of something that looked like a cross between leather and rubber, but was actually a far more advanced material known as Necron.

Gloves like hers were what kept my Word from taking hold of another body. Most of the time, my power could reach through any clothing if the fabric wasn't too thick. But it could never cross Necron, which comprised most of my clothes now. Here in the Death Factory, as I called this lab where I had all my lessons other than reading, history, and jiu-jitsu, I wore pants and boots made of the stuff, and weird sleeves that went from my wrist to my shoulder—a valid precaution, I supposed, when a stray elbow from me could kill someone. But my torso and hands were bare, so Ryse could read the Words on my back and make me kill with a touch.

Ryse herself always wore a black body suit of Necron underneath her white coat, but now the idiot had taken off her glove. In the month that I'd been meeting with her in this lab once a day, she'd pushed me, driven me, to the point of imagining her death in a thousand different ways. But she had never done something so risky or stupid as to expose herself in order to coax the Word of Death out of me.

"Are you trying to get yourself killed?" I hissed, jerking away from her.

She dropped her hand and deftly snapped the black glove back over it, like a doctor prepping for a surgery. "I'm trying to get you to acknowledge who you are," she said. "Admit it: you want to kill me."

"I would want to kill you anyway," I said, "even if the Words weren't telling me how." Which was probably true, though my own thoughts on the subject would have been less creative.

Her eyes took on an eager, almost hungry light. "What do you hear? Tell me."

I clamped my mouth closed. She'd baited me, and I'd swallowed it. I folded my oddly sleeved arms, wishing I had a shirt, and looked away from her.

"You need to be at peace with yourself. First you shouted the Words uncontrollably, and now you hold them so tightly inside that we have to force them out." She masked her frustration with concern as saccharine and fake as cheap, artificially flavored candy. "Don't make me force you."

I shook my head in disgust, still not looking at her. "You're sick, you know that?"

Ryse moved lightning-fast while my head was turned. She, too, had trained in jiu-jitsu and hand-to-hand combat, for far longer than I had. In seconds she had me pressed against the table, one of my arms twisted painfully behind my back, the other braced to keep my face from smashing into the steel surface. Startled by the commotion, the rabbit made squeaking noises in its cage, its little pink nose twitching madly just inches from my eyes on the other side of the glass.

She leaned over and whispered in my ear, "Not as sick as you. I know what's in you. I can read it in your skin." Her black hair swung forward to tickle me between the shoulder blades, brushing over the Words written there. Her breath was warm on my neck, and the perverted, mock-intimacy of the situation made my hair stand on end. I could feel her eyes tracing the dark letters in my skin, searching for and finding what she wanted.

"Don't. Don't do it," I said again, my pleas half-garbled against the table. I struggled, but it was pointless. I knew what was coming, that nothing would stop her.

She whispered again: the Words. Her voice...*slid*...into me, like her hand into the black glove, taking up the Words as her own. The sound tugged on my flesh and bones, like a current pulling me along. Even her thoughts seeped into my brain:

Death, relax.

My straining muscles responded and slackened, following her instructions.

"Reach, grasp, squeeze..." she began, speaking the Words through me.

I could only watch as my hand snaked out, whipping into the glass cage. The rabbit squealed as I seized its neck and lifted it, hind legs kicking the air in panic.

"...pressurize, burst..."

The little creature shrieked, making a noise no animal should make, and those wide brown eyes, pink nose, and long, downy ears began to bleed. It was the Words; my hand wasn't even squeezing it hard. Until...

"...tighten, pinch, crush..."

My grip was now like a vise around its throat, sealing off its screams. I felt its windpipe collapse. Its neck snapped next, vertebrae separating under the strain. The body went limp, head drooping and red-stained eyes staring, its fur soft and wet between my fingers. Still warm. My hand was covered in blood.

Ryse stopped godspeaking, her voice releasing me. She always let me go right after a kill so she could see the raw expression of what I was feeling inside.

I didn't know what she saw in my face, but she smiled again. The Word of Death could kill in a split second with the lightest touch, but she'd drawn it out and made my hand do the bulk of the dirty work. I sagged against the table now that she no longer held me up and stumbled away from her, too unhinged to even drop the rabbit. My knees hit the floor and I vomited all over the white tiles.

So much for enjoying more solid meals.

"There, that wasn't so bad now, was it?" she said behind me.

Blind and burning rage flooded me. Before I could stop myself, I turned and hurled the bloody corpse at her. It hit her chest with a wet smack and bounced off, splattering red all over her white jacket. I wanted to shout at her, too, unleash all of the Words that were filling my throat, straining against my lips. But I ground my teeth together instead, my hands squeezing my head as if I could hold my thoughts inside. My shoulders curled around me.

Ryse's dark eyes were wide; furious. "You think that was bad?" she said, her voice barely above a whisper. "You have no idea how bad it can be."

"I'm Tavin, I'm Tavin, I'm Tavin," I said out loud, rocking back and forth.

"You are not—" She strode toward me, raising her gloved hand like she was going to strike me in the face. Never mind that I was still on my knees in front of her.

"Ryse!"

At the sound of that authoritative voice, Ryse stopped mid-stride and dropped her hand. Dr. Swanson stood framed in the sliding steel doorway to the lab. His usual tailored gray suit was draped with a white lab coat, matching Ryse—his assistant, and the Godspeaker he'd appointed to work with me in his place. He'd been viewing the proceedings through the reflective glass windows ringing the lab, as other Godspeakers and their trainees often did.

But unlike the others, he watched in order to look out for

me, not to get an "educational" or, rather, entertaining glimpse of the new freak-show: the Word of Death who hated killing.

I knew this because he was my father. My biological father, and in name only, since he hadn't raised me and I'd only recently found out he had any relation to me. But in his strangely reserved way, he cared about me. He'd tried to save me from this life, risking his career as the head of the Godspeakers and his reputation with the City Council to sneak me out of the Athenaeum as a baby. So maybe he cared about me a lot.

The feeling wasn't mutual. Especially since he was letting Ryse have her way with me.

"Ryse," Dr. Swanson continued. He almost sounded angry. "I'm willing to tolerate the use of force for the purpose of Tavin's advancement, but *not* for the purpose of revenge. You pushed him too hard. It's reasonable to allow for some backlash."

Ryse faced Swanson with a calm smile. Her voice came out perfectly measured and respectful. "We all understand why you might wish to go easier on him, sir, but I don't need to remind you—"

"No, you don't." Swanson cut her off. "We're finished here for today, Ryse."

She nodded, her expression controlled, and turned to leave. Before she did, she glanced down at me in my huddle on the floor. "See you tomorrow," she said.

In response, I threw up again.

TWO

Swanson let me have a minute to collect myself. He even offered me a damp towel for my hands and face. I tried to snatch the towel from him, but my arm was so weak that I flailed at him like I was drowning. He caught my wrist with his other hand like he was going to help me up, but his grip slipped on the black sleeve and came into contact with my skin. Recoiling as if he'd accidentally touched a poisonous snake, he dropped my hand and the towel.

"Let me get my gloves—" he began. He must have entered quickly, without adequate protection. From me.

"I'm not going to kill you," I snarled, my voice falling somewhere between feral and despairing. I seized the towel from the floor and pressed it to my face. It was cool against my hot forehead. "As much as I might want to."

"Tavin … " At least Swanson always called me by my true name. His tone was stern but apologetic, maybe even a little hurt. "You know I—" He glanced at the reflective glass windows, then at one of the many surveillance cameras along the ceiling. "You're showing remarkable control, now—too much, in a sense, bordering on stubbornness—but accidents can still happen. Let's both get ourselves situated and let the janitorial staff have the lab."

I picked myself up off the floor, my knees wobbling and my head spinning, and followed him to the door. I doubted he was in much of a rush to have the lab cleaned, since it wouldn't be used again until tomorrow—*Gods, tomorrow*, I thought, feeling another wave of nausea—so I figured he wanted to talk to me. In private.

I trailed Swanson on unsteady legs into the rooms surrounding the lab, some of which were designed for observation, others for preparation. While he retrieved his gloves from a desk, I ignored the stares of the Godspeakers who'd been watching unseen on the other side of the windows. My first impulse was to shout something at them like, *Enjoy that? Maybe I can practice on you next, make YOUR gaping eyes bleed out of your skull!* But I resisted, since they knew as well as I did that I wouldn't follow through on the threat.

Swanson guided me into the dressing room, where my own gloves and shirt were, and mercifully no other people. Not that we weren't under surveillance. My privacy wasn't exactly a top priority for anyone other than me.

It would be nice to put on a shirt again, even though I hated the thing. It was made out of Necron, of course, and it was too fitted for my comfort. Not that it was entirely uncomfortable; it was designed to flex and fold with my body and muscles, so was equally suitable for bending over a computer for hours in my attempts to decipher the keys or practicing kicks and punches in the gym. But it was as sleek and tight as spandex, and I didn't like being shown off like a pet. More degrading, it didn't zip in front like most shirts that put the wearer's convenience first. It zipped in the back for the Godspeakers' convenience only, a fact that Ryse had already demonstrated more than once. All of the Words' clothing was designed like that. Even if she wasn't around to humiliate me by proving she could gain access to my back with only a deft flick of her wrist, I still couldn't get into or out of it easily on my own, and that was humiliating enough.

Now I knew why Khaya had despised it here so much—being used, like a tool, every day. The Words were supposedly pampered and all-powerful, but there was no doubt the Godspeakers controlled every aspect of our lives. The thought of a Godspeaker doing these things to Khaya made the murderous chorus of Words rise in my head again.

Gods, Khaya. Where was she? Would I ever see her again? Did she even *want* to see me again? She was the Word of Life, and I was the Word of Death.

The Words grew louder in my head and I shut out all thought of Khaya along with them. That was my usual routine lately; beyond picturing her face, I could hardly stand thinking about her. Missing her hurt so much and sent me into the inevitable spiral that ended in the realization that she would most likely hate me now, because of what I was.

I'm Tavin, I'm Tavin, I'm Tavin...

Swanson lifted the black sleeveless shirt for me, like he was a butler helping me into a jacket, except it was all backwards. He held it in front, not behind, and I was the servant, not him. I thrust my arms through the holes, settling into it as quickly as possible, my face burning, while he stepped around me to zip it.

I didn't thank him.

"Walk with me," he said when I had my gloves on. "I want to show you something."

"Fine," I said, as if I had any choice.

We exited the lab area and headed down several brightly lit corridors until we took an elevator upward. Only then did our surroundings grow less sterile. Tame potted plants now lined the walls, interspersed with boring pictures of important people whose names I didn't know. But at least it was something. The walls themselves were painted warm cream instead of cold white, the tables and chairs in the waiting areas outside of various offices became curvy glass instead of functional steel, and a floral rather than antiseptic smell pervaded the air. I wasn't paying much attention to anything but the windows, however, which let in some sunlight and gave me a glimpse of trees planted outside.

Really, though, it wasn't outside. The building I was in, a massive structure reserved for the training, studying, and monitoring of the Words, was one of many contained within the Athenaeum—the elite heart of Eden City. The Athenaeum's colossal glass pyramid encased an entire complex of skyscrapers, offices, apartments, restaurants, and the hospital where I still had room and board, so to speak. I only ever left the hospital to come to my lessons here in the training center.

Before I'd become a Word, I'd been allowed into the Athenaeum only to collect the trash, like it was some sort of exclusive club. I now wished I hadn't been let in, because that was what had landed me in this shit-pile of a situation. I wished I was still collecting trash, back when no one even looked at me twice. Back when the Athenaeum wasn't a prison for me.

But then I wouldn't have met Khaya. And she would probably be dead now, or scheduled to die, along with the rest of the Words. I'd saved her life and ruined my own.

I wasn't sure where we were going, but I didn't complain as Swanson took us into another elevator and higher up in the building, away from all the stares. Although I was sort of a secret, nearly everyone in this place, at least, knew who I was. Their expressions weren't only curious but also afraid and excited, as if I was about to snap at any second and turn on them like a half-tamed lion at a circus. While I was in their view I pretended not to notice and walked tall, which was pretty damned tall thanks to the genes from the gray-suited guy leading me and the deceased mother I'd never met. But as soon as the two of us were back in the elevator, I slumped against the mirrored wall, trying not to look at myself. My hands were still shaking and I felt dizzy.

Swanson hadn't said anything else. He glanced at me once, and then away, standing a safe distance from me with his arms folded. The elevator continued to carry us up, past the normal gym and the now-missing Word of Earth's rock gym, which was the highest in the building I'd ever been before. When the elevator finally stopped, Swanson got off in silence and started down yet another hall.

This time we didn't have far to go. With a swipe of his keycard, Swanson opened a sliding metal door like the lab's, then gestured for me to lead the way. I stepped into a dark, vast space. I could tell the place was big just by the feel of the cool air and the sound of my feet on the floor. But it didn't echo like an empty room, and the air smelled rich. I couldn't see a thing.

"What is it you wanted to show me?" I said, squinting into the darkness.

Swanson stepped inside and the door closed, cutting us both off from the light. His silhouette was backlit by the glowing green and red buttons alongside the doorframe, marked with arrows for opening or closing. There was also the outline of an inactive keypad next to the buttons, which could be used to lock someone inside the room if that person didn't have a keycard or the code. The lab had one of those.

The sweet smell of rot was one of many in the room, and I wondered what the Godspeakers hid up here. With black humor, I imagined that Swanson had brought me here to kill me, to get rid of this kid who'd come out of the past to haunt him and become such a frustrating embarrassment. Murdering the Word of Death would be ironically fitting.

Never mind that he'd tried to save me twice already. No one but a select few knew he had anything to do with my childhood escape from the Athenaeum, or with what happened in the Alps when he'd nearly shot Herio, my half-brother and the previous Word of Death, to keep him from passing the Word to me. If only Swanson *had* shot him. He and I had never spoken about his actions since then, and sometimes I wondered if it had even happened.

"They shut down the surveillance equipment in here

a week ago because this room is no longer being used," Swanson said.

I barked a laugh, about to suggest the murder plot to him, but he interrupted me.

"Tavin, listen to me. We don't have much time to talk. There are two schools of thought on how to proceed with you." He sounded serious—deadly serious, but not in the murderous sense.

I swallowed my laughter. "And they are?"

"One is headed by Ryse. She has influence amongst the City Council, originally due to my promotion of her as my protégé, but now..." He didn't finish.

He was being delicate, like any good politician, but it was almost like he was trying to tell me he no longer supported her. Even so, withholding support didn't mean he was putting her back in her place, and I'd seen little evidence of the latter, at least in the Death Factory.

"And Andre," he continued, "or Drey, as you like to call him, is the effort behind the second group."

"Drey!" My heart convulsed in my chest. I'd been anxious for any word of him over the past month but had been too afraid to ask, in case I either made his situation worse or found out that it was already far worse than I'd thought. I hadn't seen him for well over six weeks, at my best guess, and even then I only had a hazy memory of him visiting me in the hospital. He'd reminded me what my name was, and shortly afterward, I'd been given the stylus and tablet to help me remember by writing it. Maybe he was still trying to help me now.

"He's under house arrest, isn't he?" I asked. "How does he have a say in anything?"

"He may be in quite the predicament," Swanson said, "but the man is brilliant. He's always possessed a way with words."

His wry tone made me smile. Drey had raised me in secret at Swanson's request, hiding both our identities for seventeen years, and had taught me more than any wordless kid my age had probably ever learned, all while pretending to be a wordless garbage collector. He was definitely brilliant.

"And with *Words*," Swanson added with emphasis. "That's why I chose him to be my assistant back before you were born."

Picturing Drey as a Godspeaker wiped the smile off my face.

Swanson didn't notice my expression in the dark. "People are still listening to him," he said, "even after all these years. And he has a lot to say about you."

"But no one has let him anywhere near me." Not since that one hospital visit, at least. I was nearly out of my mind then, so the City Council must have been desperate enough to ask for his help.

"Indeed they haven't. Ryse's voice is the loudest, but that's not to say that Drey has no influence. It's largely because of him that you were able to keep your name. He—and others, as a result—feel that you will better adjust to your new situation if you're eased into it, able to retain a few significant things from your past. Like your ability to see him, for example."

Hope rose within me, but it crashed and burned a few seconds later when Swanson said, "Meanwhile, Ryse, along with a powerful contingent of the Council, believes that a complete severance from your previous life is what is necessary, along with a strong hand in conducting your training."

"Yeah, I felt her hand," I said, rubbing my aching shoulder where she'd twisted it. "She...she's trying to break me. Literally! And she's gaining support?" My voice grew panicked. I stared at Swanson, trying to find his eyes in the shadows. "Where do you stand?"

His expression remained hidden, his voice flat. "It's not my place to vote."

"But you're the head of the Godspeakers and a member of the City Council! You can—"

Swanson sounded almost pained as he interrupted me. "And I'm also your father, so my ability to make objective decisions in this situation has been called into question."

"By Ryse," I said. Swanson's silhouette didn't nod, but it was obvious anyway. "I thought she was your subordinate or assistant or whatever."

"She is. But she's also revealing—how shall I say—a strong independent streak. I can't do much either way, Tavin, unless she missteps drastically."

"How can she misstep?" I asked desperately. "She'd be *happy* if I only screamed the Word of Death all day."

"That will happen only if you allow her to drive you too far."

"How can I stop her? She's trying to kill me." Maybe not physically, but there were other ways to die. A voice echoed in my head, one that was eerily similar to mine. It was the voice of Herio as he died, giving me the Word with a grim smile on his face: *I have something better than killing. A way to kill your soul.*

"No, Tavin," Swanson said. "You'll kill yourself if you don't cooperate more. Listen to me. A small minority of the council members have suggested a third, far worse alternative for what to do with you, particularly if the other two options fail. Nothing like this—you—has happened in recent memory. Some view it as fortunate that you were able to fill Herio's place, not only preserving the Word of Death but the generational pattern of the Words. You were originally meant to be the Word, after all. And some see in you further advantage, in that … "

He paused, clearly deciding against telling me something. Even if he had some sympathy for me because of the whole father-son thing, he wasn't exactly on my side. Not even close.

"But there are others, Tavin," he continued, "who would rather force you to surrender the Word of Death to someone more suitable."

For a second, I was thrilled at the thought of giving away the Word … until I remembered it would kill me.

My throat was suddenly dry and my hands clammy. "To who—whom?" I asked, hearing Drey's voice in my head correcting my grammar, even at a time like this.

"That's part of the problem," Swanson said. "There's no one currently able. No adult could take on the Word, or else they would be worse off than you in struggling to control it."

"Another Word can't take my Word on too?" I'd never

heard of that happening; individual Words always resided in separate people, but I didn't realize quite how impossible my idea was until Swanson shook his head adamantly.

"No! You could destroy both Words that way. Such a thing has been tried in the past, and both carriers nearly died before the process was stopped."

"Then who else?"

"A child would be the best, but none has been prepared. It would take six years for a female donor to come to Eden City, for her to give birth, and for the child to reach the proper age."

"A female," I repeated. "You mean you'd use *my* ... " I searched for an appropriate word. "Genetic material? Gods." Talk about the ultimate invasion of privacy.

Swanson ignored my mortification. "For as long as anyone can recall, the Words have descended from the previous Words. But to ready your successor in the usual way would take too long for those who are dissatisfied with you now. Besides, such preparations are usually undertaken for all the Words at the same time, and that wasn't due to happen to this generation for another twelve years."

"But you were happy to mess up the system in order to hand over the Words to automatons! Not that I'm arguing you should do that in my case—"

"It's a distinct possibility," he interrupted.

My breath stopped. It was a possibility that I could be forced to hand the Word of Death over to a mindless super-soldier and die in the process? A super-soldier that could then kill, in any way imaginable, on command? Such a Word wouldn't even need a Godspeaker to force him to obey.

My muscles tensed; I felt like running. But where could I even go in the dark, strange room, never mind in the Athenaeum? I couldn't get out, and they would find me in a minute flat thanks to the monitors—black tracking bracelets—on both of my wrists. They were nearly impossible to remove. Khaya had cut off a thumb in order to slip her indestructible bracelet off and make an escape, and ever since her maneuver, the remaining Words wore two. I could hardly cut off both thumbs, at least not without assistance. And even in the unlikely circumstance that someone would help me do something so treasonous and gruesome, I would probably just bleed to death in hiding without Khaya's healing touch.

"But Khaya's not here," I said. "No automatons can be brought to life without her, right?" Cruithear, the Word of Shaping, had built the automatons, but without Khaya they were just empty shells.

"That's correct," Swanson acknowledged quietly. "But as you know, we have a few remaining of those who were brought to life—'activated,' if you will. We didn't keep many after testing them, because, well, most of our tests destroyed them, and those that survived were costly to maintain. But there are a few more like the one you met."

He meant the one I'd killed in the Alps. The automaton had accompanied Swanson and Herio to help bring me and Khaya in, but then everything had gone to hell and Herio had given me the Word of Death. The automaton had still tried to capture Khaya…before I stopped it by death-touching it.

"These prototypes aren't ideal vessels for the Words," Swanson said. "They're only to be used as a last resort. They're adults, designed to be soldiers; we have no child-aged automatons activated for the Words' transferral. We were planning to have Khaya awaken the child vessels directly before we made the shift, but then she escaped. With only adult prototypes, which lack the ability to grow into the Words, we don't know if the power will overwhelm their bodies like it did yours. You, at least, could eventually be reasoned with. An out-of-control automaton driven by Death would be an even greater disaster. So this alternative is risky, riskier than keeping you as the Word of Death…thus far. But it's a possibility that's under discussion."

"How long do I have before…before this becomes more than a possibility?" It was the last thing I wanted to ask, but I'd heard it in his voice: the fatalism of a likely eventuality. And I had to know.

He didn't answer me immediately, and for a minute I thought he wasn't going to tell me. Until he exhaled and said, "You have a month to make drastic improvements, or else the possibility becomes more a plan of action."

"So I'm screwed either way," I said, horrified. "Either I cooperate and lose my mind, or the City Council kills me to replace me."

Swanson took a step closer to me. "Or you cooperate and maintain your sanity. You've managed so far—you pulled yourself back from the brink. Stay that way."

"I don't know if I can, especially now that they're asking more of me. What comes after rabbits, huh?" I gestured wildly at him. "Baby seals? Children? And I have a *month* to get used to it? I ... I can't do this."

My hands flew to Swanson's shoulders before I could stop them. Swanson gasped, but he didn't pull away. I had my gloves on, after all.

"You could get me out of here," I whispered. "You've done it before, so you could—"

Swanson extricated himself from my grip. He might have squeezed my wrists ever-so-slightly before he dropped them. "No, Tavin. You're not mine anymore, now that you're a Word. You belong to Eden City."

"Please," I said, begging for what felt like the tenth time that day. Except now I meant it more than ever before. "You can't let them have me. You can't do this to me. Please."

"I tried, Tavin, to save you. But *Herio*"—he half-growled the name—"ruined my efforts." He took a step back from me. "Now, I'm afraid, the answer is no. But you can stay alive if you heed my warning."

"Swanson!"

He shook his head, then punched the green button near the doorframe. The door slid open, blinding me with light. He stepped through before I could try to stop him, hitting another button on his way out. I debated whether or not to shout after him, call him "Father" or "Dad" to make him care more about what he was doing to me.

But I couldn't stomach it, not even to save myself.

three

It took standing there a minute, blinking against the glare and trying to swallow the bile in my throat, to realize that Swanson had turned on the lights on his way out. In a sense. Shutters were rising in a gliding whisper, letting natural light stream in all around a high-ceilinged room far bigger than the multi-truck garage I'd lived in while working with Drey. Vents began circulating fresh air, and water started trickling nearby. I looked around.

I was in an indoor garden that took up a large portion of the building's top floor. And yet it looked and felt more like outside than any place in the Athenaeum, and even more than most places in the open air of Eden City. It was magical, almost, after the Death Factory—a paradise of living things. Some plants were wilting, leaves dropping to the ground and flower petals browning at the edges, but even after a week without attention, this garden still contained more life than I'd seen in my two months as the Word of Death. It was green, fragrant, beautiful, a maze of trees and bushes and vines towering all around me, twisting up and around each other to reach for the sun.

I fell to my knees in a patch of grass, staring. Some vines caught my eye, woven in a complex pattern that would have been impossible in nature. And then I saw the trunks of three trees, braided together in a perfect wooden rope that was thicker than me.

I knew only one person who could grow things like that.

This had been Khaya's garden—her training ground. It was her equivalent to the Death Factory, and yet so vastly different. I wasn't sure why Swanson had brought me here. It had to be for reasons other than the deactivated surveillance equipment, but I couldn't guess as the whole picture blurred in my vision.

It took a while for me to wipe my eyes, as if the garden was an illusion and moving would break the spell. Khaya felt so near, closer than I'd ever let myself daydream in the past weeks. I could see her rich dark hair and eyes, feel her warm honey skin, smell her sweet, spicy scent. She was everywhere here, in the trees and flowers breathing and growing all around me. And what was better, nothing recoiled from me in horror.

Maybe I'd only imagined the awful look in her eyes the last time I saw her. She knew what I had become, but maybe she only ran because she had to, in order to escape—not from me, but from Eden City.

She'd hated Herio as the Word of Death, but so had I. I'd still hated him even after I found out that he was my half-brother and that he probably had reason to be the inhuman sociopath he was. Knowing who he was hadn't changed anything—the guy was a murderer to the core.

I wasn't a murderer, and maybe I could keep myself from becoming one. Maybe Khaya could still love me in spite of my being the new Word of Death. Because I was still Tavin. She'd loved me as Tavin first.

Mostly I see you, she'd said, looking into my eyes on that crisp sunny afternoon that felt like years ago. *And you're good.*

I'm Tavin, I said to myself, taking a deep, fragrant breath. *And I'm good.*

I didn't know if that part was true anymore, but I could hope. Hope. Hah. Not so long ago, I'd hoped that Khaya and I could hide away together, just the two of us—anonymous, isolated, and peaceful. That hope hadn't gotten me very far.

And now, if I didn't start killing, and soon, I might end up being killed. That just about put the death-touch on any hope I may have had.

What would be worse? Becoming a murderer or nothing at all?

It wasn't a thought I could dwell on for long, because neither outcome worked for me. I didn't know how, but I had to find another option. And yet, all I could do at the moment was close my eyes.

Soon my boots and gloves came off. I sprawled on the lawn in a patch of sun and spread my fingers and toes in the grass, enjoying the fact that nothing died when it touched my skin—now that no one was forcing me to speak the Word of Death.

I must have dozed, since whole hours seemed to be passing, the sun moving across the sky. A distant part of my brain was surprised they were letting me be for so long.

It wasn't like they didn't know where I was, of course. Never mind the monitor bracelets; the surveillance cameras had to be back on now that the shutters, air vents, and water pumps were running—and now that I was in here. So I took as much time as I could, even to the point of skipping my late afternoon reading lesson.

It was approaching twilight when someone finally came for me. I assumed it would be a pair of guards, armed with tranquilizer guns in case of my noncooperation. Or worse, Ryse. The thought of her in my new sanctuary made me shudder, and I jumped up as soon as I heard the door hum open.

I wasn't expecting to see who actually stood in the doorway.

He was as tall as me, but wirier and ebony-skinned, wearing a fitted silver tracksuit and white sneakers like he'd been jogging. The sheen of sweat on his forehead told me that he probably had been. I hadn't spoken to him much before, but I knew who he was. I knew most of the Words by sight. He was Brehan, the Word of Light.

He smiled without showing his teeth—gently, not standoffishly. "Hey," he said, taking a slow step into the room like I was an aggressive dog or something.

I sighed and dropped back onto the grass to put on my boots. "I won't bite, you know."

"I know," he said. "I'm just not sure if you want me in here. Is it all right?"

I wasn't sure either, but to be polite I waved a hand. "Come on in."

He moved farther into the dusky garden until he was standing right over me, putting his hands on his hips as he looked around. A few colorfully woven bracelets encircled each wrist along with the monitors. These bracelets made the black bands look less severe, more like any other decorative accessory.

"Man," he said. "I haven't been in here in a while. It's not looking so hot, without Khaya."

"It's looking pretty good to me." That came off sounding surly, so I added, "But there hasn't been enough sunlight in here."

Brehan's teeth came out in a brilliant white smile. "You called?"

Then he spoke in a language I'd never heard. What he said had power, substance, gathering into a glowing fog that condensed and grew brighter until I had to shield my eyes. When I could see again, several radiant orbs were floating in front of him. At another of his Words, they shot skyward like flares from flare guns, scattering across the high ceiling like huge sunlamps, or even miniature suns. They illuminated the entire room, burning especially bright now that night was falling. I even felt sunnier, as if the light was shining on the darkness inside of me.

"Hey," I said, blinking up at him. "Thanks."

"No problem," Brehan said, offering me his hand. "Those should last for a while, and provide enough light even when the power is off in here. I can redo them when they start to fade."

I took his hand without thinking. My Necron gloves

were still off, and my skin touched his. He pulled me to my feet before I could rip my hand away from him.

"Shit!" I said. "Sorry."

Brehan looked surprised. "What?"

"My gloves," I said, leaning over to swipe them up from the grass. "I could have ... you know."

He shrugged his lanky shoulders. "I know. But I figured you wouldn't."

"Why not?"

"As far as I know, you don't have any reason to kill me." He chuckled. "But the Gods know I've been wrong before. Anyway, *they* thought I was safe enough," he said with a nod at a surveillance camera. "They didn't stop me from coming up here."

"I'm a defective Word of Death, after all," I said with bitterness.

Brehan laughed outright. Even his laughter sounded sunny, somehow. "I wouldn't call you defective for not ending my life on first contact."

"You're about the only one."

"Not quite," he said, his words airy and vague. He abruptly turned and headed for the door.

"What are you doing here, anyway?" I asked.

"It's dinnertime." He tossed his head as he reached the doorway. "Come on. Let's go."

Bemused, I followed him. "Uh, I usually eat in my room." I didn't specify that it was a room in the hospital.

"Then it's about time you checked out the mess hall," he said, starting off down the hallway with a rangy, easy gait.

The Athenaeum spread out beneath the windows alongside us, lights now twinkling around the complex and reflecting in the glass sky of the pyramid above.

"And I have permission to do that?" I asked, lengthening my stride to keep up. Brehan might have looked languid as he walked, but the guy covered a lot of ground.

"I never really ask permission to do anything. I just try until someone stops me. That's how I learn where the boundaries are."

I respected that approach. It had been my own, growing up with Drey. "All right," I said, following him into the elevator.

We looked oddly complementary in the elevator mirrors: his dark skin and silver tracksuit, my lighter skin and black Necron suit. Like a yin-yang. I wasn't quite his opposite, like the Word of Darkness was, but close. I couldn't imagine what it would be like to be filled with light instead of death … how much nicer that would be.

"You like to run?" I asked to make conversation, nodding at his white sneakers.

"Yep." A smile twitched the corner of his mouth. Brehan nodded at my black boots. "You like to kick people?"

I glared at him, since I'd been forced to do a whole lot of hurting just a few hours ago against my will. "Trust me, I didn't pick these clothes."

"I'm just kidding, man." Brehan punched my shoulder and I teetered sideways, more imbalanced by the casual contact than the force of his mock-blow. "You need to lighten up."

"Lighten?" I said, straightening and stepping a safer distance from him. "Har har. Is that why you're here, Word of Light? To lighten me up?"

"So suspicious of other people's motives," he said in his breezy tone, without really answering me. "Why on earth would you be that way, in this place?"

Why, indeed?

Brehan stepped out of the elevator as it opened and grinned at me over his shoulder. "Here, we can make a deal: I'll try not to brighten your day if you try not to kill me. How's that?" He held out his hand to shake on it.

I scowled and batted it away. "You like to push the boundaries more than is good for your health." I brushed past him out of the elevator. "You really don't need to make me feel normal with all the hand-holding. I'm not normal."

"Is that what I'm doing? Who knows, maybe I just like you." He snickered at my expression after I jerked to halt and stared at him. "Gods, you're too easy to mess with. Relax! I'm not trying to give you any extra-special attention. You're just used to being treated like a leper." He hesitated, a sly grin on his face. "But Luft does swing that way, so *he* might give you some."

A noise of exasperation escaped me. "Luft has tried to kill me a few times, so I'm not anticipating any awkward moments."

"You might want to prepare yourself for some of those in here," Brehan muttered out of the corner of his mouth, nodding ahead. "This place breeds drama."

I looked around, only then realizing that I hadn't recognized where we'd gotten off the elevator. We were one level underground: one floor above the Death Factory and two above the vast pool, where the Word of Water had once trained. She was missing now, along with the Word of Earth—and the Word of Life, of course. I'd never stopped on this floor before, always going from the ground floor down two stories to the lab, or occasionally deeper to the pool for a swim.

After drowning in a mountain lake while on the run with Khaya, it'd taken me a couple of weeks—even after being strapped to a hospital bed for a month—to want to get near water again. But I couldn't resist swimming a few laps in that mind-blowing pool. And I figured if I practiced once in a while, maybe next time I wouldn't drown.

On this first level down, the floor was sleek with mirrors and metallic accents, but in a stylish way, unlike the lab. The floors were pieced together in intricate patterns of dark wood, weaving a path through low dividing walls and tables to a long, curving glass counter that glowed red. A team of white-suited chefs worked in the background.

"Wow," I said. "So this is the mess hall." I'd pictured something more sparse and functional, like a military mess hall, not a massive five-star restaurant. But this was the Athenaeum, so I shouldn't have been surprised. The room's capacity wasn't even close to filled. Only a few groups of people were scattered here and there at tables lit by red cylindrical lamps, talking in low voices or eating.

Brehan followed my gaze. "We're too early for the evening rush. Still, it's not usually packed," he added, as if in answer to a question. "A lot of higher-ups, the Words included, often have their meals delivered to their rooms—like you, but I figured you needed to get out more."

It was a shame that a different part of the training center counted as *out* for me. Brehan, at least, and the other Words probably got to take walks in the park once in a while, or go to a restaurant—all still within the Athenaeum, of course, but it was more than I got. I didn't complain, though, since it was nice not eating in my room for once. I wondered how the food in this place would compare to the hospital's fare. It wouldn't have to try hard to be better than bland steamed broccoli, rice, and chicken breast.

We worked our way through the mess hall, skirting a couple of tables of people who fell silent as we passed. At one table sat a team of young Godspeakers who all stopped eating to watch us—me in particular. Brehan nodded politely at them, our captors-in-training, but I didn't. The sight of them made me lose my appetite. Thank the Gods Ryse wasn't here.

"Order whatever you want," Brehan said as we reached the red glass counter. "They stock just about everything."

"Filet mignon," I said, just to be a shit. "And lobster." It was the most expensive thing I could think of. I'd never eaten it before.

The person taking my order only asked me how I wanted the dishes prepared, and then took Brehan's request for two chef salads and a loaf of whole-wheat bread. The man swept back toward the kitchen without further ado.

"You'll get sick of food like that in no time," Brehan said. "Or you should. Better watch your girlish figure."

At the rate I'd been heaving up my meals, I wasn't too worried. My stomach didn't even want anything. But I wasn't about to tell Brehan that, so I eyed him instead. "Who has the girlish figure? You run any more and you're going to turn sideways and vanish."

"People say I'm like a light pole," Brehan said with a straight face.

I burst out laughing.

Brehan's eyes widened, looking especially huge in his face. "Whoa, break out the champagne! I think that's the first time I've heard you laugh." Before that could make me sober again, he said, "So I run a lot. Maybe it's my Ethiopian genetics. Maybe it's a distraction from everything else. What do you do to distract yourself?"

I shrugged as we made our way to a table. I worked out daily in the gym and went to my jiu-jitsu lessons, but those things were reminders of my strange new life, not distractions.

"Those arms of yours didn't come from thin air," Brehan said as we sat down. "What did you do before you got here?"

"Collected trash," I said shortly, toying with a red napkin folded like a fan.

Brehan stared at me from across the table. "No kidding? You're a trash boy?"

"*Was*," I clarified. "I'm sort of the Word of Death now."

"Quite a career change."

"You're telling me."

"How did it happen?"

I sighed, closing my eyes and rubbing my forehead. "I'm sure you know already. Everyone must know by now." At least the rough idea, if not the details that only Swanson and I knew.

"There are rumors, but…" Brehan trailed off, then asked abruptly, "Did you kill Herio? Leave him with no other choice but to give you the Word?"

My eyes flew open. "No! No, I didn't kill him. He killed himself to do this to me!" I was nearly standing. "Do you think I wanted this?"

"Dude, relax," Brehan said, gesturing for me to sit back down. "People are going to ask, especially the others." He meant the other Words, I realized, when he added, "Herio was one of us, after all. It's better you practice your answer with me now than with Agonya. She's, uh, a little more *fiery* than I am, get it?"

I didn't laugh this time, but I took a deep breath and sank back into my seat. I waited in silence until my lobster and steak arrived in the hands of a red-and-black-clad waiter. Both entrées dripped with butter and fat, the steak resting in a little pool of blood. It reminded me of the bunny. I shoved the plate away from me as soon as it hit the table and covered my mouth, trying to stifle a gag. Maybe they had the right idea in the hospital with all the tasteless food.

Brehan pursed his lips, considering me, then took a bite of one of his salads. "You *are* in a bad way."

"Thanks," I said into my hand.

"Want some salad?"

The diced egg and ham didn't look too appealing. I shook my head.

"Want to go back to your room?"

I was about to nod when the waiter returned, discretely setting a black tray on the table with a white rectangle of paper. He moved off without a word.

"We have to pay?" I asked incredulously, staring down at the tray. The thought almost made me laugh, in a hysterical way.

"I think that's for you," Brehan said, pointing at it with his fork.

Then I recognized that it was an envelope, not a bill. I picked it up, surprised, and slid a white plastic card out onto my hand. It had a magnetic strip along with a number and a letter printed in black: 2 F.

"What the hell is this?" I asked, holding it up for Brehan to see.

"Huh," he said. "It looks like a room key to me." He pulled an identical card out of his pocket.

"But I don't usually have a—" I stopped myself before *key*. My hospital room wasn't locked on the outside but the inside. I had to knock and wait for a guard to open my door in the morning. It wasn't information I really wanted to share ... but Brehan probably knew this already, judging by the gentle smile that reappeared on his face.

"Looks like you do now," he said. "Let's go check out your new place."

Four

The way to the Words' apartment complex was much the same as my path back and forth from the hospital: an underground tram that didn't allow for many detours. Before, I'd figured the Words just kept themselves aloof from everyone "beneath" them, such as wordless nobodies like me—or, more critically, from those who *could* read and might have illegally tried to godspeak through them. But now that I was a Word, I'd discovered that we were paraded or shuttled from place to place without coming into contact with anyone unauthorized, whether we liked it or not.

It had been a matter of extreme luck that I'd caught a glimpse of Khaya alone on her balcony during my first day collecting garbage in the Athenaeum. Well, *luck* was one way of putting it. *Fate* was another. My fate.

I wondered if my new room would be anywhere near hers. Curiosity—and sharp longing that felt almost like pain—took hold of me as we rode the tram.

A private boarding platform for the tram branched off from the mess hall, open only to Words, Godspeakers, and other uppity-ups. I hadn't recognized the guards who stood at attention outside the sliding glass doors, but they'd let us pass with only a glance. Funny—as long as we went where we were allowed to go, no one gave us any trouble. I wondered what would happen if I tried to leave the Athenaeum.

It wouldn't be pretty. My ass would probably be stuck with five tranquilizer darts in each cheek before I got within a hundred feet of the gate ... if I even made it that far. Back when I was a garbage boy, I'd just driven out.

I suppressed a sigh as I leaned against the silvery wall of the silent shuttle, which raced smoothly along at probably fifty miles per hour. Thinking how a slow, rumbling garbage truck would be preferable, if only I were free again, I flipped my new, mysterious keycard back and forth across my knuckles. The black number and letter flashed at me with each full turn.

Brehan watched me for a minute in silence, then asked, "Who taught you sleight-of-hand?"

"Drey," I answered without thinking, then looked up in alarm. "I mean ... "

Brehan gave a slight shake of his head that was almost imperceptible. A surveillance camera couldn't have caught it. So he obviously knew who Drey was, and that his situation was precarious. I hadn't wanted to talk a second ago, but now I wanted to ask Brehan a hundred different questions. And yet, I couldn't.

I stared at him, wishing I was telepathic. There had to be some way for us to speak openly. Khaya had used the pool to sneak in conversations with Pavati. But since Pavati was the Word of Water, she'd been able to manipulate a space below the surface for them to talk. If Brehan and I went to the pool and tried to speak underwater, we would only blow bubbles at each other.

There had to be another way... that was, if Brehan even wanted to talk to me in private. He wasn't looking at me, just staring at the dark blur behind the tram windows as if bored. I wasn't sure what he wanted. Not many of the Words left in the Athenaeum, if any, seemed interested in subterfuge. Those who had been had already escaped.

We arrived at a platform that opened up onto a black and cream marble lobby more opulent than any place I'd yet seen in the Athenaeum. Wide, sweeping steps rose under a crystal chandelier to a long counter, behind which were several guards, sealed off from us by a glassy, no-doubt-bulletproof divider. The only path through was a steel door, set in the wall off to one side, that looked like it could withstand a battering ram. The guards' area appeared to comprise most of the lobby, and I didn't see any way to get outside, at least not from this side of the counter... there was only an elevator with an up-arrow. There would be no chance to "accidentally" wander outdoors.

Brehan threw a casual wave in the guards' direction, and it was returned. I certainly didn't wave. Maybe if you were raised in captivity, you didn't mind it so much. Brehan pushed the arrow near the elevator, and there was a ding that signaled us into yet another mirror-covered box.

"They must think we like to look at ourselves or something," I muttered as I stepped inside. My gaze dropped to the marble-tiled floor as soon as the doors closed.

Brehan didn't respond immediately, and when I glanced up, he was giving me an almost pitying look. Before either of us could say anything, the elevator doors opened onto a lush hallway decked out in spiraling patterns of red and silvery white, a door at each end. The red door was marked with a 1A, the white one with 1B.

"Agonya and Luft live on this floor," Brehan said, then turned around. "Same with Pavati and Tu."

I spun to find that the back doors of the elevator had opened also, revealing a twin hallway in patterns of flowing blue and bronze. 1C and 1D marked a blue and a bronze door at opposite ends . . . which hid empty rooms, now that Pavati and Tu had escaped.

I asked the first inane question that came to mind. "They don't put girls on one side and boys on the other?"

"Agonya and Pavati, Fire and Water, would have killed each other as neighbors. Just like Luft and Tu, as Air and Earth. There are Words that historically get along better than others, so they pair those, regardless of gender."

"Ah," I said.

"The Tangible Words have this lower floor. Tu liked to say it was because they're more down-to-earth, of course, and not high-in-the-sky like us Intangibles. But I think it's because any fire started by Agonya could be put out easier, closer to the ground and the security guards."

There wasn't much else to see from the elevator. I spotted an emergency fire hose coiled in a glass case in each hallway. There was a place for an axe, but the axe was missing. It had probably been removed after Khaya used one to hack off her thumb, slip off her monitor, and escape.

"So, does Cruithear have the penthouse suite on the top floor to herself or something, being a Word of Power and all?" I asked.

"No. Cruithear doesn't live here," Brehan said.

That was curious. I hadn't seen the mysterious Word of Shaping yet, but maybe the other Words didn't see much of her either. Before I could ask about her, Brehan pushed a button and the elevator doors closed. My stomach felt a slight tug as we rose again. The hallway that appeared this time was shimmering charcoal gray and jet black.

"Let me guess," I said.

"Yep, Darkness and Death."

At one end of the hall was a gray door, 2G, where Mørke, the Word of Darkness, obviously lived, across from the black door, 2H—Herio's old room and likely mine now. I felt sick even though I didn't have anything in my stomach.

Until I glanced down at my card. "But wait…"

"And this is the best side," Brehan said, turning me around and pushing me into a hall of twining green and gold, lively and warm compared to its counterpart. There was a gold door at one end marked 2E, matching Brehan's card, and across from it stood a green door with a 2F, matching mine.

"They must have made a mistake," I said. But when I

swiped my card through the reader next to the green door, the door popped open with a beep and a faint click.

"Nope," Brehan said behind me. "I guess you're my new neighbor."

I stared into the room, speechless. No, it wasn't a room—it was a suite of rooms, an entire apartment. My feet carried me inside in a daze, Brehan trailing behind me as I wandered through a kitchen, a dining area, a living room with a giant flat screen TV and a sleek computer, a bathroom with a claw-foot tub, and a bedroom with a king-sized bed raised up on a dais and surrounded by curtains. The walls and furnishings came in every shade of green on the planet, from grassy to jade to bluish teal. Rich rosewood covered the floor, giving the illusion of earthen paths surrounded by foliage. It reminded me of the garden sanctuary.

"This..." I stammered eventually. "This was Khaya's apartment."

"Yep," Brehan said. "Now it's yours."

I wandered out onto a balcony—the same balcony from which Khaya had thrown herself on top of me with her severed thumb. This was the launching point where it all began: my love for Khaya, the ruination of my life. And now I was standing here instead of her.

Above me, the glass ceiling of the pyramid glinted in the night, catching the glare of a spotlight outside. In order to look down, I had to press my face against the cage of bars that now covered the balcony.

No wonder security hadn't felt it was necessary to bar the area before, and no wonder Khaya had broken an ankle when she'd jumped. It was a long drop to the grassy courtyard. She shouldn't have been able to make it far after falling, especially not with the monitor. They'd never expected her to be as resourceful and daring as she had been. Or as desperate. Nor had they expected me to be there when she landed.

I wished I could leap off and find her down there now, waiting to escape with me.

"But ... why?" I asked, turning back to Brehan. "Why Khaya's room and not Herio's? Darkness and Death supposedly get along best, not Death and Light."

Brehan scoffed. "Who cares about that? We made a deal, remember—a truce. Besides, you should see gloomy 2H, all ebony furniture and onyx floors. A guy's likely to get depressed in there."

The truth of his words struck me: no matter how nice it was, I would have been unhappy in Herio's old apartment, and angry as hell that they'd put me there. I would have preferred the hospital room, as much as I hated it.

"That's why I'm here," I murmured. That was why the Godspeakers had moved me out of the hospital and into this place. That was why Swanson had brought me to Khaya's garden, in addition to it being somewhere we could speak unheard. And that was why Brehan had found me there. Someone had sent him to cheer me up. I sighed, leaning back against the balcony bars. "They want me functional. You do too," I added, my tone accusing.

Brehan folded his arms in the balcony doorway. "Man, don't *you* want to be functional?"

"Not in the way everyone else seems to want."

He glanced up at a small black globe above his head: a camera. "You have no idea what I want," he said, without elaborating. "You don't know me."

"You're right." I shoved past him, back into the apartment. "I don't. And, like we agreed in our so-called truce, I *don't* need you to brighten my day."

Floor lamps rose in organic spirals around the living room, casting everything in a warm glow. I glared at it all, furious that Khaya's things were being used against me.

"They're just trying to buy my cooperation," I said. "Lull me into compliance." I marched underneath the nearest black semisphere of a surveillance camera, which was hovering over the TV, and scowled up at it. "You think I'll kill for, what … a damned TV?"

My hand shot out and seized the top of the flat screen. I wrenched it away from the wall and sent the giant thing crashing onto the wood floor. The noise reverberated through the apartment, the hallway, the ground.

Swanson's words echoed in my ears—his entreaties for me to cooperate in order to save my own life. I barely managed to get a grip on myself, stopping just short of shouting into the camera, *Well, I won't!*

The fallen TV probably declared my noncompliance just as well.

Brehan frowned down at the wreckage, as if thinking the same thing. "That'll get security up here in no time." He sighed and stepped around me, heading for the door. "I'll leave you to explain."

I didn't watch him go. His door soon clicked shut at the other end of the hallway.

A month, I thought. I had one month to do what they wanted, or near enough. Otherwise, I would likely be killed.

Others would pay too, if an automaton was given the Word of Death.

I sat on the jade leather couch and stayed there for a long time, staring off into space, mulling over Swanson and Brehan, Khaya's garden and her apartment, and my appointment in the lab with Ryse tomorrow. The latter thought tried to make the rest of my thoughts freeze in panic, to send me running for Khaya's bed so I could curl up under the covers and hide.

The thought of my month ticking down scared me even more.

Security never arrived. Maybe they'd been instructed to let me trash the apartment if I felt like it. All around, they seemed unusually stand-offish.

I tried to make sense of it all. This apartment, and certainly Khaya's garden, were like safe havens, and I couldn't imagine Ryse or her supporters wanting me to find comfort in them. After all, my connection to Khaya came from my past life, not this one. Now I was supposed to be Khaya's opposite. So maybe no one was trying to buy my cooperation by giving me Khaya's space. Maybe whoever was responsible was only trying to keep me from buckling under the strain of dealing with Ryse and being the Word of Death. Which meant this kindness could have come from Ryse's opposition: Drey.

What would Drey want me to do?

The room grew cooler, and I realized I'd left the balcony door open. I stretched when I stood to close it, yawning so widely I thought my jaw would unhinge. Gods, I was tired. I could think tomorrow.

Never mind that tomorrow would be worse than today. And so on.

I suddenly wished Brehan was still here to cheer me up. I considered going down the hall to apologize, but figured he would probably be asleep by now. So I closed the balcony door, stripped off the layers of Necron with a lot of contorting and cursing, and crawled between the silk sheets of the massive, green-swathed bed. Maybe it was my imagination, but it still smelled like Khaya. I dropped off to sleep, dreaming she was lying there next to me.

———————

I woke up the next morning, disoriented. With sunlight filtering through the gauzy green curtains around the bed, I briefly thought I had awoken from my nap in Khaya's leafy garden. Then I remembered everything that had led me to this apartment yesterday.

I stumbled out of bed, tripping over the fallen TV, and discovered that, in addition to the absurd claw-foot tub, the bathroom was equipped with the basic necessities: a toilet and a shower, soap and shampoo, and a toothbrush and toothpaste.

My bedroom also had a walk-in closet bigger than my old room in Drey's garage, all of it lined with clothes. The clothes were my size and mostly black. I briefly considered wearing a gray undershirt, sweatpants and sneakers for the day, since they were about the only things in the closet that weren't black and fitted, but I reconsidered when I pictured Ryse's reaction. It was best not to make things worse than they already would be, so I cursed my way back into another Necron suit.

Before leaving, I checked the glossy, spaceship-like fridge and rosewood cupboards in the kitchen. To my disproportionate delight, I found milk and Captain Crunch cereal, my all-time favorite import from America. After I had a giant bowl-full in my stomach, I almost felt like I could handle whatever was to come. Almost.

In my jiu-jitsu class later that morning, I asked my trainer to show me how to twist out of the armlock Ryse had forced me into the day before. I didn't explain why, of course, and he showed me without hesitation, happy that I was exhibiting more interest in having him beat the crap out of me—or in my self-defense, as he saw it. Words had to be able to protect themselves from abductors or assassins, after all. He wouldn't think I was trying to protect myself from my Godspeaker. We practiced several times before I was sure I could get out of the hold if Ryse tried it again. Not that I knew what I would do at that point.

Run? I couldn't run.

My stomach felt too jittery for lunch, so after my jiu-jitsu lesson, I went to Khaya's garden instead of the mess hall. Anything I ate would probably come right back up after my lesson with Ryse, anyway.

Swanson had left the door unlocked, so I let myself in with the push of a button. Even standing in the sunlight and trees for a few minutes, smelling the rich scent of leaves and earth all around me, I felt stronger. Maybe I could do this. Maybe I could face Ryse and not lose the remnants of my breakfast ... or another part of my soul.

Or so I hoped. When I heard the sudden hum of the door opening behind me, I expected to see Brehan again, or maybe even Swanson.

Not her.

The sight of Ryse ahead of schedule nearly made me shout in alarm. She stood in the entryway to Khaya's garden, her usual lab coat not yet draped around her shoulders. But her Necron bodysuit, made for the purpose of dealing with me, was tightly in place. She smiled, her pale face framed by the severe cut of her straight black hair, her dark eyes as cruel as ever. She took a step inside, and the sunlight around me seemed to freeze.

"No, no, no," she said in a tone meant for scolding a five-year-old. "We can't have this, now can we?"

Five

Ryse's gaze flickered around Khaya's garden, as sharp as a knife—or a machete, mentally slicing and chopping—before cutting back to me. "It's not appropriate for you to be here," she said. "As your Godspeaker, I can't allow this."

"We can leave," I whispered, choked. Every muscle in my body was tense, frozen like a deer's at the sight of a predator. Gods, I was the Word of Death, and yet this woman terrified me.

Oddly, the Words were silent. Usually they started speaking up whenever Ryse was around. Maybe it was Khaya's vibrant greenery or Brehan's light suppressing them. Or maybe it was my willpower, because I didn't want to hear them whispering anywhere near even a single blade of grass in this garden.

At least I knew for sure now that Ryse had nothing to do with giving me these places that had belonged to Khaya. Maybe they really had been given to me for solace, not bribery. But now that Ryse knew about them...

"We'll leave," she said, and I relaxed a fraction of a

millimeter. "But first you must do something for me, so this never happens again."

The word left my throat as if wrenched out. "No."

"No?" Ryse echoed coldly. She never liked it when I said that.

I took a step back, but then corrected, forcing myself toward her. I had to get her out.

The challenge in my movement didn't escape her, and she looked me up and down, assessing the weight of it. Her eyes glittered with anger and something else, like excitement. Gods, she really was sick if breaking my resistance *excited* her.

"You think that's a smart move?" she asked, her voice low and dangerous.

I didn't answer. She bit her bottom lip as if she couldn't wait to sink her teeth into me and moved forward to meet me. I had height and muscle mass on her, but she had years of training. If I could avoid some of her trickier moves and block the rest, maybe I could shove her aside and get out the door. She would catch up with me, of course, and there would be hell to pay, but at least Khaya's garden wouldn't bear the brunt of it.

We were ten feet away from each other when she pulled out a black, plastic-looking gun and aimed it at my chest. I should have known Ryse wouldn't fight fair.

For a split second, I was relieved. I wouldn't have minded if she'd dropped me with tranquilizers. I wouldn't have to deal with this situation, and I'd likely still be knocked out for our lesson in the lab. I'd wake up groggy and with a killer head-ache later this evening, but it would be a small price to pay.

When the two darts thudded into me with thin cables attached, I realized she wasn't going to let me off so easy. Those weren't tranquilizers darts.

I hit the ground a split second later, every muscle in my body screaming. I couldn't scream, though, because my jaw was wired closed from the electric current running through it.

"This is an EMD," Ryse said, standing above me, "an Electro-Muscular Disruption device. You should find your muscular and nervous functions ... disrupted."

It only lasted about five seconds, but those five second could have been a half an hour. My mind went numb with that same buzzing pain as when I smashed my knee or elbow, that "funny" bone pain that wasn't so funny, except it was as if every square inch of me had a funny bone with a hammer hitting it over and over again.

When it stopped, my entire body tingled like mad, burning and itching. I tried to tug the darts out of my chest, but my hand flopped like a fish on a line with no coordi-nation whatsoever, my arms more cramped and exhausted than if I had pumped iron for ten hours straight. My brain wasn't even functioning enough for me to curse at Ryse. I just stared at her, stunned, as she crouched down beside me.

She set a black leather bag on the grass nearby, in which she calmly and efficiently stowed the gun after pull-ing the darts out of my chest for me. Then she slipped a syringe out of a side pocket, popped off the cap, and ejected a few droplets of clear liquid into the air.

"Wait," I managed to say drunkenly, regaining some control of my mouth.

But she didn't wait. She jammed the syringe into my thigh.

I couldn't stop her in time. My numb hand moved to intercept her about two seconds too late. She let me rip the syringe out, only smiling down at me as the tube came up with the plunger depressed: empty. I hadn't even felt the sting with all the pins and needles assaulting my muscles, but I felt what came after.

My body went from hot and prickly to warm and fuzzy, the cramped tension draining out of me as if a plug had been pulled. While it didn't leave me more functional, it was decidedly more relaxing—a feeling I'd experienced regularly when I'd first arrived at the hospital. My arms now felt like they were made out of jelly instead of static electricity, falling to my sides. The syringe rolled from my limp grasp.

"Feels better, doesn't it?" Ryse said as I tried to lift my head and failed. She brushed the hair out of my eyes and I had the vague inclination, if not the ability, to recoil. "See, it's not my goal to cause you pain. Not *too* much, anyway."

That was horseshit, in my humble, drugged-out opinion. I tried to tell her so but only groaned incoherently.

She shushed me. "Don't try to talk. You don't need to. Let me."

My eyes couldn't focus on anything but one of Brehan's lights drifting in the treetops near the ceiling. I wanted to ask it for help as I felt Ryse peeling off my gloves. I'd never been able to speak the Words while sedated, but then, no one had ever tried to use me to godspeak while I was drugged. I'd accidentally godspoken through Khaya once when she was asleep, though, so maybe Ryse could use me now.

Her hands gripped my arm, rolling me over onto my stomach, and then the zipper of my shirt parted near the back of my neck and down my spine. I tried to say no, but it came out more like "Ngh." My fingers flexed, making a weak fist in the grass. I attempted to push myself to my knees but she knocked me flat with a gentle shove.

"We're going to try something new for today," she said, above me. "Now, I also prefer it when you're able to conduct yourself with more dignity than this, but if you're going to be uncooperative, then dignity must be sacrificed."

No, Ryse definitely wasn't behind me getting my own apartment. She would prefer me drugged into obedience, not bribed, and locked in my hospital room until the day I died.

"I hope the dosage is correct," she continued, her fingers brushing the skin of my shoulders. "Not so much that you lose all motor functions, but not so little that you can resist. Now let's see."

At the sound of her voice reading from my back, I hoped my muscles wouldn't respond, that they were too drowsy to hear even the call of the Words.

No such luck. Even after I'd been electrocuted and doped, the Words stirred inside. Her voice flowed into me, filling my body like water in a hose. At her urging, I hauled myself to my feet. Even so, I couldn't move all that well, only well enough to stumble to the nearest tree and flatten my palm against the trunk. It was actually three trees—the three Khaya had braided together.

Ryse's voice spoke behind me, *through* me: "Wither, desiccate…"

The trees shuddered, leaves dropping in a rustling rain of death, bark wrinkling under my fingertips.

And then I lurched to the next tree. We went on like that, through the entire garden, touching every trunk, shrub, and flower. It took hours. At the end she let me drop to my knees on my patch of lawn, but not to rest, not yet. The hands that had so recently run their fingers through the grass, savoring the life, thrust downward now until they touched roots. Ryse whispered over my shoulder until every blade had curled in on itself, shrinking into brown, brittle knots.

By the time she stopped godspeaking and I looked up on my own, the late-afternoon sunlight seemed less warm, leeching color from the world. Maybe that was because the trunks of all the trees looked like bleached bones, their rasping leaves as dry and crumbled as sand on the ground, their naked branches and the gnarled twigs of bushes straining skyward like skeletal fingers, never reaching the release they sought. The garden was now devoid of life.

The sound I made wasn't intelligible, but I hadn't meant it to be. Still on my knees, I fell forward, not wanting to see anymore. I rested my face on my forearms to keep from touching my hands, which I held as far away from my body as I could. Even my eyes felt like a desert, too hot and dusty for tears to trickle out. But my shoulders shook.

"You're crying?" Ryse asked, behind me. "Nothing you've killed has made you cry, but this? Hmm." She sounded thoughtful, not concerned. "Well, we'll see how you feel today in the lab."

I raised my wobbling head enough to look up at her. I tried to form the words on my tongue, but they wouldn't come. My body was still too sedated.

"Yes, we're still going to the lab," she said, staring down at me with her pitiless eyes. "Don't think you can use this as an excuse to miss our session. Really, the harder it is right now, the sooner you'll get used to it."

SIX

Ryse turned for the exit of the now-dead garden, her boots crunching through the dry grass, sending up puffs of dust. If she expected me to follow on legs that felt like half-peeled string cheese, she was in for disappointment. But then she motioned for the guards who'd been standing outside the garden's entrance.

They entered hesitantly, and Ryse said, "Don't worry, he's immobilized. Even if he touches you he can't speak, so don't bother with his gloves. Just bring him."

Only then did they shoulder their dart guns.

I wouldn't have hurt the guards even if I was capable of speaking, but maybe she didn't want them to know that. Perhaps the Godspeakers were trying to keep the fact that I was defective from getting out, pretending I was still a tool to be feared.

And maybe I was, in the hands of Ryse.

The guards were definitely wary as they gripped my arms, careful to touch only my Necron sleeves. They lifted me to my feet, then half-helped, half-dragged me to the doorway. I wanted to look back at the garden, search for some shred of green that I hadn't withered and destroyed, but my head hung forward, too heavy to lift. I was pretty sure I'd left nothing alive anyway.

And I was pretty sure I hated myself.

Lucky for the guards, they didn't have to drag me all the way to the lab. A wheelchair sat in the hallway, where they deposited me like a sack of trash. Unlucky for me, they buckled me in with a seat belt so I couldn't fall out. I would have happily thrown myself through the windows and plummeted the ten or so stories to the pavement outside than ride down to the lab with Ryse. But it was likely that my legs wouldn't have worked long enough to close the short distance, and that the windows were shatterproof. At least a dart in the back would have knocked me out completely.

As if sensing my thoughts, Ryse wheeled me away from the windows and ordered the guards to go back to their other duties. She didn't head for the main set of elevators but down a long hallway that ran deeper into the building, apparently taking a back way down to the lab. She probably didn't want anyone to see me like this, for the same reason she'd put on a show for the guards.

I certainly didn't feel very fearsome or intimidating, and I doubted I looked it with my head lolling, my eyes either on the light fixtures flashing past on the ceiling or on my repulsive hands in my lap. I vaguely wondered if I was drooling.

We entered a more functional, white-walled elevator that required a swipe of Ryse's keycard to open. At least

I wouldn't have any of the Godspeakers' trainees or other underlings gawking at me.

Or so I thought. But then the elevator slowed, halting on the fourth floor. We were headed down to the second floor of the basement, so it was someone else who was stopping it.

Ryse wheeled me back and stepped partially in front of the chair, as if to block me from view. She looked irritated, even more so when the doors opened and she saw who was waiting.

Luft, the Word of Air, stood before us: tall, blond and athletic in a loose pair of pants and nothing else, his jaw square enough to measure other men's. His bright blue eyes looked as surprised to see me as I was to see him, glancing up at Ryse then back down at me. His hand shot out to keep the elevator doors from closing.

"What's going on?" he asked.

Gods, I wished I could have spoken to Ryse like that without getting my ass kicked. Ryse looked like she wanted to kick Luft's, but she refrained.

"What are you doing in here?" she demanded. "This elevator is for Godspeaker use only. Does Carlin know you're—"

Luft held up a keycard in one hand. "Carlin gave this to me. *And,*" he added when she opened her mouth, cutting her off again, "whether or not you think he should have isn't your prerogative. He's my Godspeaker, Ryse, not you."

"You will address me as *Dr. Winters*," Ryse snapped. "But I am the Word of Death's, so none of this is your—"

"No, *Dr. Winters*, technically Eli is Tavin's Godspeaker, and you're Eli's assistant."

It took my foggy mind a second to realize he meant Swanson. Luft was on a first-name basis with my father. Not many people were. Not even me.

Ryse's eyes went wide and her tone dropped to icy depths of fury. "I will not be put in place by—"

"Not even by Eli? Does he know about this?" Luft glanced down at me again, and my head fell forward so I could peer blearily up at him. My disheveled hair was partially in my face, but it was better than gaping at him with my head back and my mouth hanging open.

Luft's eyes didn't betray anything other than distaste for Ryse. That alone shouldn't have been enough for him to stick his neck out for me. I doubted he was doing it for my sake, since we'd only seen each other a few times and at least one of those times he'd definitely tried to suffocate me. Or steal my air at the bottom of a lake to drown me, but same difference.

"He looks like hell," Luft pronounced, then turned back to Ryse. "And he can't speak for himself. What did you do to him? Where are you taking him?"

In response, Ryse jabbed the button to close the elevator. Instead of blocking the doors again, Luft sidestepped into the elevator with us, keeping his back turned away from Ryse.

"Tread carefully, Word of Air," Ryse said softly as the elevator started to descend again. "If you think you can regulate my actions like you do the temperature, you have another thing coming. I am far more dangerous than the weather. In fact, why don't I send you off to play..." She lifted her hand as if to brush Luft's shoulder, where the dark lettering began to curve around his muscled back.

"Touch me and I'll kill you," Luft said, and her hand froze. "Not that you could do much even if you tried—you don't know the Word of Air. So you'd better step back onto safer ground, or else you might find yourself falling off the roof of this building with the oxygen vacuumed out of your lungs to keep you from screaming."

Ryse sucked in a breath in shock—maybe to make sure she still could—and hissed, "What would Carlin have to say if he knew you were threatening another Godspeaker?"

Luft shrugged, with an unconcerned smile on his face that didn't quite reach his eyes. "He's used to it. As long as I don't threaten him, of course. And I never would."

He seemed to have a tolerable working relationship with his Godspeaker, if not a close one. I couldn't imagine ever achieving such a state with Ryse. It probably helped that Carlin didn't seem to be a sadistic psychopath like her. At least, he had to be nicer than she was if he was passing on keycards that let Luft get around without constantly being on display. Now that I thought about it, I'd spotted Luft nearly as infrequently as Cruithear, the mysterious Word of Shaping who I'd never laid eyes on.

It also probably helped that Luft didn't believe the City Council was out to destroy him. After all, using the Word of Air probably didn't kill him a little bit inside every day. Nor did he know about the Council's mostly thwarted plan to replace even the obedient Words with unthinking, unfeeling automatons—a plan that still might be put into action, just for me, in less than a month.

The sub-zero silence of our ride continued to the basement, where Luft had apparently decided he was going. I would have made some joke to piss Ryse off if I could have articulated it better than a fall-down drunk on the street. And if I could have mustered the humor for joking. My humor was in the negative. The silence was broken only by the ding of the elevator as it opened onto a tucked-away hallway of the greater lab facility, which led to the outer observation room.

Luft backed out of the elevator first, keeping Ryse in front of him, and paused to wait for us as if being polite. But I knew it was to keep her from seeing his back. Ryse's eyes narrowed.

"You're not authorized to be in here," she said, wheeling me past him and down the sterile white hallway.

"We'll see." Luft followed us, hanging only slightly behind Ryse.

A scent-wave of antiseptic hit me in the nose, and my hands tightened into fists ... fists! They were still weak, but stronger than they had been. Maybe the sedative was wearing off. That was an upside—the only one—to spending hours painstakingly destroying Khaya's garden: the drug had had some time to work its way out of my system.

The lab was quiet, the lights dim. It must have been later than I'd thought, far later in the day than my usual training session. My leaden stomach grew heavier when I realized no one was in here. For once, I wanted witnesses.

We stopped outside the locked door leading to the outer observation room. I shot Luft a desperate look, silently begging him to stay. I might have even whimpered. Speaking was maybe possible at this point, but I didn't want to try in front of Ryse and let her know that I could.

Ryse was about to reach out and swipe her card when Luft beat her to it, swiping his own. A light on the card-reader turned green and the door slid open. He gestured the way forward for us.

"After you," he said with a slight smile.

Ryse shoved me into the observation room and whipped around to face Luft, blocking the doorway. "This is absurd. I don't know what Carlin was thinking giving you that key-card. Only Godspeakers are allowed in here—"

"Tavin's not a Godspeaker," Luft pointed out. "He's a Word, and so am I—"

"He's the Word of Death, and this is his training area. I'm his trainer. No one else needs to be here."

Luft shrugged. "I often have observers, both God-speakers and Words, when I'm training."

"The Word of Death is at a precarious stage in his devel-opment, unlike you. The circumstances are different—"

"Different because you're doing something … uncon-ventional … with Tavin?" Luft asked with dark insinuation.

Ryse was nearly shaking with fury, her white hand grip-ping the doorframe like a claw. "How *dare* you question my—"

"Then, if this is a normal training session, what does it matter if I stay and watch? Either you let me, or you delay your training to call Carlin and Eli down here. Otherwise I'm not leaving." Luft folded his formidable arms across his chest. "And don't try to close that door in my face unless you want it blown back in yours."

"There will be repercussions for this," Ryse said in her softest, deadliest voice. "I promise you that."

He only shrugged. "Maybe."

Gods, he knew how to throw his weight around. Maybe Words weren't so powerless with the Godspeakers if they knew how to play their cards right. I would have cheered Luft on if I could have.

Ryse stormed out of his way, thrusting my wheelchair through the observation room toward the inner lab. She marched me inside it and the steel door slid shut, the room closing around me like a cage of white tile and reflective windows. The chair's rubber wheels squeaked to a halt while she punched a numerical sequence into the keypad next to the door, then there was a metallic thunk as the door's bolt slid into place. I was locked in with her.

At least Luft was outside, able to watch through the windows. It would be bad, but maybe not as bad with a witness to keep her in check. Then again, Ryse was more furious than I'd ever seen her.

Maybe it would be worse.

That was when I heard the soft whining, and then a high-pitched yap. Something rattled its cage.

Oh, Gods.

The heels of Ryse's boots clicked on the tile as she walked in a slow circle around my chair, her hand trailing along my bare shoulder. My shirt was still open in the back, the Words exposed. She dropped her hand to the seat belt and unbuckled it, then strolled across the lab and knelt behind a counter. I heard the click of a latch being released.

A floppy-eared puppy burst out from behind the counter, slipping on the slick floor. A mix of black and white splotches covered its short coat of fur, and a whip-thin tail was tucked as far as possible between its back legs, curling around to point at its belly. It ran away from Ryse, then skittered to a halt when it saw me in the wheelchair. As if it could sense the Words that started whispering in the back of my mind, a whimper of fear leaked out of it, along with a trickle of urine.

So I had graduated from bunnies to puppies. Ryse was going to make me kill a puppy, for the Gods' sake. A terrified puppy.

I didn't like full-sized dogs, the kind with sharp teeth and long legs that had chased me when I'd hung off the back of the garbage truck. Or the sniffer-variety that the Athenaeum had sent to track down me and Khaya. I'd killed one of those, not with Words but a pocketknife. But that was for survival. This was just a scrawny little thing, the kind I used to find half-dead in a trash bin and spend weeks nursing back to life in Drey's garage.

It didn't matter that I had less than a month to become a functional Word of Death. I couldn't do it, or let Ryse make me.

I lurched, trying to stand, but all I did was topple sideways, knocking the wheelchair over with a crash and spilling myself out on the tiles—closer to the puppy, who shied away, its eyes wide in fear and confusion. I dragged myself to my hands and knees and started crawling for the door. It was locked, I knew, but I didn't have another plan.

"Luft," I groaned, "help me!"

A cold hand seized the back of my neck. I tried to wrench it off and roll away, but Ryse twisted my arm behind my back and slammed my face into the ground. Blood burst from my nose in a hot flood.

My blood was fine. I didn't care about that. But it wouldn't only be mine for long.

Ryse started to read the Words, and the strength of their intent flooded me—but then she cut off with an abrupt scream and a snarling yelp from the puppy. Perhaps it had bitten her, but I didn't wait to find out. I writhed, spinning out of her armlock like I'd been taught, and threw her off of me. Her head slammed into the nearby wall and she cried out.

My body was stronger, reinvigorated by the Words and a massive dose of adrenaline. Instead of running nowhere, I leapt on top of her, straddling her with my weight so she couldn't kick me off. My bare hands found her throat.

This was the only way I could escape her.

Her eyes bulged and she made gurgling noises, her fingers clawing at my wrists hard enough to draw blood. Again, I didn't care about my blood. She tried to go for my eyes, but my arms were longer and she couldn't reach when I leaned back. Her legs thrashed, but the heels of her boots only scraped frantically against the tiles.

A chorus of Words sang in my head as my grip tightened and Ryse's pale face reddened: *Squeeze, asphyxiate, crush . . .* I ignored them, choking her with my own hands.

I wasn't a murderer, but her death was the only way to stop her. And if I killed her, I wanted it to be me that did it, not the Words; Tavin, not Death.

I might have killed her, too, if the door hadn't exploded. The force tossed me off Ryse, cracking my skull on the floor when I landed. My vision blurred.

Through the dust and wreckage, I eventually made out Luft standing in the warped steel doorway. Not only him. Swanson and another man came rapidly up behind him, arriving with too many guards to count—but I might have been seeing double as they slipped into the lab, in and out of focus. The room began to fade around the edges.

The tranquilizer dart wasn't even necessary, though a guard shot one into my shoulder at practically point-blank range.

SEVEN

I felt like death when I awoke. That precise figure of speech made me laugh grimly, and then I wished it hadn't because my head exploded. A tranquilizer hangover was one thing, but this was a whole new level of skull-splitting agony—a side effect of a concussion, most likely. I tried to lift a hand to feel my head, but my arm jerked to a halt.

It was cuffed with leather straps to a metal bedrail. I looked around to discover I was back in the hospital.

"Shit," I said.

"Did I raise you to talk like that?"

I whipped my head in the direction of that voice—and cursed again as my head exploded a second time.

Drey only smiled and folded his hands in his lap, where a magazine rested. He was seated at my bedside, wearing a white button-down shirt and tweed slacks. A squat pair of reading glasses perched on his nose, and for once his chin was free of grizzled stubble. He'd never looked so clean-cut while driving the garbage truck. Nor had he ever read a magazine.

As odd as it was, seeing Drey after so long quieted all the

fears that had been clamoring just outside the sphere of my immediate attention. If he was near, that meant Ryse wasn't.

"Nice outfit," I said, wincing. "You look like a nerdy professor."

"And you look like a madman."

"Thanks." It was probably true, with my restraints and the hospital gown I was wearing. I gingerly leaned my head back against my pillows and stared at him, unable to contain the hope bursting in my chest. "Gods, it's good to see you. I've missed you—I mean, since I've been here, never mind all that time I thought you were dead. I'd hug you, but..." I waggled my cuffed hand at him.

Drey stood up and moved closer to the bed's rails. "Not because you're worried about killing me?"

I frowned at him. "Well, a little. Not really." If I could keep from unleashing the Words on Ryse during the most out-of-control moment of my life, then I wasn't too worried about how I'd be with Drey. Especially not with this headache pounding too loud for me to even hear my own thoughts, let alone the sinister, ever-present whisperings in the back of my mind. Still, it was a first to not have to worry about killing someone. "I think I've got it mostly under control now—"

"Too much control," Drey said, echoing Swanson in a disturbing way. But then he lifted his hand and took mine. His fingers were as rough as sandpaper and as gnarled as always, which was somehow comforting.

I pretended to shake his hand with the limited range the cuff gave me. "Hi. Nice to meet you. I'm the Word of Death. What was your name again?"

Drey blew out an exasperated breath. "It's Andre Bernstein, as you must know by now, judging by that petulant smirk on your face. Though you don't get to call me anything but Drey. Or Mr. Barnes, if you keep smirking at me like that."

"I've never once called you Mr. Barnes, and I'm not about to start now, old man." I hesitated, the so-called smirk dropping off my face. "What does everyone else call you? *Dr.* Bernstein?"

Drey's smile faded too. "I haven't been called that for a long time. But yes."

"So why are you here?" That sounded harsher than I'd meant, so I asked, "Why are you allowed to see me now? Is this goodbye or something? Have they already decided to replace me?" My fears began to interject again, making me sound like how I felt inside: not like a scary, powerful Word but a kid, scared shitless.

"Not yet," Drey said. "But they will, if you keep running your mouth about their ability to do so. That project is a secret, known only to a few Godspeakers and the City Council."

I took the hint, not even needing to look for the surveillance cameras to know they were there. "Why, then? They're not … they're not getting rid of you now that I've screwed up so badly, right?" My voice came out more and more panicked. "What I did wasn't your fault!"

"Shh, Tavin, don't worry," Drey said, patting my hand. "You haven't done anything wrong. But this *is* my fault. I can't tell you how sorry I am that this happened to you." Tears glazed his eyes. I couldn't remember a time I'd seen

Drey cry. "If only I hadn't gotten you that job that sent you in here... Please believe me, I just wanted Swanson to see the man you'd become, and maybe give you a future—but, Gods, not this future. Not the one I thought I'd averted."

He was still careful to avoid mentioning Swanson's role in everything, even as emotional as he was. While people now knew that I was Swanson's biological son, hardly anyone knew that Swanson had orchestrated my original escape as a baby. Most everyone thought it had only been Em, my mother and the former Word of Death, and Hayat, Khaya's father and the former Word of Life, who'd faked my death and convinced Drey to smuggle me out of the Athenaeum.

"I thought you were safe from your fate as the Word of Death," he continued. "Never in a million years did I think you would end up like this. But you did, and it's my fault."

Now I was really freaked out. This definitely sounded like a goodbye, or a confession before death.

"No, Drey, I was the one who broke Khaya out of here! I was the one who got her out of the city." I searched for a camera, as if I could talk directly to whoever was watching on the other end, convince them.

It wasn't entirely the truth, of course. Drey had helped us escape Eden City by providing supplies and a safe house; Chantelle, a prostitute I'd known most of my life, had hidden me and Khaya in an old utility room under a bridge; and Jacques, captain of a trash barge, had smuggled us out on his boat. But no one needed to know how much I owed those three.

"And I'm the one who's deciding to be a shitty Word

of Death now," I went on. "Do you hear me? It was all me! They can't punish you for—"

Drey shushed me again. "Tavin, Tavin. Listen to me. You need to worry about yourself, not me. I'm not going anywhere. In fact, you and I are going to be spending a lot more time together."

"How?" I demanded. "What about Ryse?"

"Swanson suspended Ryse."

"What?" I sat up in surprise, my back straightening as if I'd been zapped by Ryse's stun-gun. I let out something halfway between a groan and a shout. "Gods, my head hurts!"

Drey plucked a pill bottle off the stand next to my bed, unscrewed it, and shook a couple pills into his palm. "Think you can swallow these?"

I was about to nod but stopped myself in time. "Yes. Now tell me what's going on."

"Stop talking and open up."

I obliged him, impatient. He tipped the pills into my mouth and held a glass of water up to my lips like I was six years old again and he was giving me something for a fever, not for a concussion after a fight with a Godspeaker. I swallowed as quickly as possible and said, "Tell me."

Drey sighed, setting down the glass and leaning both hands against the bed rails. "Ryse was pushing you too far, driving you insane. She was impatient because ... "

He didn't finish, but I knew why Ryse was in a hurry with my training, other than just being a sadist. She had a deadline to get me functioning before her godspeaking would be rendered unnecessary. If an automaton was given the Word of Death, it would obey the Council's commands without her special brand of urging—unless, of course, it went nuts and tried to kill everyone.

"Well, her methods were too harsh," Drey said. "I knew it, but finally everyone had to acknowledge it after the debacle in the lab two days ago."

"Two days?" I glanced down at myself. No wonder I felt as fresh as rotting road kill. "I've been out for a while."

"You received quite the blow to the head when Luft blasted the door open."

"He helped me," I said with renewed surprise. "Or, wait . . . did he bust in to save Ryse's life?"

"Both," Drey said, looking down at his hands. "By saving Ryse's life, he saved yours. If you'd killed your God-speaker, it would have been a lot harder for me to argue with the City Council to give you a second chance as the Word of Death."

"A second chance?" I repeated, both relieved and alarmed. "With *Ryse*? But I thought Swanson suspended her!"

"He did, Tavin," Drey said quietly, meeting my eyes. "I don't mean Ryse. I convinced them to let me try."

I blinked at him. "Try what?"

"To save both of our necks. I know you better than anyone, and now that Ryse is suspended, I'm the most qualified, no matter how much they hate me for abducting you."

"Qualified for what?" My voice rose, but he couldn't mean what I thought he meant. There was no way.

Drey scowled at me. "Damn it, Tavin, don't play dumb. This is hard enough as it is. I haven't been a Godspeaker for almost two decades, but when I was, I was the best. I—I told the City Council that I could train you to do anything they want, like Ryse claimed she could do, but without driving you insane. And I can."

I stared at him in horror. He shifted in my mind, like he'd done in the past when I remembered he'd been a God-speaker, but this time, the shift was sickeningly disorienting … and permanent, even though in reality, Drey hadn't moved from his place at my bedside. My hands jerked against their cuffs, fighting to get free—away from him. It was futile, of course. "How could you?"

Drey winced and averted his eyes. "Son, don't look at me like that. I'm trying to help you."

My head shook in denial, over and over, and the pain didn't matter. It didn't hold a candle to what I felt inside. All of my hope was tortured and dying, as if I'd used the Word of Death on it. "You can't call me 'son' if you're going to do to me what Ryse did."

"Would you rather work with Ryse, then?" Drey growled, rounding on me.

"No!" I shouted. "Hell no! But why not … why not Swanson or something?" I would rather destroy my relationship with Swanson, since there wasn't much to destroy. Drey was far more of a father to me than my biological one, by far. I would have chosen anyone but Drey.

Except maybe Ryse.

"He can't," Drey said, his tone impatient now. "As the head of the Godspeakers, Swanson doesn't work much with individual Words; he oversees all of them and their God-speakers. Of course, he's always had particular interest in Life and Shaping. And Death came under his direct purview as well, shortly before you were born. But he appoints those Words with Godspeakers who report directly to him."

I knew why Swanson had special interest in those Words. Life and Shaping, of course, had been the creative force behind the automatons, the creatures that would replace the Words against their will. And it was the Words' *will* that had been the reason why the Council started building automatons in the first place—they wanted to get rid of the Words' free will entirely, since it was a barrier to the Godspeakers' full access to the Words' power. We could still subtly resist the Godspeakers—and even resist our Words—through reluctance, stubbornness, fear, hatred, etcetera. Automatons, on the other hand, had no feelings, no will. It would almost be like the Godspeakers were Words themselves when godspeaking through the automatons. Minus the forced servitude, obviously. If they had the option, the Godspeakers would do things with the Words that we would never dare do. Things we didn't even know we could do.

I also knew why Swanson had a special interest in the Word of Death. Although physical interaction between Words and Godspeakers was strictly prohibited—all pregnancies being the result of artificial insemination using genetic material donated by competing countries—Swanson had broken all the rules and gotten Em (a nickname for the Italian-inspired *Morte*) pregnant with me. So, naturally, he assumed more direct control of the situation in order to keep the secret from getting out.

"Swanson never actually took over any individual training himself," Drey continued. "And in the case of the Word of Death, it's a particularly challenging position that not many are willing to fill. At Swanson's request, I worked as Em's Godspeaker before I left the Athenaeum with you. Prior to that, I'd worked with Hayat, the Word of Life, and I found the change… disturbing. It was one of the many reasons I was happy to leave with you. After I was gone, a man took over, finishing up Em's tenure as Death and then working with Herio until… there was an accident."

I snorted. "*Accident*, my ass."

Drey folded his arms, looking both stern and defensive. "You see why it's not a popular position. With the Word of Death, there are occupational hazards beyond your average Word, and it requires a certain personality type: someone who likes toying with death. Not many people are like that. I'm not. The position was never again filled for Herio, since Herio always went above and beyond what was required of him. He didn't need a Godspeaker to guide him."

So that was why Herio had been able to keep his shirt on most of the time. Lucky bastard. Or not so lucky, seeing as he was dead.

"Swanson kept a personal eye on him," Drey added, "but that was it. So while Ryse built a career studying the Word of Death, she never gained any practical experience until she was assigned to you, as your Godspeaker."

"I'll bet she couldn't wait," I said with disgust. "I

mean, come on. Don't they *test* for psychosis or sadism before hiring these people? Gods."

"There weren't many candidates to choose from. Not that I approve of their choice. That woman … " He blew out a breath. "I don't want to say what she is."

"She's a horrible bitch."

"Watch your mouth," Drey said, but without conviction. "And say what you will about Ryse, but the woman is sharp. No one else, Swanson included, has the depth of knowledge or skill necessary for your case. Except me." He paused. "And besides, Swanson can't work with you for other reasons."

Drey's expression filled in the gaps in what he was saying: Swanson couldn't work with me after everything he'd done to try to save me from this life. It would be like digging his son's grave.

"But *you* can?" I demanded.

Drey sighed heavily and took a step back from my bed. "It's me or Ryse. Tavin, as much as you don't want me to do this—as much as *I* don't want to do this—wouldn't you rather it be me instead of her?"

Silence hung between us.

"I figured you'd say yes, which is why I approached the City Council. Even if you say no, I might become your Godspeaker anyway, just to keep you from going the way you were headed." He paused, letting silence fall again, but only for a few seconds.

The way I'd been headed was toward either insanity or death, and in less than a month's time. Maybe this was my other option. I didn't know *how* it was yet, but hope stirred feebly in me. It was battered by my other tumultuous thoughts, and yet it wasn't quite dead, like me *or* my soul.

Drey half-turned for the door. "So, what's your answer? Do you prefer me as your Godspeaker over Ryse?"

I hesitated. "Well, yeah. But you said it yourself—you don't want this job either."

"And I also said that you need to think about yourself right now. I'm willing to do a few things I'd rather not do … for you, Tavin. And what I'm asking in return is: will you do a few things for me that you'd rather not do?"

Apprehension wrung my empty stomach like a rag. This wasn't yet sounding like a third option, just a more pleasant version of option one or two. "Maybe … it depends … "

Drey slapped his leg, his usual motion to hustle me into the garbage truck for work in the morning. "That's a good start," he said. Then he asked abruptly, "How's your headache?"

I squinted, as if I could somehow see inside my skull. "Better now. Why? Where are you going? We're not going to work on anything right this second, are we?"

"Not exactly," he said with a mysterious smile, and then moved for the door. "Let me introduce you to someone. She's going to be your new partner."

"She? *Drey!*" I hissed at his back, highly conscious of my hospital gown and the straps on my arms. "I can't meet anyone like this. Look at me!"

"Trust me," he said, knocking on the door with a chuckle. "She won't care. In fact, she probably prefers you this way. You can't defend yourself."

My hiss rose to a rasp. "*What?*"

He didn't answer because he was halfway out the door, speaking to someone else. Then he was backing into the room, something in his arms. He turned, and before I knew what was happening, he dumped a writhing, whining ball of fur into my lap.

It—she—was the puppy. The one I'd refused to kill. And she wasn't scared of me now, especially in my vulnerable state. Her thin tail whipped like mad, wagging her scrawny body back and forth and beating against my arms and shoulders as she clambered her way up my chest.

"What's she doing here?" I asked in alarm, craning my neck to look at her. "You're not going to make me...?"

Drey's smile faltered for a second. "No, Tavin, nothing like that. Not her," he added, giving me the sense of darker things to come. He'd promised to make me a good Word of Death, after all, not the Word of Butterflies and Rainbows. My hope faltered, too, but then he continued. "I saved her because she saved you, in a way. She's yours."

Saved me how? I wondered. How was my fate any different other than Drey was now the deliverer of it instead of Ryse? But I couldn't focus on much beyond his reassurances because the puppy had reached my face and was trying to lick it off.

"Gods!" I sputtered, spitting as she licked my lips. I twisted away, but not far enough with my hands pinned, so she only staggered and wriggled her way back in for another attack. "Get her off me!"

Drey only laughed, a great booming guffaw that I hadn't heard in a while. By the time he'd finished with it, the puppy had coated one cheek in slobber, and then my neck as I'd tried to tilt my face out of reach.

"I'll pick her up when you name her," Drey said, when he could draw enough breath to speak. "You know how important names are, so think long and hard."

"Bastard!" I wailed helplessly.

"An inappropriate name … because she's a girl!" Drey wheezed, tears of a different sort in his eyes. And then he bent over, having to brace himself against the bed.

I swallowed more curses to save time. "Okay, uh … " I strained my neck even farther, hoping the white ceiling would give me inspiration. But the puppy blocked even that when she tried to climb on my face. Her short fur, which was about all I could see, was a splotchy black and white: piebald.

" … Pie!" I shouted around the fur trying to work its way into my mouth. "Her name is Pie! Now get her the hell off me!"

"Pi, like the mathematical constant?" Drey asked in surprise.

"No, like the dessert!"

He finally rescued me, picking up the puppy and giving me a skeptical look over her squirming back. "Pie? That's the best you can do?"

I scowled at him and tried to wipe my face on my shoulder, but my hospital gown was askew and I ended up only smearing slobber on the inky beginnings of the Word of Death. "I was under pressure, thanks to you. And what's wrong with Pie? It's good, it's sweet, and it doesn't usually attack my face. It's a hopeful name."

Pie could keep my remaining hope alive for me, in whatever pitiful state it was.

"Pie it is, then." Drey set her down on the floor, and I heard nails scratching on metal as she immediately tried to scale the bedrails to get at me.

"She's energetic," I said, dropping back on my pillows. It was the understatement of the century. "And I think my headache is back."

Drey cleared his throat, a funny tone coming into his voice. "Call her a belated birthday present if you want. You ... uh ... turned eighteen a month ago, on December 13th."

I stared at him in bewilderment. "I have a birthday?" It sounded dumb as soon as I said it, but I was used to not having one.

"Of course. It's only about a month earlier than the other Words' birthdays, which traditionally fall in January after the New Year ... though Herio's was about nine months later than the rest because of your supposed still-birth." He cleared his throat again. "Anyway, I've always known the date, but I could never tell you until now."

A month ago, they'd barely started letting me out of restraints or my hospital room—though perhaps not much had changed, seeing as I was back in both. I was officially an adult, a time when I was supposed to be free to make my own decisions, and yet I was anything but free.

Not to mention that in another month, I might still end up dead no matter who my Godspeaker was.

This meant that somewhere, Khaya was turning eighteen. At least *she* was free. I closed my eyes again. "Just when I thought the day couldn't get any weirder."

"I thought you might want to know," he said, sounding hesitant.

I opened my eyes. "Of course I do. And thanks for telling me, and for Pie, and ... the rest. I'm just a little overwhelmed by everything. Not to mention dizzy." I felt oddly stretched—filled too full, and yet somehow hollow at the same time, like a balloon.

A fitting image, as far as birthdays went.

"You need some fresh air. How about you take Pie for a walk?" Drey began unbuckling the cuff on my nearest wrist.

I shot him a glare. "You could have let me go from the beginning."

That probably wasn't true. He'd likely been told to wait to release me until I'd agreed to have him as my Godspeaker. I didn't know what would have happened if I hadn't agreed, and I was glad I didn't have to find out.

"But then I wouldn't have been nearly as entertained." Drey's tone was both diplomatic and far too amused for diplomacy.

As soon as one hand was free, I attacked the other cuff, ripping it off me as fast as possible. I sat up all the way and sourly rubbed my wrists, then my face, wincing as I chafed a sutured cut high on my cheekbone. I was lucky the puppy hadn't clawed it, and I shot Drey another glare for good measure.

"Come on," he said, clapping me on the shoulder with a grin. "Let's get the hell out of here."

eight

Drey brought me some clothes, black of course, and left the room with Pie while I changed out of the hospital gown. At least the long-sleeved shirt was cotton and slightly less fitted than my Necron suit, and the pants were even looser canvas.

I still winced and hissed as I put them on, more bruises and cuts coming to light on my legs and arms. I would have traded a box of Captain Crunch for a quick heal from Khaya ... and every box in the world to be with her, wherever she was. The lump on my head and the cut on my cheek seemed to be the worst of the damage I'd taken, and I was grateful for the soft, stretchy neckline as I gingerly maneuvered it over my head. There was a zipper along the back but I ignored it, pretending the shirt was normal.

I rapped on the door when I was ready to go, and Drey opened it.

"With any luck," he said, "you'll never have to knock to leave your room again."

"I didn't lose my apartment after my little screw-up?" I asked, stepping out into the white hospital hallway.

Pie promptly assaulted my shins. She was now on a purple leash, a purple collar around her neck. I wouldn't have picked that color, or a collar period, which reminded me too much of my monitor bracelets. But at least Drey hadn't chosen pink.

He shook his head, though he didn't look congratulatory. "Never mind that your 'little screw-up' almost cost you a lot more. And just so you know, Khaya's apartment wasn't easy to secure in the first place."

So it *had* been Drey's doing.

"But your living arrangement is entirely up to me now," he continued, "as is whether or not you have to wear protective clothing. There are quite a few Godspeakers, Ryse chief among them, who believe you're going to hang yourself with all the slack I'm giving you. So ... don't. Treat your relative freedom like a hard-won and easily lost privilege. Don't abuse it."

"Right. No noisy late-night parties at my place. Although I *am* an adult now ... "

He shot me a look and started down the hall. "Tavin. Take me seriously."

I was, more than he knew. But there was no denying my mood had significantly improved, and thus my ability to be an ass. I followed him, picking up Pie after her twig-like legs became tangled in the leash and she craned her neck to chew on it in irritation.

"You should teach her to heel," Drey said with mild disapproval as I caught up. "She needs to learn the leash."

"Like me?" I asked in a casual tone, without looking at

him. I kissed the top of Pie's silky head and nearly got my nose nipped.

He sighed.

"Anyway, Pie needs to put on some poundage before she has to drag me around," I said. "She's half-starved."

"No, she's not." Drey reached over to pet her. Instead of allowing him, she chewed on his fingers. "She's naturally thin. She's a greyhound, purebred."

"Really?" I held Pie up in surprise, turning her around to study her shape until she squirmed in discomfort. She obviously didn't like being so exposed. I cradled her against my chest again with an apologetic squeeze. Being on display wasn't my favorite thing either.

Life probably wasn't reaching peak potential when you could relate to a puppy.

"But she was in line to be ... you know," I said, not letting myself think about what I could have done to her. "Why on earth would Ryse use a purebred?"

"Why does Ryse do anything she does?"

"Because she's twisted," I said without hesitation. "And whatever she destroys has to be worthy of her attention." I also didn't let myself think about Khaya's garden. I couldn't, not yet. Or maybe ever.

"Worthy of the Word of Death," Drey said, his expression grim.

"Ugh. A purebred victim for her special killer." I looked down at the little bundle in my arms. Pie latched onto my gaze and yapped excitedly until I lifted her onto my shoulder. Her tail whipped me in the face a few times until I pinned it against her hindquarters with my hand. "Well, you were too good for me, huh, Pie?" I said as she snuffled my ear with a cool, damp nose. "Now I'll have to prove I'm worthy of you. Feeding you is probably a good first step." My stomach gurgled. "And feeding myself, so I'm alive enough to feed you."

"It's nearing lunch. Why don't you go to the mess hall?" Drey suggested as we rounded a corner, approaching the glass doors of the tram boarding platform. "I'll take Pie to your apartment and feed her, since I think the City Council would likely draw the line at allowing her into the mess hall. Her presence here is unorthodox enough."

"All right," I said, unable to resist the thought of food served to me without any effort on my part. My appetite had suddenly and exuberantly returned, now that Ryse was out of the picture.

Not that it would necessarily last. Just because Drey was now my Godspeaker didn't mean I could escape what the Council wanted me to do … or their deadline. Which was why I needed to eat as much as possible, while I could.

Neither Drey nor I acknowledged the guards at the doors, nor did they acknowledge us, weird as we were: the brilliant Godspeaker back from seventeen—eighteen—years of hiding and the new, squeamish Word of Death with his still-breathing puppy. They obviously had to be well-trained to see what they saw every day and not stare, let alone shout about it all over Eden City. The Athenaeum was a veritable obedience school.

When my tram arrived, I reluctantly passed Pie to Drey. "Uh, be careful with her. And be nice—especially nice."

Drey smiled at me in a way that could only be described as tender, maybe even sad. He held her securely with both hands, looping the purple leash over his arm. "I will."

Speeding away from the hospital ten seconds later, I already missed Pie. And yet I felt lighter than I had in two months. That had likely been Drey's intention in giving her to me, but I felt so much better that I didn't even care I was being manipulated—albeit in a gentle rather than a brutal way.

Really, I wasn't about to complain. Drey had gotten me my own apartment, less humiliating clothes, and a puppy. Aside from the killing, I could almost do this.

As the elevator opened onto the sleek surroundings of the mess hall, I felt unarmed in spite of the fact that my pinky finger was a lethal weapon. Brehan had been with me the last time to make it all easier, even though I'd probably acted like a petulant ass. Now I was on my own. I took a deep breath and squared my shoulders, then started for the glowing red counter to order.

This time I tried a chef salad like Brehan's, plus a BLT and fries, my stomach growling. I'd always passed a snazzy café on my trash run that had a menu posted in the window featuring an American-style BLT and fries. It didn't help that I was usually there right when I was getting hungry for lunch, and that it was in the nicest part of town and therefore astronomically expensive, but I'd been wanting to try it since forever … unlike the pâté, escargot, foie gras, and whatever else it was that filled the menu. Because Eden City shared a border with France and Switzerland, having supplanted a town called Geneva when the Words took it over a couple of centuries ago, the French influenced a lot of our food. Which usually meant it was completely unaffordable and revolting to boot.

I was going to eat that BLT now. Maybe not that exact one, but it was a small victory, and I would take what I could get. What was more, I was going to enjoy the hell out of it, unlike the fillet mignon and lobster I'd ordered before.

I sat at an unoccupied table and raised the sandwich to my lips, about to dig in ... but then Luft slid into the seat across from me. I nearly dropped the BLT, and then opted for setting it back on my plate instead of stuffing my face.

Luft had helped me, and I was grateful to him, but we hadn't exactly spoken when I was drugged in the wheelchair. And before that, there'd been the whole trying-to-suffocate-me thing, back when I wasn't yet the Word of Death.

I didn't quite know what to say, so I cleared my throat in the awkward silence. "I hear it's just about your birthday. Congratulations."

His lips quirked in a half-smile. "Yesterday. And thanks, though there usually isn't much fanfare around here, especially not with what's just happened. How's the head?" he asked, his blue eyes serious. His blond hair was damp from a shower. Maybe he'd just worked out. The rest of him sure looked like he had.

"Sore," I said honestly. "But thank you for stepping in. Really."

He nodded, accepting my thanks.

"Are you ... uh, in trouble?" I asked.

"I should be asking you that. But since you're sitting here and not with armed guards in the hospital, I'm guessing you've agreed to have Dr. Bernstein as your Godspeaker." He shrugged, toying with the corner of my thick paper napkin. "As for me, I got a lecture about abuse of privilege from Carlin and had to return my keycard. Big deal. So I have to ride the normal elevator now."

I figured he'd lost access to more than the elevator with the keycard—such as to the other Words' training areas, including the Death Factory—but was downplaying it for my benefit. Some birthday he'd had. At least I'd gotten a puppy out of the deal.

"I might have been in more trouble," he admitted, pulling the napkin across the table toward himself, "if this whole thing with Eli—er, Dr. Swanson—and Ryse didn't eclipse what I did. He put his whole reputation on the line by suspending her and supporting Dr. Bernstein's return."

It occurred to me that Drey might be trying to save more than only *our* necks: it was now mine, his own, and Swanson's. And then I decided to hell with it and took a massive bite of my BLT. Everything else on the planet was conspiring against my ability to eat it, so I wouldn't let Luft's presence stop me.

He smiled slightly, as if he knew what I was thinking. "And while I royally pissed Ryse off, I also saved her life." He held my eyes as I chewed. "You *were* going to kill her, right?"

I nodded.

He grinned, but it seemed as hard and serious as ever. It said what he couldn't say out loud: *Good.*

I couldn't smile back, both because I didn't feel like it and because I had food in my mouth, so I saluted him with my sandwich and took another bite. It was then I noticed what he was doing with his hands, even though he was still staring at my face.

He was writing on the napkin with a pen, which shocked me. Pens and pencils weren't impossible to find, but none of the Words were allowed to have them. The pen went back up his sleeve before I was even sure I'd seen it, and he cupped his hand in such a way that only I could see what was under it: a small, neatly scrawled message. Thank the Gods it was short and simple enough for me to read.

Reach Khaya. Important.

My heart started jackhammering in my chest. I opened my mouth, but Luft gave a sharp, single shake of his head and coughed, discreetly crumpling the napkin in his hand. It vanished up his sleeve with the pen.

He wanted me to contact Khaya. Never mind that I had no clue how to do that, but *why*? Maybe he'd found out about the automatons. Maybe his Godspeaker had told him. He and Carlin were close, after all. But then why would Luft want me to risk revealing Khaya's location when she was the key to that plan's success?

Maybe she was in danger and needed help. But no, there was no way for me to help her from in here. *I* was the one who needed help.

Then it hit me. Maybe Luft was trying to help me— again. Maybe he knew just how precarious my situation was. Khaya might not even know for sure if I was still alive, but if I could signal her somehow, maybe she could form a plan to come get me. Maybe she already had one. She could never risk coming herself, of course, since the world's stability relied on her staying out of the City Council's hands, but Pavati and Tu could possibly break me out. If only…

"Someone's hungry now."

Brehan collapsed into the seat next to Luft before I had a chance to look up. I tried to pretend like Luft and I were having a normal conversation, though I couldn't imagine what one of those would even sound like. *Think about Khaya later,* I commanded myself, and took another hurried bite of my BLT.

The fact that I owed Brehan an apology for my outburst at the apartment didn't help the awkward factor, but he didn't give me the chance to apologize. "I hear you had an even bigger tantrum since I saw you last and that you almost killed your Godspeaker—or ex-Godspeaker." He squinted at me with a teasing glint in his eyes as I chewed, staring particularly at my cheek where it was sutured. For a second I was grateful even for *that* topic of conversation until he added, "Without Khaya to heal you, that cut might actually scar your pretty face. What do you think, Luffy, is he less handsome? Or maybe more handsome, in that rugged sort of—"

I swallowed quickly, about to tell Brehan to shut the hell up, when Luft whispered a word in German. Brehan's voice choked off and his eyes bulged in his face.

I laughed. "Much better."

Luft grinned at me again, then said another Word that released Brehan's air.

"Asshole," Brehan croaked amiably after gasping for breath. "Don't make me blind you. Or worse, sneak in your apartment tonight while you're sleeping and set up a strobe light above your bed."

"Are you sure you won't be sneaking in for something else?" Luft asked, turning his sharp grin on Brehan. "Have you come to the dark side, Light Boy?"

I choked, laughing, on a bite of salad. Luft obviously knew what people said about him behind his back and was happy to beat them at their own game.

I was liking him more and more, in spite of the danger of suffocation. *Gods*, I thought, *could he actually be helping me more than he already has?*

"Man, they won't even let me pick a side," Brehan complained. "What's a guy got to do to get some action around here?"

A scathing voice spoke over my shoulder. "I hate to interrupt this charming discussion with my female presence … but if I didn't, you guys might devolve into filthy cavemen right here at the table."

Agonya walked around the table until she stood over Luft's and Brehan's shoulders, her hands on her hips. Her light brown hair was pulled high and tight on her head, her cheekbones sharp. Her brown eyes were even sharper—she could have been carving me as she stared down at me.

Now I had an audience. Gods, my lunch just couldn't get any better. Actually, the BLT was amazing, but the rest was just ridiculous. If I'd known *she* would sneak up behind me, I would've been looking over my shoulder a lot more often. Agonya was probably the last Word I wanted to see.

"Me want woman," Brehan grunted in his best caveman voice, then swiped at her. She dodged his hand easily and shot him a look that should have killed him. If she weren't so suited for the Word of Fire, I would have nominated her for the Word of Death. It was too bad that two Words couldn't share one body . . . and that it would have killed me to give it to her.

She wedged herself between Luft and Brehan, which wasn't too hard with her slim figure, and sat down. They both scooted over quickly to accommodate her, and then the three of them suddenly seemed like a panel of judges facing me.

My sandwich had officially lost its appeal, and I wanted to think about Luft's message in private. "Well, I'm done. I guess I'll see you later."

"Not so fast!" Agonya said, slamming my plate down as I half-stood with it. "So what is this?" She glared at the guys on either side of her. "You two eat lunch with murdering thieves? I thought you both had more class than that."

"Excuse me?" My ass thumped back down onto my chair as my voice rose with incredulity. "I'm the thief now? Last I checked, *I* was the one who had my life stolen from me."

"Right," she scoffed. "You were a trash boy. Who wouldn't want something better than that? You probably couldn't wait to get your hands on the Word of Death."

I felt the first dark stirrings in my head since I'd been knocked out, and I forced myself to calm down. The best alternative to rage was sarcasm, so I tapped my chin and gave her a sympathetic look. "Hmm, so you *are* completely insane. I suspected as much."

In response, Agonya only said a word in Russian I couldn't understand. A *Word*. Her hand was still touching my plate, and the remains of my sandwich and fries went up in flames. The fire didn't last long—only a second—but it was strong enough to heat my face and leave only greasy black char on the plate.

I raised an eyebrow. "You're only proving me right. What, did you have a crush on Herio or something? It would make sense, since he was a psychopath too."

Fast as a striking snake, her hand shot across the table and seized my bare wrist. "I can burn you next."

I didn't pull away. "Gods, now you're stupid on top of crazy. You're touching Death, you realize." I barked a laugh. "I wonder who would die quicker, me or you? We can always test, and then—*poof*—two precious Words gone, just like that. Not that I care, but I'm sure the rest of the world would."

Like they cared about the Words who had been lost already—three of the strongest Words, the Words of Power. Movement had vanished centuries ago, never to resurface; Naming was assassinated in the nineteenth century; and Time died by suicide in the early twentieth, around World War I. Their loss was viewed as one of humanity's greatest failings. But Words had never killed one another, and if that happened at this mess hall table, I couldn't imagine that Eden City's prestige would ever recover. It was almost tempting to go through with it for that reason alone.

"Agonya," Luft warned. Brehan looked just as tense.

"And if you knew *anything*," I added, unable to help myself, "you'd know this Word was the last thing I ever wanted, and that Herio's last wish was to damn me as thoroughly as possible, not kill me. So go ahead, do it. You'd practically be doing me a favor."

But then Khaya and Drey flashed before my eyes, and absurdly, Pie, and I knew I didn't mean it. Not anymore. It was almost a relief to know this.

I was the Word of Death, but somehow I still had a few reasons to live. Especially if I had the slightest chance of seeing Khaya again.

I wrenched my hand away then. "Don't touch me," I said to her. "Ever."

There was an implied *or else*, though I didn't know what it was. All I knew was that I was damned sick of people touching me without my permission.

Agonya's eyes were narrowed, her mouth slightly open. She was obviously still angry, but I didn't think she'd been expecting my reaction. She probably thought I'd get defensive and flustered, after which she would have pounced on me with all the reasons why I was a liar. But death was sort of a game-changer, I'd realized.

She stood in a rush, maybe since I was no longer going anywhere. "Just remember," she snapped, "you're not one of us and you never will be, so don't even try. Stay out of our way."

"You all sat down at *my* table," I reminded her swinging ponytail as she stalked away.

She flipped me off over her shoulder.

I relaxed in my chair and turned back to my food. At least she hadn't torched my salad. There was still some left. I picked up my fork and looked up at Brehan and Luft. "Don't mind me. Feel free to storm away too, whenever you want."

Brehan raised his hands. "Hey, Agonya should speak for herself. I don't find your company as unbearable as she seems to ... though fewer tantrums on your part would be nice." Again, before I could apologize, he added, "And I'm *sure* Luft here doesn't want you to stay out of his way."

Luft rolled his eyes. "Don't you have any other angle? My witty comebacks are wasted on such crap. Besides, Tavin's not my type."

"Really? Who is? We're all dying to know."

Luft winked at him and waggled his blond eyebrows.

Brehan laughed. "I *know* that's not true."

"Do you? Are you so sure?" Luft slid closer to him. His coy expression looked absolutely absurd on him, but it did the trick.

"Okay, okay, you win!" Brehan leapt up. "I'm hungry, but not for fruitcake." He headed for the red counter.

"Must get old," I said after he was out of earshot, my mouth full of salad.

"There are limited sources of entertainment in here, you'll notice," Luft said, studying his hands as he folded them together on the table. "And Brehan uses whatever's available to lighten the mood. I don't really fault him for it." His lips twisted in distaste. "*Lighten*, Gods ..."

"Yeah, we've already been over that joke too." I swallowed. "Still, you won't hear it from me."

He seemed to know I wasn't talking about light-related puns, because he looked up at me, squinting for half a second as if trying to see me better. "Thanks," he said. Then he tapped the table with his fingers and abruptly stood. "I have to meet Carlin. Try not to get yourself killed within the next few hours … I'm busy."

So he *was* looking out for me. I couldn't help smirking at his cockiness, but it turned into a grimace on my face. "It's not *me* dying I'm worried about." At least not for the immediate future—the next month, to be exact. "Only everything else," I added.

Luft gave me that searching look again before he left. "Right, that's quite the conundrum. Good luck."

He didn't sound sarcastic. And it didn't sound like he meant just the one conundrum, either.

Because reaching Khaya would be another.

nine

I waited at my table in the mess hall for Brehan to return with his food, the questions banging around in my skull louder than the Word of Death. Now that Agonya had stormed away, and even Luft had left, I wasn't sure if I wanted to be alone with my thoughts. More than anything, I wished I could talk to Brehan.

Well, I talked to him once he sat down with his meal, but we didn't really *talk*. He chattered on between bites of food, and sometimes during bites of food, about what he was doing in his own training—lots of stuff with light, no surprise—while my thoughts buzzed, keeping me from giving him more than short, distracted answers or comments.

How could I contact Khaya from inside the Athenaeum? More importantly, *should* I contact her? It had never occurred to me as an option before Luft's message. I was in here, and she was out there somewhere, just like I was the Word of Death and she was the Word of Life. But maybe the walls between us weren't as impenetrable as I'd thought. I desperately *wanted* to believe they weren't.

The thing was, I wasn't sure if I could trust Luft, not yet. He'd helped me, but he'd also tried to kill me before. And he was still here in the Athenaeum. Unlike Khaya and Tu and Pavati, he'd never tried to escape, and like Agonya and Mørke, he'd been on the team to bring them back.

Brehan hadn't been. Maybe that was because the Word of Light would not have been useful in that situation, but still, it made me want to trust him. Besides, he'd been nice to me from the beginning.

A hand waved in front of my eyes. "I can see you're orbiting the solar system."

"Huh?" I said, blinking and looking at Brehan.

He took his hand back, smirking. "All you need is one of those bubble helmets and the white jumpsuit and you'd be a real space man."

I leaned back in my chair. "I was listening. Sort of. Sorry."

"It's okay, man. You've had a rough couple of days. You might even still have a concussion, which I hear increases spaciness—also drooling."

I wiped at my mouth in alarm, only to find nothing aside from Brehan's renewed grin across the table. I glared at him, and then I cracked up. He laughed too, and it was then that I really decided to trust him.

"Yeah," I said, getting an idea. "I'm kind of tired. I might head back to the apartment. Do you...uh..." Even though we'd just been laughing, the words were suddenly awkward on my tongue, like a mouthful of gravel. "Want to hang out?" My face flushed what had to be a humiliating hue, and I hurried on before he could answer. "I mean, I've been an ass, and I want to apologize—"

Brehan chuckled and waved off the rest of my verbal fumbling. "No worries. I have some time before physics. And you know what, I managed to talk Mira—my Godspeaker—into getting me that new gaming system for my birthday…" And then he launched into a description of a car racing game he had, which didn't sound terribly exciting to me—why pretend to drive when you could just go out and do it?—until I remembered that the Words weren't taught or allowed to drive. I might not know a thing about physics or the latest video games, but at least I could operate a motor vehicle.

I made a sincere effort to follow Brehan's game-talk on the way to the Words' apartment complex, but once we were on the tram, I tuned him out while I searched for what I needed—and then found it. For once, I was thankful for our elite mode of transportation; the man near the doors obviously wasn't wordless, based on the gold pen in the front pocket of his sleek button-up shirt.

The tram began to slow to a stop as it neared our exit. I reached up to scratch my nose, as we turned to get off, and bumped into the man, my hand hitting his chest. I made eye contact and smiled apologetically. The beginnings of a smile froze on his face as he recognized the unstable new Word of Death—or, at least, the twin monitor bracelets around my wrists—and he took several steps back.

Perfect. He was too flustered about me touching him to notice his pen was missing—the pen that was now up my sleeve. I silently thanked Luft for the idea.

Brehan and I were quiet as we walked through the black-and-cream marble lobby of our apartment complex. When the elevator doors closed us inside the shining box, he nudged me with this shoulder, grinning at me in the floor-to-ceiling mirrors.

"That guy just didn't know how cuddly you can be," he said.

I realized he was trying to make me feel better for the pen-man flinching away from me. For about the first time ever, recognition and fear had been exactly what I'd wanted, but Brehan must have been taking my silence for gloominess instead of what it actually was: me trying to come up with the rest of my plan. I needed to do a better job of pretending nothing was up, or more people than Brehan might notice before I got the chance to enact it.

"Oh, hey," I said, remembering something with a rush of genuine happiness. My face broke out in such a smile that it surprised even me, never mind Brehan. "You're going to be jealous. I have a new lady in my life now. In fact, she's waiting for me in my apartment."

Brehan looked at me like I was crazy. "What, do you get conjugal visits now or something?" His voice went falsetto. "'I'm Tavin and I'm so depressed that the only way to make me feel better is...'" He started mock-caressing his chest, his hand sliding south, as the elevator doors opened on the green and gold of our floor.

I winked at him before I stepped out into the hallway. "She has an amazing tongue." His jaw dropped, and I tossed the *coup de grâce* over my shoulder: "Maybe she can come over to your place soon."

"Bullsh—" Brehan began, and then I swiped my keycard and opened my door.

Pie came skittering and sliding along the rosewood floor of the apartment and then burst onto the hallway carpet. She made a sharp turn and immediately threw her wiry body at my legs.

I scooped her up in my arms while Brehan stared, dumbfounded. I nuzzled her warm silky face, breathing in that amazing puppy smell that hadn't yet morphed into stinky-dog, while she alternately licked and nipped my cheek—the one that wasn't sutured. I held her up at eye level for Brehan.

"Pie, Brehan. Brehan, Pie. He's the Word of Light, and Pie is the Word of Licking."

A laugh burst out of him. "Good with her tongue, huh?"

"The best. Want to verify?" I held her out to him, and she struggled against my hands to get at him, her tongue lapping the air. Brehan took her in his arms, and she promptly coated his cheek with puppy slobber while he laughed and cursed and tried to tilt his face out of reach. Pie liking him so much reaffirmed my decision to trust him. She'd been terrified of Ryse and had even bitten her. Clearly, she was a good judge of character.

The fact that she also liked me gave me more confidence in myself, I wasn't ashamed to admit—admit only to myself, at any rate. Like several things about me, that wasn't really information I wanted to share.

Brehan wiped his cheek with a sleeve, setting Pie on the ground with his other hand. She bounded back over to me and leapt in a circle around my feet, trying to get me to play.

"She can *definitely* come over to my place," he said, smiling at her. He looked like he was about to ask how I'd gotten her and then thought better of it. He nodded toward his door. "Speaking of awesome new additions to our lives, you want to race?"

"One second," I said, seizing my chance. "Need to piss."

I dodged into Khaya's—my—apartment and slipped into the bathroom, being especially careful to close the door behind me. I would have anyway, since there were cameras right outside the bathroom... but not, as far as I could tell, inside. That was too much of an invasion of privacy for even the Godspeakers to sanction. I turned on the faucet to at least sound like I was doing something ordinary, ripped off a piece of toilet paper, and scrawled in the most childlike penmanship imaginable with the stolen pen:

I trust you. Can I trust Luft? Flush this.

Then I actually pissed for good measure, washed my hands, and headed back toward the hallway. En route, I noticed that someone had cleaned up and replaced the giant flat screen TV I'd broken with a brand new one. I nearly laughed but swallowed it instead. I didn't want whoever was watching to feel they should keep a closer eye on me, and mocking the outcome of my miniature insurrection would likely be all the incentive they'd need.

When I stepped into the hall, Brehan was on his back

on the green and gold carpet with Pie, letting her climb all over him. He sat up when he saw me.

Before he could suggest the video game again, I said, "So, you were telling me about that 'flare' technique you were practicing." At least it was true in case anyone felt like cross-checking the facts; I remembered *that* much from his lunchtime conversation. But then I flicked my eyes at the black semisphere casing of the camera set into the hallway ceiling. "Now that no one else is around to freak out, you should show me."

If he caught my look, he didn't let it show on his face. He only grinned. "You sure you're ready for this? It's going to be bright."

"Hit me with it."

It nearly felt like an actual hit when it happened, right in the eyeballs. He uttered a few Words—in Amharic, he'd told me at lunch—and the hallway flared like the sun had stumbled and fallen inside of it. I couldn't even see him, or anything else for that matter, so I wasn't worried about what the camera saw. The "flare" was brighter than I'd hoped. I reached forward blindly, caught Brehan's hand, and stuffed the tissue into his palm. His fingers closed around it. Then I threw myself away from him, laughing and shouting, "Okay, okay, I get it! Pie is scared!"

It was true; Pie was whining in a way that made me pick her up and nuzzle her in apology once the light faded. Brehan grinned from his seat on the floor, as if I hadn't just shoved something into his hand. His arms were folded in his lap.

"You're sure that it's not *you* who's scared?" he asked.

I grinned back. "Okay, I would have pissed my pants if I hadn't just gone." I widened my eyes at him ever-so-slightly.

"That sounds more like it. And speaking of which ... " He unfolded his lanky frame from the floor. "I could use a bathroom break myself. Mind? I want to check out your setup, see if they upgraded the girls' tubs with Jacuzzi jets or something. You know, since their apartments apparently come with puppies."

I could picture Khaya fuming over such a notion, even if it was just Brehan's excuse to get into my bathroom—where I'd left the pen on the toilet tank. But at least the request didn't sound so strange when he put it that way, and, odd or not, we were slightly closer to my apartment and my door was conveniently open. I didn't know if Brehan had a pen hidden away somewhere at his place, but even if he did, it might raise suspicions if he went looking for it. He must have been thinking the same thing.

I forced a laugh. "Go for it."

I played with Pie in the hallway, trying not to reveal my nervousness. It seemed like Brehan was in the bathroom forever. I suppressed a jump when I heard the bathroom door open.

He stuck his head out into the hallway. "Do you know your tablet is beeping in here? I think you have a message."

My stomach lurched into my throat. Was someone onto us? I stood, wiping my sweaty palms on my pants, and stepped into the apartment. Pie followed, yapping. I headed for the tablet I used to practice writing, which was resting on the kitchen counter and, now that I listened for it, emitting a faint beep. I woke it up and pushed the flashing icon that signaled a videomail.

To my immense relief, Drey's lined face appeared with my rosewood cupboards in the background and with a time signature from a couple of hours ago. "I just fed Pie," the recording began. "Your other studies can wait for today, but meet me in the lab at four p.m. Don't be late." The video cut out.

I glanced at the tablet's clock: 3:47.

My stomach twisted again, but for a different reason. "Damn. I have to be in the lab in about ten minutes." Not only did I have to face using the Word of Death again, but I had to do it with Drey as my Godspeaker. And how was I going to get Brehan's reply, assuming he'd written me one? The apprehension was audible in my voice.

Brehan gave me a sympathetic look. "I shouldn't make you late. Some other time on the game, yeah?"

He held out his hand for me to shake. I couldn't tell for sure, but it looked like his pinky finger might have been curled into his palm ... pinching something.

Perfect. But I didn't usually shake hands, especially not without gloves on. I made a show of eyeing his hand. "Are you sure you don't have a death wish?"

"Aw, but I thought you were starting to trust me."

I trust you, I'd written.

I smirked. "I haven't *quite* thrown out killing you just yet." I took his hand.

"I still count that as progress." He released what felt exactly like a folded-up piece of toilet paper into my palm.

"Later, man. Good luck." He clapped me on the shoulder with his other hand and sauntered out of my apartment.

Luft had wished me luck too. They were probably saying that because they couldn't do anything else to help me deal with being the Word of Death. I was on my own—only luck could help me now.

Or maybe Khaya could too, in a perfect universe ... with a little assistance from the Words of Earth and Water. If anyone could get me out of here, it was Tu and Pavati.

I wanted more than anything to read the note, but I didn't have time to pretend I needed to use the bathroom again. I dinked around only long enough to crouch behind the counter, kiss Pie goodbye—I wasn't about to take her back to the lab where she'd been so close to death—and slip the scrap of toilet paper into my pocket. Then I headed out the door myself.

My route to the Death Factory passed in a haze of anxiety. Fortunately, or maybe unfortunately, I didn't have long to wait. The tram and the elevators delivered me there just in time. Drey was already waiting inside the shining white-and-metallic lab. He looked out of place in his tweed slacks.

Before I could even get out a hello, he said, "I noticed your pulse doubled during lunch. Others did too."

Shit. He was warning me to be careful, even though he probably had no idea what had made me so excited.

I took a deep breath, trying not to think about Khaya and hoping my heart rate wasn't skyrocketing again. I made my voice irked, even angry. "If you know that, then you should know about Agonya crashing my lunch. If *they*"—I pointed to one of the surveillance cameras nestled in the corner of the lab's ceiling—"want me to be stable, then they should keep her the hell away from me." I actually meant the last part, even if that wasn't what my monitor bracelets had picked up.

"Should Luft be kept away from you too? Because, according to the report I received, your pulse reached peak elevation while you were talking to him—before Agonya showed up."

Double shit. The surveillance on me was too good. But at least, I hoped to the Gods, it still wasn't quite good enough to reach inside the bathroom. Even if my pulse became elevated *in there*, no one in their right mind should want to ask why. Or at least no one who knew the first thing about young guys, especially those condemned to a life of celibacy. So no one should know about the notes.

I wanted to wink at Drey or something, let him know that he didn't need to worry about this—but then, I had no idea how he would feel about me possibly conspiring with Luft to contact Khaya.

I opened my mouth and hesitated. "Luft and I are cool. Enough, anyway. He makes me nervous."

Drey nodded without pressing me. "Just keep yourself in check. I don't need to remind you that any accidents, especially any involving the Word of Death, are to be avoided at all costs. Letting yourself get riled up in public won't give the City Council any much-needed confidence in you. *I'm* confident in you," he added, "but it's not me you need to convince."

I wanted to retort that I'd *kept* myself from getting too riled up with Agonya, but then using her as an excuse for my heart rate would have sounded even lamer.

"Right," I said, looking around and feeling that familiar dread resettle in my stomach. "Which is why we're here: for me to become the best Word of Death ever."

Drey stepped aside, and I finally saw what was on the table behind him: a smallish furry shape laid out on a white towel. A cat, with gray tabby stripes. Its eyes were closed, but it was still breathing.

The dread tightened like a fist in my guts. "You think it'll make it any easier just because it's asleep—"

"Sedated," Drey corrected.

"Even so—"

"And dying."

That gave me pause. Now that I looked at the cat, I noticed its ribs jutting out. Its fur was thin and dull, even gone in spots. It definitely looked sick. "Then we should just let it—"

"It's in a lot of pain. Feline leukemia."

"You're a bastard," I said, already knowing what was coming.

"I won't make you, Tavin . . . and I won't do this for you, either. I won't Godspeak through you. But if you don't do it yourself, the sedative will wear off. You'll be abandoning this cat to a lot of suffering it doesn't deserve."

I clenched my jaw so hard my teeth creaked and made a fist at my sides as I looked at the cat. The Words were already straining, reaching . . .

Because that was the problem. I *did* want to kill the damned cat. A part of me wanted to kill everything I could touch. The Words were like an addiction, a seductive voice in my head—actually speaking to me, in my case—trying to convince me to give in. As long as I could ignore the voice, I would still be me. But if I let it take over, what would be left?

But I'd told Drey I would work with him, and he was definitely working with me. This was as far from a cruel death as anything could get. This would be mercy. I couldn't say no or turn back now, not if I wanted to survive this. And yet it was the first step down a very dark, twisting road—one that I had only a month to walk.

Or one that I had to follow just long enough to figure out how to contact Khaya and get the hell out of here somehow. I could dream, at least.

I exhaled, and my fists relaxed. I voluntarily opened myself up to the Word of Death for about the first time, and it seeped into my thoughts like tendrils of black smoke.

Asphyxiate, bleed, burn, crush . . .

With equally black humor, I wondered if the Words were coming out in alphabetical order after being pent up for so long. I waited while the morbid parade went by in my mind, until I heard—or *felt*—the Word I wanted.

I reached out and pet the cat, stroking its thin fur. I thought my hand might shake, but it was completely steady.

"Stop," I murmured.

The cat stopped breathing.

I raised my hand and let it fall to my side. I gave Drey

a grim smile as I turned my back on the table. "I imagine I'll be seeing more dying animals in the near future."

Drey was watching me, his eyes careful. "Yes. Until you get used to it."

"Your friendly neighborhood pet euthanizer," I said with a low chuckle.

His eyes grew more scrutinizing. "You seem to be taking this rather well."

He was right. I was completely calm. No crying or vomiting. Maybe when I wasn't forced to use the Words or carried away by them, when I was in control ... *this* gave me peace. Using the Word of Death was what I wanted, deep down.

I shuddered, tucking my hand behind my back. "Are we done for the day, then?"

"Yes. Tav, I—"

"See you tomorrow." I headed for the lab door, but then I remembered I couldn't get out on my own.

Luckily, Drey was right behind me, swiping his keycard for me. "I'll get you one of these," he said right before I bolted.

I didn't bother stopping by the mess hall, not even to order something to go, because my appetite had already vanished and I didn't anticipate its return. I wanted to hold Pie. I wanted to read what Brehan had written on the scrap of toilet paper in my pocket.

I *needed* to.

ten

On the tram back to my apartment, I kept my right hand behind my back, my left hand gripping it above the wrist, as if restraining it. I almost wanted to cut it off. It probably wasn't fair of me to blame my hand for the darkness inside of me, even if it had been the deliverer. After all, the Words were in my head—or at least, that was where I heard them—but I didn't want to cut my *head* off. At least, not yet.

Gods, I hoped it wouldn't come to that. I wondered, briefly, if I could use the Word of Death against myself. The Word of Time had killed himself, taking his Word with him, but *Time* hadn't been the thing that killed him. I doubted my own Word would work on my body, since it seemed to exist inside of me happily enough without killing me. The possibility was something I was better off not considering, anyway.

It wasn't until I was back in the privacy of my bathroom that I dared to take Brehan's note out of my pocket and open it. Written as it was on delicate toilet paper, it was battered but still readable:

Tentative yes. He's loyal to Carlin but not the rest. Why?

As I flushed it, I couldn't keep the hope from rising in my chest. Brehan's endorsement was enough for me to trust Luft.

Now I had a new mission, in addition to learning how to kill—or, rather, in addition to learning how to *love* killing: *Reach Khaya.*

I vigorously scrubbed my hands in the bathroom sink. Pie had been too distracted by what must have been the smell of the cat on my hand to stay still enough to let me hold her. But at least she hadn't shied away. In fact, she was scratching on the bathroom door, trying to get in.

I opened the door to another puppy-sized assault on my shins. Crouching down in front of Pie, I let her sniff my hands. When she didn't seem to find anything interesting and started chewing on them instead, I rubbed her down and play-fought on the floor with her until she eventually stopped attacking me and sprawled out, falling asleep in five seconds flat.

Man, if only life were that easy for me. It could be, I supposed, if I let it. All I had to do was pretend this was a game, kill whomever I had to, like the good attack dog they wanted me to be, and then sleep soundly at night.

Yeah, right.

After Pie was completely out, I got up, stretched, and sat down in front of the wooden desk, so dark green it was almost black, and the sleek computer that sat on it. I tried to look like I did this every day, even though it was just about the first computer I'd voluntarily touched in my life. In the hospital, I'd practiced typing in conjunction with my reading and writing lessons, but like most of my activities, it hadn't been optional. Typing was a milder form of torture, but it was still torture.

My incentive now was that since this might have been Khaya's computer, maybe I could somehow contact her from it. My personal surveillance team would of course be monitoring anything I did on it, let alone any voicemails I sent or emails if I could've even managed to write one. But maybe Khaya had sent a message *here*. Probably not to anyplace obvious like the email inbox, but maybe I could discover a less-obvious place.

I still had the reading level of an eight-year-old, so after the screen blinked to life I was happy to discover that I could click most words for an audio prompt, just like I could on my old videophone back when I'd been totally wordless. I could also cue the computer with audio prompts, but I didn't want to make my search so obvious as to announce it to the room.

Instead, I browsed some random folders filled with articles I didn't even bother attempting to read, but which looked like they had to do with biology. A good sign that this had indeed been Khaya's computer. Then I launched a game of Solitaire and promptly closed it. I'd always found it too dull, but maybe Khaya had liked it. Finally I launched the web browser and idly clicked on a bunch of news articles that I once again didn't read, until whoever was watching me had probably died of boredom. Or at least started watching something else. That was when I opened up the browser's history.

There was nothing from the past two months or so, but there were quite a few sites recorded before Khaya escaped. I read the titles as quickly as I could, which wasn't as fast as I would've preferred, and made a mental note to try harder during my reading lessons.

Oddly enough, there wasn't much to do with anything other than birds: bird websites, bird articles, bird photos. The last thing listed was *The Physical Characteristics of Blue Finches*. "Physical characteristics" was a pain in my ass to puzzle out, and yet it told me nothing.

I closed the web browser, my heavy disappointment sinking me into the chair. I could see that the history included no external messaging sites or forums. And I was pretty sure there was no hidden code within the bird sites, or at least not one that I'd be able to decipher.

For some reason, the fact that Khaya liked birds was an extra weight on my mood. It made sense, caged as she'd been, but I hadn't known she liked them. I didn't know all sorts of things about her. I supposed these things would maybe come with time... if I ever saw her again.

Would Khaya even want me rescued? What if she thought I belonged in here, locked up like a rabid animal? What if she'd already met someone else? We hadn't known each other for that long. Since we'd met, we'd been apart longer than we'd been together, never mind all the years *before* we'd met. What if her liking me had just been a matter of happenstance, and I'd only been the first person she could get close to?

But that didn't say much for her powers of discernment or for her regard for me... or for people in general, if she'd just used the first person she came across. *I* regarded *her* more highly than that. Even from the depths of my doom and gloom, I couldn't really go there. But there was still the problem: even if she'd loved me then, would she love me now?

Probably only if I could keep it together and stay true to myself until I somehow managed to get out of here. And that involved focusing, not acting like a whiny baby.

By now it was long past dark, so I shut the computer down and went to bed, taking Pie with me. I didn't care about letting her roll around in the silk sheets. If all of my stuff became coated with puppy fur, especially my all-black wardrobe, so much the better.

———————

The week wore on and Drey kept bringing sick animals to the lab for me to kill—mostly dogs and cats that were about to be put down anyway, collected from animal shelters throughout the city. At least, that was what Drey assured me. That wasn't even the bad part, since, after the fourth animal, I wondered if I'd even care if they were terminally ill anymore. The Word of Death certainly didn't, as I used it to stop their hearts.

What was bad was when Agonya sauntered by my table one day during lunch in the mess hall, before my usual afternoon lab session with Drey, and said, "You know what they're calling you around here? *Merciful Death, Liberator of Aging Pets.* Way to make a fool out of yourself—and the rest of us, at this rate. Can't you just suck it up and do your job?"

I mustered a grin. "But you yourself said I'm not one of you. And you're right. I'd *much* rather be a fool than that."

She stormed off, predictably. But I didn't feel as confident as my grin had made me look. I wasn't even sure why I was in the mess hall. Brehan wasn't even here, or Luft. Now that I knew I could trust Luft, I especially wanted to talk to him again and try to glean if he had any clues as to *how* I might contact Khaya. But he hadn't made a second appearance in the mess hall all week.

As I stood from my table, clearing my half-full plate even though everyone else left their plates for the bussers, I couldn't help but feel like eyes were on me. More than usual, anyway. It was probably bad enough that given the dog hair on my clothes I wasn't hiding the fact that I had a cuddly puppy, but now…

Merciful Death? Gods. The City Council wasn't going to let that image of me last for long.

It was then I met a particular dark pair of eyes watching me from across the mess hall. I only caught a glimpse of her pale face and straight black hair before she turned away to talk to someone else, but it was enough for me to see she was smiling.

It wasn't a pleasant smile. Smiles never were, with Ryse. She might be suspended and banned from working with me, but she was still in the know. And if she was smiling, it meant things would be bad for me.

Sure enough, when I showed up at the Death Factory that afternoon, Drey was standing on the other side of the steel table, a glass cage resting on the shiny surface between us. The guinea pig inside of the cage wasn't sedated, and didn't look anything close to sick and dying. It didn't even look old.

"I'm not sure—" I began, but Drey spoke before I could finish.

"The City Council wants to see more progress with you, and I think you're ready. You have to be ready, Tavin."

This sounded serious, and I looked at the guinea pig with mounting anxiety. Its twitching little nose reminded me of the bunny Ryse had made me kill. It was like she was insinuating herself in my life again, even from far away. "What do I have to do?"

Drey put his hands on the edge of the table and stared at me levelly. "You have to kill it, Tavin, and not just by stopping its heart. Or else we'll do this again and again until you kill it how they want you to."

So this was how it was going to be. My anxiety twisted into anger. "Do *this*? What, stand here?" I folded my arms. "Fine, I'll stand here. We'll see who gets tired first, old man."

Drey's eyes dropped. "I told you that I was willing to do things for you I'd rather not do, as long as you were willing to do them for me in return. And I meant it." He unfolded part of a white towel lying behind the cage. More steel, sharp steel, shined in the fluorescent lights. A scalpel rested on the towel. "You won't do anything I don't have to do myself. We're in this together."

"Wait, what are *you* doing?" I demanded.

That was all I had time to get out before Drey seized the guinea pig by the scruff of its neck in one hand, the scalpel in the other, and stabbed it in its fat little belly.

The creature screeched. I just about screeched too, crying out and lunging for Drey. But he kept the table between us and held the bleeding, squealing guinea pig aloft, so I could see it but not reach it. Its tiny limbs flailed and spun in the air, scattering droplets of blood.

"*What are you doing?*" I shouted again. "Gods damn you!"

"I won't give it to you, Tavin, until you agree to make it bleed. You can kill it quickly, but nevertheless ... "

I couldn't stand the sight, but I couldn't look away. The anger in my chest rose to my face in a burning wave and the word exploded out of my throat. "Fine!"

Drey held the struggling creature out over the table and I snatched it from him, trying to ignore the feeling of the warm little body squirming in my grip. The squealing was scrambling my brain, and I used the first Word to come to me.

"Open, open, open!" I shouted at it.

At its veins, rather.

Red spots appeared all over it, soaking its fur. A brief rainstorm of blood pattered onto the steel tabletop. I dropped the stained, twitching corpse back in its cage and held up my shaking hand, smeared with blood. It was just like it had been with Ryse. Except this time, I'd done it myself.

The City Council wasn't going to let me get away with clean hands anymore, literally or figuratively.

"This is sick," I said, my voice shaking like my hand. I turned on Drey. "You're sick."

But then I realized how pale Drey was. He looked about ready to throw up. He swallowed, tossed the scalpel down on the table, and wiped his own hands on the white towel.

My shaking subsided as I watched him, a cold realization filling me like water in my lungs—like drowning and not being able to do anything about it.

I couldn't let him do this. But I didn't want Ryse to step in either. Nor did I particularly want to die.

So I had to do it on my own.

"That was still a mercy killing," I said, swallowing my own bile. "I was still putting it out of its misery because of what you did, and that's not good enough for them. You don't have to hurt them anymore. I'll ... I'll do it without your help. That's what they want, anyway."

Drey nodded, not looking at me. That was no doubt what he wanted too. Whether he'd known what my decision would be before this session in the lab—whether this had all been yet another manipulation—I preferred not to know.

I didn't want to have to hate him.

eleven

Even when I woke up the next morning in my green canopy bed, I wanted to look at my hands and make sure they no longer had blood on them. Never mind that I'd scrubbed them so hard the evening before—*after* already washing them at the lab—that they were nearly bleeding themselves.

I didn't want to get out of bed, but Pie had already peed on the floor. I supposed at some point I should probably start potty-training her instead of simply cleaning up her messes. I didn't like the *training* aspect of it, but even human kids had to be potty-trained at some point. And picking up poop was probably something I could live without.

I rolled out of bed, refusing to allow myself to check my hands again. I scooped up Pie, showed her the puddle with an obligatory "No," and dodged said puddle as I left the bedroom. I deposited her outside on the balcony, where someone—Drey—had laid down some old paper, and hoped she would get the picture. She mostly just started shredding the paper, and also yelped in alarm when she nearly got her head stuck in the wrought-iron bars of the balcony railing. At least she couldn't fit through.

Poop aside, I didn't know what I'd do without her.

I still didn't feel like facing the day. But before I could estimate how long it would take my various instructors to track me down if I didn't show up to my lessons, there was a knock on the door.

When I opened it, Drey stood there in the green and gold hallway. He was half-turned away like he was deep in thought, but looked up immediately.

"Put on one of your Necron suits. I know you hate them, but it was the only way I could get the City Council to agree."

I was still rubbing sleep from my eyes. "Agree to what?" Whatever it was, it couldn't be all that good if it involved death-proof clothing.

"To let me take you out into Eden City, for us to get some fresh air. Don't bother with gloves."

Or, I was wrong. I blinked at him, stepping back in the doorway in surprise. Drey took it as an invitation to come inside.

"And they agreed to this even *with* me wearing that stupid outfit?" I asked as he walked into the kitchen and started filling the pot of the coffeemaker from the tap.

"Well, that plus four armed guards and an extra Godspeaker. Not Ryse, so don't worry. We'll have to take a van."

"But ... why?" I sputtered, still standing in the entryway.

"Like I said, I thought it would be good for you. For *us*, even. And the City Council decided to listen." Maybe they liked the progress he was making with me, but I didn't ask. He poured the water into the coffeemaker and turned it on. "I'll make you some breakfast while you get ready. Eggs and bacon sound good?" He was already pulling the ingredients out of the fridge, which he must have stocked when he put down the paper for Pie.

I hadn't had someone take care of me like this for months. At least, not counting the hospital staff, who were paid to feed me bland food and change my bed sheets. It was almost like Drey and I were back at the old garage, complete with too-bitter coffee by the looks of the tar already hissing and dribbling out of the machine.

Almost. But not quite. Nothing felt the same anymore. Or right. Not even this, which was shaping up to be the best morning I'd had since becoming the Word of Death—and the best chance I had to "bump into" Tu and Pavati and get rescued. Maybe Drey was in on it, and that was why this all felt like a ruse. It might be a ruse in our favor for once.

"Can Pie come?" I asked before I turned to get dressed.

Drey frowned slightly. "Best not."

That sounded even less right, but I couldn't argue. I got dressed and ate breakfast mostly in silence. If I opened my mouth, I knew I would start asking too many questions and ruin any plans Drey might have.

It was as if Drey knew my hopes were running wild, because on the elevator ride down to the apartment lobby, he told me, "I've sworn, on pain of execution for treason, to use either godspeaking, a stun gun, or tranquilizers on you if you try to escape. So have the others. And all of the guards will also have loaded assault rifles and handguns. For your ostensible protection, of course, but nevertheless... don't try to escape. You never know if one of the guards will confuse which gun to use in the heat of the moment."

Or if they hated me for whatever reason, or if Ryse had bribed one of them to turn me into a paraplegic to make my life that much more difficult, etcetera. In any case, I got the drift.

This wasn't an escape attempt.

Maybe the point of this venture was purely for us to get outside for a while. But if escape was impossible today, maybe I could still find a way to get word to Khaya that I was alive and desperately in need of an escape. This would be my best chance.

I wasn't sure how even that would be possible when I saw the four guards gathered in the marble lobby. They looked more like soldiers with their Necron uniforms, bulletproof vests, and assault rifles. There was also a brown-haired woman, a Godspeaker I had seen only every once in a while, who didn't look much friendlier, standing behind a very pale girl with nearly white hair. Maybe the girl was wearing the black tutu and so much black eyeliner to try to counteract her paleness, but mostly it served to accentuate it, making her look like an undead ballerina.

Drey had failed to mention that the extra Godspeaker would come with a Word.

Ever since our showdown in the Alps, I'd only seen Mørke from afar. Now she was close enough to ... wink at me? At least that was what I thought she did as soon as she spotted me.

Their choice of the Word of Darkness made sense.

Agonya or Luft's powers would be more likely to kill me than keep me from escaping, and if the City Council wanted me dead, it would have happened ages ago. Although Brehan could blind me, he'd also blind everyone else in the vicinity; Mørke could likely blind*fold* me without everyone else experiencing the same effect. I couldn't run very far like that.

Running became even less of an option after we walked up to the group and a guard handcuffed me to Drey. As the metal cinched tight and cold around my left wrist, I noted that while I might not have gloves, the guards did.

"Is this necessary?" I asked. "Don't you know I could cut off his hand with a Word if I really wanted to get away?" At least I was pretty sure I could; but doing that would also likely kill Drey. I wondered why they didn't just handcuff both my hands together until I remembered that Drey was still under some type of house arrest and they probably didn't want him running either.

Drey answered for the guard, who had barely acknowledged me except to cuff me. "They're betting on the likelihood that you don't want to cut off my hand."

I was tempted to say that was a lousy bet, but I swallowed it. "So," I said, "thank you all for joining us."

"You're welcome," Mørke said. Her lip quirked up in a half-smile.

I hadn't expected a response, not even her mildly sarcastic one, though I supposed my sarcasm deserved some in return.

"You here to blindfold me if I try to run?" I asked her.

"Check."

"Awesome."

Drey sighed and shared an exasperated look with the other Godspeaker—Angelina was her name. Mostly I knew that because Brehan jokingly called her "Angel of Darkness" as a tribute to her general lack of cheer and, of course, because she was Mørke's Godspeaker.

"Let's go," Drey said, pulling me after him by our handcuffs.

We all exited into a parking garage, through a heavily guarded door hidden behind the lobby desk, which was already sealed off from the rest of the lobby by the glass screen and another ridiculously thick door. A white van with black-tinted windows was waiting against the curb in the garage. Angelina, Mørke, and a guard ducked into the back row. Drey slid into the middle row first, followed by me—as if I had a choice—and then a second guard sat between me and the door. The other two guards sat up front, one of them driving. I wondered if they'd drawn straws to pick who had to sit next to me.

I couldn't see much as we pulled out of the garage onto a discreet side street in the Athenaeum—only through the windshield, since the back and side windows were so tinted. Even with my limited view, my stomach still clenched in anticipation as we drove up to the gate that would take us outside. I could see Eden City rising beyond the glass pyramid wall, its pale stone and shining metal buildings gleaming in the sunlight.

I leaned forward in my seat to talk to the guys up front, ignoring the guard who tensed next to me. "Can we roll down a window?"

"That would go against protocol, sir," the driver said. "These windows are bulletproofed for your protection."

Funny that he called me *sir* when he'd been the one to handcuff me to Drey.

"Is there going to be any fresh air involved in this trip outside for fresh air?" I muttered to Drey.

"Soon." Then Drey leaned forward to give the driver directions, and we drove through the gate and out into the city.

Before Drey had his first sentence out, I knew where we were headed. We drove for a while through the richest section of the city, crossing over the Nectar River on one of its more ornate bridges, but soon the buildings grew drabber, turning into brick and concrete instead of marble and glass.

In no time at all we pulled to a stop in front of the garage where I'd lived and worked with Drey since I was six years old. Even before, as a toddler, I'd lived at his bachelor pad of a tiny apartment and ridden in the front seat of the garbage truck with him while he was working. This was practically the only home I'd ever known.

It was ridiculous that it was such a short drive away, and yet it felt a world away. The last time I'd been here, Drey had been lying in a pool of gore on the floor. I thought he'd died, but he'd only been in the process of it. Now, one of the garage's two huge doors was rolled up, and guys I didn't recognize were tinkering with one of the green trucks inside. Drey had cycled through employees quickly, probably so no one could start asking too many questions about either of us. That gave me hope that the guys who used to work there with us had just been transferred as usual, not arrested when everything went down.

"See, the place is getting along without us just fine," Drey said, staring out the window. He sounded nearly as homesick as I felt.

"Indeed," Angelina said dismissively from the back seat. "The outside world is beneath you, Tavin."

Mørke cupped her hands around her face as she peered out the window. Even her nails were painted black. "I think it's cool."

I almost felt grateful for her presence, then.

"You don't need this anymore," her Godspeaker insisted to me.

"No, the outside world doesn't need *me* anymore," I snapped. "Only sick people do." I felt a pang as I said it. Khaya definitely didn't number among those people. I changed the subject. "Will I be able to get out of the car at some point? Not here," I added. It was too painful looking at my old home, let alone walking around it.

Even if Drey and Angelina were saying it in different ways, their point was the same: I didn't belong here anymore. Maybe Drey hadn't meant it *quite* like that, but it still felt like a punch to the stomach. And yet as I looked out the window, I knew it was true.

I was someone else now—*something* else—no matter how much I wanted to be the same old Tavin.

Drey gave further directions, and after that we drove to the edge of Eden City. There, without too many eyes around, I was able to get out of the car and walk along the river, with

Angelina and Mørke following behind us and the four guards forming a loose perimeter. A breeze blew more strongly than it ever did in the Athenaeum, and the river smelled like a real river: like algae and rank mud, nothing artificial. Better yet, the sunshine wasn't filtered through the Athenaeum's panes of glass. There were only shipyards and graffiti-covered storage containers within sight, but it was still almost nice.

There was that word again: *almost*. It was *almost* nice. It was *almost* like the old days with Drey. It was *almost* bearable being the Word of Death. But not quite. Drey was doing his best to make my life less miserable, but it wasn't good enough.

Then again, it could also be worse.

I was just thinking that at least I wouldn't have to kill anything today when Drey stopped in front of a chain-link fence. We'd veered away from the mud of the riverbank, walking up a heavily potholed road until we were bordering what looked like a junkyard on the other side of the fence.

Drey held up his handcuffed wrist, and the guard unlocked it. The guard unlocked my handcuff too.

I shot Drey a questioning glance. "What's going on?"

Drey didn't answer. He only lifted the metal hatch on a gate—which was unlocked, oddly, in this neighborhood—and said, "After you."

I stepped through, feeling nervous for some reason. With *good* reason, I discovered, when one of the guards closed the gate right behind me and held the latch down. Reflexively I tried to lift it, but the guard had better a grip than I could get with my bare hand. And his gloves were Necron, so I couldn't even pretend to threaten him.

If the whole area hadn't been fenced in, and the fence crowned with spirals of razor wire, I would've thought this was my chance to escape. As it was ...

"What the hell?" I demanded.

"You were right," Drey said from the other side of the fence. "We're done with mercy killings. But I'm not going to let you go straight from that to ... harder things."

"Wait—what is this?"

A snarling growl answered for him and I spun against the fence, the metal links biting into my fingers. I would have scaled the stupid thing if not for the razor wire, because a massive Rottweiler had come out from between cars—a classic junkyard dog, big tendrils of drool hanging from its mouth and a spiked collar around its neck and everything.

This was why the City Council had let me leave my gloves off.

"Killing in self-defense should be easier for you at this stage ... " Drey began after a pause. But even he sounded hesitant at the sight of the dog.

"Oh, you're doing this out of *kindness*? How stupid of me." I edged along the fence, trying to position a rusty car between the dog and me, but it lunged and feinted, sticking too close. All too soon, it would be near enough to sink its teeth into me. I already knew what that felt like and I didn't care to experience it again.

I would have to move fast.

"Stop trying to run, Tavin," Drey said, recognizing my stance. "You're the Word of Death; you just need to—"

I was the Word of Death, and I ran my ass off. Throwing

myself into a sprint, I headed for a close formation of old vehicles, the dog at my heels. I launched myself onto the hood of a car, and then scrambled onto the roof. My boots drummed on metal, denting the surface, but I didn't slow down to step more lightly. I leapt from the car onto a nearby bus, using my arms to heave myself up. The dog jumped and nipped at my ankles, but I hauled myself out of his reach just in time, scooting away from the roof's edge for good measure.

I stood, dusted flecks of rusty paint from my palms, and took stock of my situation. Yep, indeed, I was stuck on the top of a bus with a crazed dog and a razor-wire fence between me and safety. The river glimmered prettily in the distance.

"Your reaction should be offensive, not defensive," Drey called from behind the safety of the chain links. The gang of guards with their guns stood on either side of him. They looked even less interested in helping me than Drey did. If anything, they looked entertained. Angelina appeared disinterested, while Mørke was chewing nervously on one of her black-painted fingernails.

"Want to demonstrate for me?" I called back at him, shielding my eyes. The sun was bright out here, and the sky so blue. The roof of the bus was even kind of nice, a place I would have climbed up on to hang out as a kid growing up in the city. Too bad there was a ravenous beast thirsting for my blood circling it, snarling and barking at me. Gods, why couldn't I have been the Word of Flight instead of the Word of Death? All I had to do was lift off, and I would be free.

But no. And if Pavati and Tu were going to rescue me, this would have been their best possible opportunity.

I wanted to leap around and shout for help on the off-chance they would come swooping down in a helicopter or something, but I'd be making myself look like an idiot for no good reason. Besides, Tu would probably tunnel up from the ground, anyway.

They weren't coming. I was on my own. The ruse of this whole outing had definitely been on me.

"So this dog's owner doesn't mind that we're here to kill it?" I asked, watching the dog pace back and forth beneath me.

"He called a shelter," Drey answered, "to report that it was acting too aggressively even toward him, so he wanted it to be picked up and exterminated. I've been in touch with Eden City's animal services since . . . well, since I took over as your Godspeaker, so—"

"So now I'm here. Great. Was that the whole point of this? Not to actually let me breathe some fresh air for once, but to sic a demented dog on me?"

"The purpose was two-fold."

"Nice. Sort of like killing two birds with one stone. Except one of the birds is a dog."

"Sarcasm isn't going to help."

No, only killing the dog would. It circled the bus in a frenzy, kicking up dust. It even let out a whine between its growls, it was so eager to get at me.

In another lifetime, this dog could have been as cute and cuddly as Pie. Okay, maybe not *quite* as cute, but certainly as nice. Instead, it had been made into a monster. And now another monster-in-the-making was here to kill it. I was sure the Athenaeum would argue that they needed me, just like the dog's owner had probably argued that he needed a dog like this. It was an endless cycle of monsters making monsters to supposedly kill *other* monsters.

There wasn't much else for me to do.

I considered stretching an arm down the side of the bus to reach for the dog from a safe distance, but I'd likely get my hand chomped before I could speak a Word. The only way for me to get close enough yet still avoid its teeth was to get back down on the ground.

I banged the roof on one side of the bus, the clangor echoing around the yard. "Hey, dog. Hey!"

The dog trotted quickly over to that side, growling deep in its throat. I spun and jumped off the first side, rolling as I hit the dirt. I came up fast, but only fast enough to see the dog racing around the hood, coming straight for me.

It leapt for my face before I had time to think. I meant to shout *Gods!* as my hands tried to stop it in mid-air, but the word twisted in my mouth. It became a Word.

"Gut!"

The dog careened into me, making a stranger, *wetter* sound than I would have expected. It still flattened me to the ground, but didn't seem to have any more interest in biting off my face. It took a few steps to one side and collapsed. When I saw all the blood staining the dirt beneath it, I lifted my head to look at my chest.

The dog had left its entrails on top of me.

I sat up, heaving the hot stinking mass away. Half of it seemed to stay behind, sticking to my Necron suit and leaking under my sleeves. And I'd been worried about only my *hands* getting dirty.

The gate squeaked open behind me, but I was too occupied to bother looking.

"Interesting choice of Words." Drey stood over me.

"Not my choice," I muttered. "Apparently the Word of Death goes into auto-defense mode when I'm under attack. Good to know." I took another minute trying to wipe off the red goop before realizing it was somehow in my hair too, at which point I gave up. I was almost glad Khaya couldn't see me like this. "So we've had mercy killings and now a self-defense killing." I squinted up at Drey. "I imagine the next step is cold-blooded murder."

His expression might have been stoic if not for the eyes that betrayed him. "They're going to expect it of you someday soon, Tavin. You have to know that."

"Oh no, all this time I was thinking they wanted me to plant the damned flowerbeds." I spat and tried to wipe my mouth off with a black sleeve that turned out to be even bloodier. I spat again. "This blood was a little warm for my taste, anyway."

Drey offered me his hand, but I ignored it as I stood up and looked down at myself. I laughed.

He raised a questioning eyebrow.

"Looks like I get the front seat." I glanced at the guards, who were taking in the gore spattering my clothes. Even Angelina's face was twisted up in disgust. "Unless anyone wants to sit next to me?"

They gave up the front seat. And they didn't even cuff me for the ride back to the Athenaeum.

Twelve

I'd been right that the next step in my training would involve cold-blooded killing, if not yet murder. The Death Factory truly began to live up to its name. And even though I'd managed to leave the Athenaeum for a few hours, I was no closer to contacting Khaya. But I wasn't even sure if I should anymore.

Over the next several days, I killed other animals. Some were cute and cuddly, others scary. None were sick, and most were getting bigger in size. I half-wondered if they'd make me work my way through a zoo, all the way up to elephants or something. But I knew we wouldn't get that far. The end-goal would come before then … something more human-sized.

One afternoon, about a week after the junkyard, I showed up at the lab to find a chimpanzee sitting in a wire cage that was nearly too small for it. It was holding the bars, its long face looking like it wore a deep frown. Like it knew it couldn't run.

"For the Gods' sake!" I shouted as soon as I saw it, my voice exploding into the too-still, antiseptic air. The chimp startled, looking around the lab in alarm. "This thing is probably smarter than half the City Council, and I'm supposed to kill it?"

Drey glanced at the surveillance cameras with a grimace, but he didn't chastise me for insulting the Council. "I think that's the point."

Right, I was *supposed* to feel bad about it...and then get over it. Because how bad would I feel when I had to kill a person? The plan was for me to get over that too.

"How do they want me to do it?"

When he hesitated, I knew it would be bad. "Slowly, to prove you're capable of carrying out orders. The City Council is impressed with your progress, but they have to know you can do whatever is asked of you. You have to *learn* how to use the Word at some point, and not just practice what you already know intuitively. Organic bodies are complex, and there are many ways to take them apart."

They wanted me to torture it. I closed my eyes. "This is horrible."

"It's life." Before I could object that this was precisely the opposite, Drey continued. "Death is always intertwined with life. And of all the horrible things going on in the world right now, this is actually pretty small in comparison."

"Keep telling yourself that if it'll help you sleep better at night."

He only stared at me. I doubted he was sleeping too peacefully.

My hands were suddenly in my hair, squeezing the sides of my head. "*How* slowly?"

"They didn't specify, but I would think at least a few minutes."

Ryse had probably suggested this to the City Council. Rage consumed me before I could drop my hands—I'd begun pulling out my hair. I wanted to hit the wall, punch Drey, throw something across the room, do anything other than what they wanted me to do. What *she* wanted me to do. But the lab was too tidy and there wasn't much to throw. There was only smooth metal, glass and white tile, and the chimpanzee in the cage, watching me with wary dark eyes.

Instead, I held out my hand to Drey. "Give me your videophone."

"Why?"

"Don't worry, I'm not going to try to call anyone. Or smash it on the ground," I added in case he could see how much I wanted to break something.

He handed it over, eyeing me as warily as the chimp. I pushed a few buttons on the screen, found what I needed, and held it ready at my side. Then I turned to the poor creature. I walked slowly up to the bars, holding its gaze. It pulled its lips back in sort of a weird grin as I bent my head to put myself level with it. I doubted it was a happy grin.

"I'm sorry," I said. And then I touched one of the hairy knuckles protruding through the bars.

My eyes closed, and the Word of Death filled me. My rage was gone in an instant, replaced by a cool deep river flowing through me—a river of death. It was a place where things dissolved and joined the rest of the endless flow. It was a place where I didn't have to fight, where I didn't have to fear myself, where I could just relax. Just *be*. Too bad it was a place where I was alone, since, by definition, nothing else could live there with me. In spite of that, I heard myself sigh in what was nearly pleasure.

It didn't bother me, because I was already too focused on listening to something else to care—the whispers. The Words.

Something was different this time. The longer I touched the chimp with the Words murmuring through me, the more I heard *it*, too. The chimp's thumping heartbeat, its huffing breath, the blood thrumming it its veins. The music of life. And after even longer, I *saw*: the golden strings playing the music, connecting it all together and vibrating with vitality. They were the same strings I'd seen once when I'd godspoken through Khaya.

But *I* was different now. I was seeing them from a new angle. Not how to weave them together, like the Word of Life, but how to cut them. How to silence their music.

I was learning. The Word of Death could be like a pillow, smothering all the humming strings at once, or like a pair of scissors, picking and choosing. I saw exactly what I needed to do.

"Numb." The center of the brain for pain—*snip*. "Weaken." Blood flow and oxygen levels—*snip, snip*. But those I only cut a little bit. I tried to say the Words under my breath, as quietly as possible. But after the chimp blinked at me and sagged in the cage, I knew I could speak louder. Say what I wanted to say.

Recreating the effect of a hemorrhagic fever was pretty easy. Blood soon leaked from its nose, ears, mouth, and eyes. The chimp couldn't feel anything—I'd made sure of that—but it still looked horrendous. The City Council wanted blood, after all. And a part of me, a part that was getting stronger every day, did too.

I didn't turn away until the chimp breathed its final gurgling breath, just after its third seizure. I wasn't sure how long I'd stood there watching it die. But that was what a timer was for. I slammed Drey's videophone onto the steel table, with a force just shy of breaking it.

The red numbers of the digital clock had stopped at 15:36.

I turned around to look at Drey, who was pale and staring at me as if he wasn't sure who I was anymore. I looked at the reflective windows where I knew people were watching, and the nearest surveillance camera too. "Fifteen minutes and thirty-six seconds," I said. "Is that long enough?"

I was calm, so calm. I still couldn't help feeling like I was in a cage just like the chimp, with a timer ticking down to my demise. And not even one that was counting down from a month, not now that I was doing so well. No, this would be another sort of death.

I have a way to kill your soul, Herio had said.

Drey didn't try to stop me or even say anything when I moved for the door out of the lab this time. He probably didn't know that I'd killed the chimp's pain receptors, but even so ... I paused before I reached the door and glanced back at him over my shoulder. "This is what a monster looks like. Don't act so surprised. You're creating it."

I passed the usual audience outside the room, safe

behind their windows from whatever went on in the lab. As much as people liked a good show, their numbers had dwindled recently. Now that I was cooperating, it must have grown too repetitive to just watch animals die in gruesome ways, over and over again. But if ever there was a human waiting for me in the lab, I was sure they'd return in a mob, like ancient Roman spectators for a gladiator match. Human blood was always more exciting.

Even for the Word of Death. The murmuring in my head increased just at the thought of human blood. It *wanted* it.

I hurried out into the hallway without looking at anyone. I needed to get away.

Pie was my usual solace when my mood was this dark, but I couldn't face her right now. I couldn't face anyone else either, not even my friends—if that was what Brehan and Luft were these days. I didn't want to see their lively eyes, hear their laughter, or feel the warmth emanating from them.

Because I wasn't sure if I could resist stopping it—the warmth, the laughter, the life—with a Word or two.

I wanted to sink myself again into that deep, dark river floating inexorably in the back of my mind. It was calling to me, and I couldn't ignore it this time as it drew me with that siren's song to the edge. But I couldn't be around anything living when I gave in. I'd be too dangerous.

I told the elevator to take me to the very top of the training center. Nobody tried to follow me inside the elevator car, thank the Gods, so I had the ride to myself. It passed with my fists clenched at my sides. Then the doors opened onto a familiar hallway lined with windows that looked out over the Athenaeum, with *that* view encased by the glass pyramid. I imagined a flood rising inside the glass walls and drowning everyone. Not a literal flood, of course. That would take Pavati. But I wondered if I could somehow make the Word of Death contagious, similar to a communicable plague like an actual hemorrhagic fever, or a flesh-eating virus. Maybe I could kill an entire city. There would be a river of blood…

I threw myself toward the sliding door down the hallway and practically hammered on the button to get in before the Words straining against my lips could get out. I was losing control again. I needed to find that peace of the river but not let it carry me away.

The door slid open, dumping me inside. Bristles poked my palms and dust rose when I landed. I was kneeling on a very dead lawn. I crawled farther away from the door as it slid shut behind me, closing me in. At least in here, I was surrounded by death.

Khaya's garden. I definitely hadn't left anything alive, not even accidentally.

When I was far enough inside, away from where someone could theoretically trip over me unaware, I collapsed on my back in the middle of the indoor wasteland. Dead trees rose around me like bleached bones in a desert. Brehan's lights no longer floated around the ceiling, so there was only the late afternoon sun slanting through the high windows. It would start getting dark soon.

I wanted darkness. I didn't want to have to see what I was becoming. I wanted to give up and let the Words rip through me, destroy me, and reform me into whatever they wanted.

Which was about the worst possible moment for Luft to walk in. The door whooshed open and footsteps crunched through the desiccated grass toward me. Then his voice entered the cavernous space.

"Hey." There was a pause, and I took in his presence, the Word of Death swelling toward him like a wave about to break. "I won't ask how you're doing. You didn't seem to see me, but I was watching at the lab today."

I didn't sit up. "You want to leave." My voice was dead calm. *Dead*, indeed. I could hear the Words underneath my own words, wanting to turn them into something else.

"Do I?" There was the same confidence in his voice as when he'd stood up to Ryse. "What if I don't?"

"This isn't the time to be brave. Not now."

"You think I'm brave?" He actually sounded flattered.

I tilted my head to look up at him from the ground. The sunlight on his blond hair was the brightest thing in the room—the most alive. "Luft. I'm very serious."

He drew air through his teeth when he met my eyes. "That bad, huh?"

"You have no idea."

"I do, actually," he said. He wasn't leaving, but at least he wasn't coming any closer. "Not *exactly* like you, but the Words do something like this in all of us, every so often. Sometimes they're just . . . too much, and they try to overflow. Too much of anything isn't good."

"What—do you get really bad gas? Does Khaya want to grow a forest? Does Brehan, I don't know, try to light up the city at night?" I rolled over, watching him from a half-crouch.

Some part of my mind registered my stance as the crouch of a predator. "I want to make the city bleed."

Luft shrugged. "Agonya often wants to light the city on fire. I sometimes want to flatten it with a hurricane. Mørke occasionally wants to lock them all in darkness."

He hadn't risen to the bait of my insult, which gave me no easy excuse to go at him. Not yet.

He held my eyes again. "You've actually been handling it incredibly well lately, but these are the Words of the Gods. Did you think they'd ride easily in mortal bodies?"

"But this isn't … it's not … " I didn't know what to say about the feeling trying to overtake me. *Not the Gods? Not me? Not okay?*

"I heard what you said in the lab. You're not a monster."

My laugh came out as short and sharp as a razor. "Tell that to my victims."

Luft folded his arms. "*You're* the victim, Tavin. No, listen to me. I knew Herio. I saw what this Word did to him. You're right, it's worse than the others—it's like poison. Your body can process it, but not fast enough sometimes. Even Herio needed help every so often. And when he stopped asking for help, that was when the Word of Death sort of … ate him up inside."

"Who could help him? Could … Khaya?" I hoped that was where this conversation was heading, anyway. That would be the only reason for me to continue having it. That and waiting for the opportunity to lunge at him.

"No. She mostly stayed away from him. And for good reason, other than her personal dislike of him."

Dislike was putting it mildly, from what I had seen of the two of them.

Luft continued. "The presence of your opposite can agitate you instead of balance you, make you want to lash out even more or try to suppress your power, which never ends well. It's the Word most related to you that can sometimes calm you down, make you feel more stable. Khaya... wouldn't be good for you right now."

I tried to absorb that. He'd told me to reach out to her, so what the hell did this mean? Maybe it meant what I was already starting to think: not even Khaya could help me anymore.

"I'm not here about Khaya," he said. "For the most part, anyway, except to suggest something else with regard to her."

My eyes shot to the surveillance cameras in alarm.

"They're not on," Luft said quickly. "I had Carlin ask for them to be shut off, since the garden is even less used than ever, now that it's... " He gestured around. "Or at least that's the reason Carlin gave to security, and since he's a Godspeaker, they listened. I've been waiting for you to come up here again."

"So we can talk? Where's Khaya? How can I find her?" I edged closer to Luft in my anticipation.

He took a step back in the dead grass, raising a hand as if to stop me. "I don't know. You're the only one who might be able to contact her—the only one she would trust."

Suspicion flashed through me again. Or maybe I was just *really* looking for a reason to try to kill him. "Why risk telling me to reach her if you don't have anything more to give me? Why do you think I should?"

He dropped his hand. "I thought it might be for your own good, but now ... I'm not so sure."

"You're being pretty damned vague."

"For a reason."

"But if she could've helped me before, why can't she now?" Then again, *I* had been the one hoping she could help me or get me out of here; Luft had never actually said anything about that. "Did you want me to find her for another reason? If you're working with the City Council ... "

"I'm not," Luft said, glancing almost nervously at the door. "Only with Carlin. But I shouldn't talk about that, not even here. Just listen to me—I don't think it's a good idea anymore. Trust me."

"I'm not sure I can."

"Then don't. But it sounds like you don't know where she is anyway, so it's moot."

Now I really wanted to kill him. He'd gotten my hopes up and then brought them crashing back down. "I'm supposed to just ... *forget* about seeing Khaya again?"

Luft gestured at me. "Look at yourself! Do you think you really belong anywhere near her right now? You're having a hard enough time not coming at me ... which I don't recommend, by the way."

I actually looked down at myself. My hands were buried in the dead grass, either to hold myself back or to claw my way forward to get at him. I had no idea what my expression looked like, but it probably wasn't any better. Maybe that was all this was about. Before, he'd been looking out for me in thinking I should contact Khaya, but now he was looking out for *her*. I was too dangerous. My legs folded under me and I sat back down in a puff of dust, putting my face in my hands.

"The more pressing issue is you," Luft said, as if confirming my theory. "You need to take care of yourself and not go off the deep end."

I'd heard this before, from Swanson, Brehan, and Drey: *Stay in line, don't lose it, keep killing.* Luft had been the only one to tell me any different, but now this. I didn't know if I should trust what he'd been saying before, or what he was saying now.

"So," I said through my hands, "if Khaya can't help me, who can?"

"Which Word is most like Death?" he asked. "Who was supposed to be your neighbor, before Andre and Brehan worked something else out? I think what they did helped cheer you up, but this kind of affinity between the Words runs even deeper than brain chemistry."

It was interesting that Brehan had apparently played a role in getting me Khaya's apartment, but I couldn't focus on that for long. I dropped my hands. "*Mørke*? You really think more darkness would do me good right now?"

Luft shrugged. "Like I said, Agonya helps me, and vice versa. It was the same with Brehan and Khaya, Pavati and Tu … and Herio and Mørke. You don't even have to like the other person. But with them around, you just feel stronger, more stable."

"So I just ask Mørke to come hang out with me when I'm feeling most murderous?" I laughed. "I'm sure she'd love that."

Luft glanced at the door. "She's outside right now."

I sat up straight. "When the hell were you planning on telling me that?"

"I've been *trying* to tell you. I asked her to come watch your lab session today with me. She recognized the signs of you getting a little … borderline … and agreed to come up here." His fingers tapped out a beat on his jeans as he studied me. "So, can I let her in?"

I flopped back on the ground, sending up the biggest cloud of dust yet, which swirled in the fading sunlight. "This is somehow embarrassing."

"Then I'll take it as a compliment that you're not embarrassed around *me*."

"When two people have shared homicidal feelings for each other … you know," I told the high ceiling.

Luft threw his head back and laughed. "I'll go get her and leave you two alone." He took a few steps, then paused to look back at me. "You'll be fine, you know."

"Right," I said with no conviction whatsoever.

He only shook his head, smiling slightly, and headed for the door. I didn't watch him leave, or her come in. It really *was* embarrassing, needing someone you didn't even know to help handle the darkness inside of you. Although I supposed she *was* the Word of Darkness.

Still, in place of Khaya and a vibrant garden, I was getting Mørke and darkness. Not a great trade. I felt like a complete jerk for thinking it, but there it was.

The door to the hallway slid open and closed. Her steps crunched over the dry grass. She stopped within twenty feet of me, though I could likely run faster than her. Then again, she could just blind me and run in a different direction.

"Hey again," she said, in a voice that seemed to be in a permanent state of mild sarcasm.

"Hey," I said tentatively. I took my first glance at her. This time she was wearing a lacy black dress and gloves ... with very high-heeled black boots. "You'll definitely want to keep a safe distance. Safer than that."

"Nah." She sat down in the dead grass, arranging her skirt over her knees. If Luft's hair had been bright, hers *glowed* in the remaining sunlight.

"You don't think I'll try to kill you?" I purposefully didn't get up off my back, even at the risk of appearing rude. I'd probably slip into a runners' starting position if I did, like I had with Luft.

"Nope."

"And why the hell is that?"

"You like me." When I lifted my head to give her an incredulous—and probably asshole-ish—look, she added, "Or at least your Word does. See?" And then she said a few things in what I assumed was Norwegian, since that was where her donor parent was from.

Black tendrils shot out over the ground, weaving like snakes until they were twining around me. I wanted to pull away until ... something happened. The Words relaxed inside of me. Kind of like how the normal part of me relaxed around Pie. I suddenly didn't feel the need to pull away or do much of anything, such as drown the city in blood.

"That's … incredibly weird," I said, laying my head back down. She didn't say anything, just let the darkness dance over the dead grass, and over me. "So the Word of Death helps you like this, too?" I asked.

"Yeah, sort of. I haven't needed it lately, but Death just, I don't know, gives Darkness more substance or something, so I don't get lost in it as much."

"Sorry. There's nothing left around here for me to kill." Except her. But she was right—I didn't feel the urge to kill her anymore. It was as if the Word of Death had recognized a friend.

She met my eyes through all of her black eyeliner. "You don't have to kill anything. Just let the Words run through you, and I'll feel it."

That was exactly what the Words inside of me wanted to do. I closed my eyes—needlessly, with the darkness beginning to slip over my face—and I opened my mind. Death seemed to well up from the dry ground like water, running over my body. The river was all around me again. But it was only the calm that I'd found before, that floating feeling, rather than the deep tug trying to drag me under, down to somewhere frightening. If Death grounded her for whatever reason, Darkness seemed to free me. Float me on top.

I closed my eyes and let the river carry me.

thirteen

I almost felt normal when I left Khaya's dead garden with Mørke—as normal as I could feel as the Word of Death. The Word was fully present inside of me but calm, leaving me steady and sure rather than homicidal.

Maybe Tavin and Death could finally begin to coexist peacefully together. Perhaps the Word was like a tool, and could be used either to put old cats to sleep or to eviscerate people. Obviously there were times when it was more dangerous than others, but trying to deny it only seemed to make it hungrier. It seemed better for me to just ride out those moments in privacy...and maybe with a little help from Mørke.

"Thanks," I said to her, blinking in the electric light of the hallway outside the garden. The sun had set, and the Athenaeum twinkled below us through the windows, and yet it looked bright to eyes that had been shrouded in total darkness for over an hour.

She flashed a smile up me—she was a good foot shorter than me. "So...where are you headed? To the mess hall?"

"Nah, I think I'll eat in my apartment." Which probably meant I'd eat a bowl of Captain Crunch for dinner. "I need to hang out with my dog and make sure she hasn't started chewing on the couch again. And I owe Brehan a session on this racing game of his." I said all of this before realizing she might have been wanting to hang out with me ... beyond sitting next to me in silence and blanketing me in darkness, rather. "Uh, want to come?" I added.

She made a face before I barely had the invitation out. "Better not."

"Oh ... because of the whole Darkness versus Light thing?"

She nodded. "Brehan's all right. We're both just kind of ... on edge around each other, is all."

"Ah, well," I said, trying not to think how Khaya and I were opposites too now. "Some other time, then?"

"I'm sure." She arched a pale eyebrow at me. "Let me know if you need me."

"Um ... likewise." It felt odd saying that, seeing as we hardly knew each other, but it was the least I could offer.

She took my bare hand, which made me blink in surprise. But then she did something vastly more shocking. She stood up on her tiptoes and hugged me. It was quick, but her slight body pressed into mine. And then, before I could do or say anything, she was walking away.

She headed for the main elevators as if nothing had happened, high-heeled black boots clicking down the hall and black lace dress swishing around her legs. I stared after her in astonishment for a second, and then I bolted for the less-used back elevator. Drey had given me a keycard to access it. That was about all I could access, other than the Death Factory, but I still appreciated it. I especially appreciated the privacy now.

Okay, that didn't really mean anything, I told myself as I ducked into the elevator and dragged a hand through my hair. The hand stayed there, squeezing the skull that had had a little too much crammed into it for one day. People often hugged as a way to say hello or goodbye. That was all that was ... except that I was the Word of Death and I couldn't remember the last time someone had hugged me.

So what the hell *could* it mean? Mørke and I obviously got along easily, so easily it was almost strange. Which probably had more to do with the fact that our Words got along well.

My hand squeezed my head even tighter, pulling hairs at their roots, but it was nothing compared to the hand that gripped my heart. It would be all too easy: Spend more and more time with Mørke. Do better and better as the Word of Death. Forget about Khaya completely, because everything with Khaya was so hard it was maybe impossible.

I didn't know if I *could* forget about Khaya, but everyone seemed to be telling me that I should try. And yet, without her, without even the thought of her to help me resist the Word of Death—rather than help me get along with it, like Mørke did—where would I end up? Who would I be?

I wasn't sure I would be Tavin anymore. But maybe being Tavin was just too hard. Maybe I was fooling myself and hadn't entirely been him for a while now.

I dropped my hand. I couldn't start thinking like that. I didn't know what I should do, but I was right on one count— I'd had enough for one day. I needed to turn off my brain.

By the time I visited Brehan's end of our hallway a half-hour later, with Pie in my arms, I'd just about shoved the horror of the chimpanzee and the confusing situation with Mørke out of my mind. Pie had helped with that. I was still picking couch fluff out of her mouth when Brehan opened the door.

"Is she so sweet she spits up cotton candy?" he asked, holding the door open for me.

"Want to try some?" I held out a slobbery piece and he cringed away, as I'd hoped. "It's couch-stuffing. Pie has reached the adorable stage where she eats furniture."

"Man, the jade leather one? That's a nice couch."

"She thinks so too."

"Well, let's see how she likes mine," Brehan said, closing the door behind us. "I'm joking. If she eats my couch, I'll turn into the Word of Dog Slippers. Shit will hit the fan."

"I'm sure she could help you out with the shit too. There's no shortage at my place."

He laughed and then led the way into his apartment.

Although Brehan and I had hung out a few times in the past week, this was the first time I'd managed to get Pie and myself to his place, as close as it was. His apartment was pretty awesome, bright and open with spherical, ornate brass lamps hanging all over the place that looked like small suns. Gold shot through the creamy marble of his counter tops, and shades of yellow were in abundance on the walls and furniture.

"It's ... sunny in here, for lack of a better word," I said, grinning. I set Pie down and she immediately ran to sniff everything in the vicinity. "Kind of reminds me of ... never mind, that's a stupid comparison."

"No, what?" Brehan said, leaning against the kitchen counter. "Spit it out."

"I guess it reminds me of the garage where I grew up with Drey. Obviously not in how that place looked," I said quickly, "but he painted the walls bright yellow, kind of like that shade in the living room, because he said I needed more sunlight in there." Before Brehan could say it sounded cool or something, even though it didn't, I added, "We drove by there when Drey and I got to leave the Athenaeum last week, which is probably why I thought of it."

"Was that when you got jumped by the junkyard dog?" Brehan said, turning for the fridge.

"Yep. More like when I jumped it. It wasn't doing anything but being a vicious psycho in its own home before I got there. In any case, I definitely haven't gotten out since then, and I probably won't ever aga—is that *beer*?"

Brehan had already pulled two brown bottles out of the fridge, set them on the counter, and dug a bottle opener out of a drawer by the time I recognized the logo. He grinned as he popped off the caps and handed me an open bottle before the metallic clatter had died.

"Cheers," he said, raising his beer to clink with mine.

I still couldn't quite get over what I was seeing and holding. "They allow you to have *beer*?"

"It's all about how politely you ask. You've seen my gaming setup, right?" He pointed with his bottle toward the living room and then took a swallow. He tilted the beer back, as if examining the contents. "There's some concern about alcohol and lack of judgment with how we might use the Words, but Mira trusts me. What, Drey wouldn't get you any?"

"He'd only just started offering me one once in a while when ... well, when 'shit hit the fan' and my career in garbage was cut short. I guess I hadn't thought to ask him for some here yet." I hesitated, eyeing my bottle, cold with condensation in my hand. "Probably because he'd say no, since lack of judgment and the Word of Death especially don't go well together."

At that, I laughed and took a massive swallow. What better way to take my mind off of things? Crisp, slightly bitter liquid fizzed its way down my throat. Stifling a burp, I said, "Gods, that's good."

"So tell me about the garage."

I shook my head. "You don't want to hear about that."

Brehan rolled his eyes. "That's why I *asked*. So, sunny yellow walls and ... ?"

I took another fizzing gulp and moved into the living room. "I can't. I just need to forget about it. After all, *sunny* apparently doesn't do it for me anymore. Only darkness."

"Ah, so you found out about that," he said, following me. "All of that just has to do with the Words, man, not you. You can still like sunshine even if the Word of Death likes the dark." He gave me a mock-suggestive grin.

I shrugged, not wanting to go into the details about Mørke whatsoever, and threw myself down on the couch, careful not to spill my beer on the tapestry-like upholstery. It looked like it actually had gold thread in there with all the creamy silk. "So show me this gaming system of yours."

Brehan sighed. But he showed me, turning on the flat screen TV and the black box nearby.

As a joke I chose, from among our ridiculous options, a car with huge chrome tailpipes, shiny black paint, and a skull-and-crossbones plastered across the hood. As if to make a point, Brehan chose an incongruous blue one with white speed-stripes. In no time at all I was laughing my ass off trying to ram him off the road. And then a couple—or four—more beers might have left the fridge while we raced around what was supposedly the city of L.A. at insane speeds.

At some point, driving a virtual car down a virtual street, I was struck again by the feeling that I didn't belong in the world anymore. I was something inhuman, external … eternal. Or at least the Word was—the Word of one of the Two Nameless Gods who'd created everything. Part of me wanted to shudder, and part of me was in awe. Or maybe that was just the beer going to my head.

And then I remembered my mortality when I accidentally careened into a wall at top speed and blew up.

Brehan stretched, yawning wide. I tossed my controller down on the couch next to me and rubbed my bleary eyes. Pie was already asleep between us.

"It must be that time," I said. I stood and stretched too ... and then promptly sat back down. "Gods, I guess I don't have much of a tolerance. Three beers and I'm done."

He laughed. "We'll practice."

I nodded. "Practice drinking beer. Practice torturing intelligent mammals to death. All in a day's work." I was surprised I said that. I doubted I would have if I hadn't been drunk.

"That sucks," Brehan said, his face growing serious. For once he wasn't trying to cheer me up.

I attempted standing again with reasonable success, and picked up Pie as I did. "Yeah. But I'll be fine. I'm already getting the hang of it. Getting used to it."

Getting used to death. All I needed was enough practice to condition me, enough darkness to blind me, and enough beer to lull me, and apparently I could get used to anything.

Brehan's nod was grim. For a second, it looked like he wanted to say something, but he didn't.

"What?" I asked.

He shrugged. "I just have this feeling, you know. That everything's going to be all right for you."

"Weird." I hiccupped. "People keep telling me that, and I keep not believing them. Anyway, I'm going to crash."

When I stepped out into the hallway and closed the door behind me, I realized I was wrong about crashing. And "people" were definitely wrong, on top of that. Because Drey stood in the hallway, which at this time of night meant I wouldn't be all right.

It hit me like a punch in the kidney that I was starting to dread the sight of him. It didn't help that he had a small entourage: Swanson and Carlin. Luft's Godspeaker was of medium height and skin-tone, with a widow's peak and a black goatee that gave his face a sharp, angular appearance. My biological father looked the same as usual: tall and pale with neat silver-streaked hair and an immaculate gray suit. No wonder he didn't want to be my Godspeaker. He would have had to get dirty.

"I didn't do anything," I blurted out first thing, which was about as good as shouting, *I've been drinking beer!*

"I know," Drey said.

So it wasn't about the beer. Drey looked nervous, which made me fifty times more nervous than if it had just been about the beer.

"It's good that you're still up," he continued, "otherwise I would have had to wake you. Put Pie inside your apartment and let's go."

"No," I said, but I walked down the hall and slipped Pie in the door anyway. I didn't want her to get mixed up in whatever was going on. Marching back to Drey, I practically hissed, "I already killed a damned chimpanzee today, and it's after midnight. What do you want with me?"

In the past, I would never have spoken to him like that. It was another sign of how far we'd come—how far we'd fallen.

I rounded on Swanson. "And what the hell do *you* want?"

Swanson only gave me a stony look, which was as much as I expected.

"You shouldn't take that tone with your father," Drey said, but he sounded awkward and half-hearted. Everyone knew he was way more of a father to me … or, at least, he used to be.

I wasn't concerned about awkwardness, not at this hour. "He hasn't exactly been around enough lately—or *ever*—for me to give a rat's—"

"A situation has arisen," Swanson interrupted, just as I was getting warmed up. He gestured down the hall, toward the elevator. "And you need to come with us. I'm afraid you don't have a choice in the matter."

fourteen

Drey shot Swanson a stern look, as if they were a bickering married couple, which would have made me laugh under normal circumstances. But he didn't challenge Swanson's edict that I had to go with them, in spite of the fact that it was middle of the night and I was headed to bed. Not to mention that I was exhausted and a bit drunk.

"Come on," Drey said, gesturing down the hallway to the elevator like Swanson had. "I'll explain on the way."

"This can't be good." It was another thing I wouldn't have said aloud if not under the influence...and not the last thing. "So why are they here?" I nodded at Swanson and Carlin.

Drey didn't answer. Neither did the other two, but there was an awkwardness lingering between all of them as they moved for the elevator with me in their wake. Swanson must've been there to make sure Drey did whatever he was supposed to do, and maybe Carlin was backup. The first step was to drag me out of bed, obviously, and I wondered what the rest of it would involve.

I only waited as long as it took the mirrored elevator doors to close on the four of us to say, "So?"

Drey cleared his throat. "The situation is that one of Cruithear's and Khaya's automatons is … malfunctioning … and the City Council decided it should be exterminated immediately."

I suddenly felt dizzy. "And they want me to do it."

They all nodded in the mirrors.

I'd finally reached the stage where I had to kill something human-sized. An automaton might not actually be human, but it sure as hell looked like one. This was the penultimate stage before the real thing. No, not a *thing*—an actual human.

I'd already killed an automaton, months ago in the Alps, but I'd been damned-near out of my mind from the Word of Death at the time and hardly remembered it. This definitely didn't feel familiar.

"And this couldn't wait until morning?" I wished it could have waited forever, though even I knew that was an impossibility.

"It was acting unpredictably and had to be sedated," Swanson said.

Carlin spoke up, in a surprisingly deep voice. "The City Council thought it would be best to deal with it immediately, to avoid any embarrassing indiscretions."

"Oh, like, the *truth* that they exist?" My words were heavy with sarcasm.

"Something like that," Drey said.

They almost sounded like they'd rehearsed this. An uncomfortable idea began to form in the fog of my mind.

What if this was planned? What if they wanted me near the automaton for a different reason? What if the City Council had determined I'd failed at being the Word of Death, never mind that I was just getting a grip on it? These three had come late at night so I'd be confused and sleepy, all the easier to lure into the same room with it...

But that didn't make sense either. Why bother waking me up first? They could have just sneaked into my room and shot me with a decent dose of whatever Ryse had given me when she'd made me kill Khaya's garden. Then I would have done whatever they'd told me to do—even kill myself to hand the Word of Death over to an automaton.

Besides, however far Drey's and my relationship was deteriorating, I couldn't believe he'd cooperate with a plan like that.

Maybe this all felt weird because it *was* weird to get dragged out of your apartment at night in order to put down a dysfunctional automaton. The three of them had probably come with their show of authority and their explanations ready because they knew I wouldn't want to do this. Drey especially knew, which was likely why he was so antsy.

And I didn't want to do it. But Swanson was right: I didn't really have a choice.

We trekked the rest of the way to the lab in silence. We mostly had the tram to ourselves, and the one person who was in our car excused herself quickly and quietly when she saw three of the top Godspeakers and the Word of Death get on board. Smart lady.

The observation room was nearly as empty. I was surprised, since I'd assumed that the first time I killed anything remotely human-like, a crowd would gather. Although it *was* about one in the morning. And, as Carlin had said, the City Council preferred not to advertise their remaining automatons, especially a malfunctioning one. At least I wouldn't have an audience.

And, at the very least, another automaton would be gone. Swanson had said there were only a few left, which meant the chances of one replacing me would be smaller.

Only Luft and Mørke sat outside the lab, facing the windows, with Angelina sitting behind Mørke. Damage control, I imagined. Luft could keep me from speaking the Word of Death by vacuuming the oxygen out of my lungs if things got out of hand, and Mørke could calm me down... or blind me. I tried not to think about her hug the instant I saw her, and only partly succeeded. If I hadn't already had the stress of what I was about to face, I would have failed altogether.

Carlin seemed relieved to get away from Swanson and Drey and took a seat next to Luft. I didn't blame him. The tension was thick enough to slice and spread with butter. That left only the three of us to head into the lab. Luft was giving me a strange, almost worried look, but I didn't have time to think about it before I stepped inside.

Even though I'd been expecting it, the sight was still shocking. The usual steel table had been moved aside to accommodate a gurney. A man—an automaton, I reminded myself—was strapped on top of it, with a white sheet pulled nearly above its bare shoulders and an IV tube running underneath the sheet. Its features were nondescript, blank-looking. It was knocked out, of course, but its face wouldn't have looked any different had it been awake.

Drey and Swanson flanked me as I walked up to the gurney. A machine measured out the slow, steady pace of the automaton's heart with regular beeps and a line-graph to illustrate it. I took a deep breath, but I didn't feel any less dizzy.

Drey touched my shoulder and murmured, "Remember, it's barely even alive. You've done this before, and you don't have to do anything... showy. Just stop its heart."

I nodded, relieved. At least human-*like* blood wouldn't have to fly all over the room... or worse than blood. I tried to remember how it'd felt to kill the one in the Alps. But it had all happened too fast for me to recall much of anything.

"I'm... I guess I'm just going to go for it," I said.

Both Drey and Swanson nodded. I almost wanted to make a crack about how both my fathers were here for me on this momentous occasion, but I didn't have it in me, not even with the beer's help. I was mostly starting to feel queasy.

Just do it quickly, I told myself. I put a shaky hand on the white sheet—it wasn't death-proof material, so I didn't even have to touch any skin—and took another deep breath. When I closed my eyes, the Words were ready and waiting.

They heightened my awareness, like with the chimpanzee. I could hear and feel, and almost *see*, everything going on inside of it. The whole circulatory system buzzed in endless loops, like Brehan's and my cars racing around the streets of L.A. I ignored everything else, narrowing my focus and going for the source of all the motion: the heart pounding out a beat at the center of it all. And then I saw it—a flaw. The heart was already weak, and it took only the slightest Word to send it faltering. Something tugged on my focus, but I ignored it. I just wanted to get this over with and then go to sleep.

The beeping grew erratic, slow, and then held steady in one endless, high-pitched whine while the beating of the heart stopped. The whirling motion throughout the body ceased, and I opened my eyes to see a flat-lining graph.

I pulled my hand away. Other than the annoyingly prolonged beep, the room was incredibly quiet. I turned to look at Drey and Swanson. They were both watching me.

"That wasn't so bad," I said, only a little unsteadily.

But they were still looking at me expectantly, as if waiting for some other reaction.

"What?" I said, getting irritated. "Would you rather I freak out? Don't you want me to be calm? It's not like it was a hum—"

And then I realized what I should have realized earlier, as soon as Drey had told me to come with him and he was so nervous that he had to have Swanson and Carlin there with him. And I definitely should have realized it when I'd felt the flaw in the man's heart.

The *man's*, not the automaton's. Because why would a perfectly designed body have had a flaw? Why would it have even been malfunctioning in the first place?

How could I have been so *stupid*?

"Oh, Gods," I said, looking back and forth between the two of them. I shook my head. "You didn't. You didn't just do that to me."

Neither one said anything. Drey flinched, but I didn't see his expression for long before I bent over and emptied the beer-flavored contents of my stomach all over the floor. Swanson jumped back when the vomit splattered their shoes, but Drey didn't.

"Oh, Gods," I repeated to the mess on the tiles. "Oh, holy shit." I stayed bent over, my hands on my knees, because the room was spinning around me. Wiping my mouth, I glanced up at Drey. "You knew all along."

He nodded. "This was the only way to get you to do it. To accustom you to … this." He hesitated. "He was a murderer, if that helps."

"I'm a murderer now," I said with a dark laugh. "Should I kill myself?"

"Don't ever suggest anything like that again. Not even as a joke. This man was a lowlife, Tavin—"

"*We* were lowlifes!" I shouted, straightening and taking a rapid step toward him. He stepped back now. "Maybe we didn't sleep on the street, but we spent all day out there, picking up trash! Or have you already forgotten? Has being a prestigious Godspeaker again made you forget everyone and everything that ever mattered to us?"

"You were the only one who mattered to me—"

I couldn't believe it—either that no one else mattered to him, or that I mattered to him all that much. Not if he could do this to me. "What if that was Jacques? He's just the captain of a trash barge. Or one of the ladies under the bridge, like Chantelle? They're just prostitutes! They saved my life, Drey, and Khaya's life."

He reached forward to put a hand on my shoulder, his other hand gesturing for me to be quiet. "You're saying too much."

"Don't touch me!" I shoved him off, and the violence of it made his eyes go wide. I shoved him again, square in the chest, and he staggered back, grabbing the gurney for support and nearly falling. For a split second I felt ashamed, until I saw the body behind him—a man's body.

"I hate you," I spat. "I *hate* you."

His face closed off. "I knew you would."

"Then why are you *doing this to me*?" I yelled so loud that he leaned back, even though he couldn't step back any more. Out of the corner of my eye, I saw Swanson slide a syringe from his pocket, keeping it half-hidden in his palm. I pointed at him, and he froze. "Don't even try it. The *least* you people owe me is an explanation."

"I did it because... because it was better me than..." Drey swallowed and held my eyes. His eyes were so blue, so clear. "Because I love you like a son, and I would do anything for you. I would even let you blame me—let you hate me, if it made you hate yourself less." He took a breath. "You didn't know he wasn't an automaton, Tavin, so you can't blame yourself."

It was too much. I couldn't take it anymore. I backed away from him, then spun, heading for the door. I glared at Swanson as I went by, counting on the ferocity of my look to warn him not to stick me with anything. His own expression was apologetic, but it wasn't nearly apologetic enough.

"No more surprises or lies," Drey said behind me, right

before I reached the door. "I'll be straight with you from now on. They want you to assassinate someone."

That stopped me in my tracks.

"Who? Where?" My words were breathless.

The Words in my head were eager. They coiled inside in anticipation, like a snake ready to strike. I wished I could cut them out of my skull, out of my skin.

"You'll get a debriefing tomorrow," Swanson said, his voice reluctant. Regretful, even. "And you'll be flying out soon after that."

Flying out? So I'd not only be leaving the Athenaeum, but Eden City.

But only to kill someone else.

I couldn't even think about that right now. I had to get out of this room. I frantically swiped my keycard and, thank the Gods, it worked. As soon as the door slid open, I was gone, speed-walking through the outer rooms, past Luft and Carlin and Mørke and Angelina without looking at any of them. When I hit the white basement hallway, I broke into a run.

I wondered if they'd try to stop me, give me a sedative, or at least make sure I wasn't about to do something stupid. But they didn't. No doubt they were watching, ready to leap out at a second's notice, but they didn't get in my way.

I didn't know where I wanted to go other than out, far and away, but that wasn't an option. I headed for my apartment, since it was the only place I really had to go where I could lose it with a shred of privacy. There was Khaya's dead garden too, but it was too close, in the same building where

I'd just ended a human being's life. Besides, Luft and Mørke had followed me there once, and they might do it again.

I would have run all the way to my apartment, but I had to take the tram. At least I had it to myself at this late hour. I paced back and forth through the cars, alternating between biting my nails and making fists so hard I thought my hand would break.

I hadn't known. Maybe I should have, but I hadn't. I hadn't known it wasn't an automaton.

If I'd knowingly killed another human being in cold blood, that would've been it. I would've been done. I wasn't sure quite what that meant, but I felt it. That was why they'd come in the middle of the night. They knew I wouldn't do it under normal circumstances, or what passed for normal circumstances around here. They'd wanted me to be too thrown off to question what was going on, tired enough ... and maybe drunk enough to be fooled.

Brehan's words suddenly flashed through my mind: *There's some concern about alcohol and lack of judgment with how we might use the Words* ... By the sound of it, the Godspeakers didn't often let the Words drink. Except they'd let Brehan and me get drunk tonight. Did they only take advantage of the situation, or had it been a setup? Was Brehan in on all of this?

Once the idea occurred to me, I couldn't think of anything else. At least it gave me something to think about other than what I'd done.

I didn't know, I didn't know ...

Drey had given me that much, at least: ignorance. And

someone to blame other than myself. But he'd still betrayed me in the worst possible way. And, Gods help him, if Brehan had betrayed me too...

I punched the wall of the tram, leaving a huge dent in the shiny silver siding. The rest of the way back to the apartment passed in a blur. When I reached our green-and-gold hallway, I marched up to the golden door opposite mine and hammered on it without hesitating. I kept pounding, never mind what time it was, until Brehan opened it.

He barely had time to squint at me, yawn, and say, "Tav—" before I grabbed the front of his white undershirt, yanked him out into the hall, and slammed him up against the wall.

"Did you do it on purpose?" I shouted, practically nose-to-nose with him. "Did you give me beer on purpose, so I wouldn't think about what I was doing later?"

"No! What the—why? What happened to you?" His eyes were wide. But with the Word of Death in his face, he wasn't even afraid for himself.

Only for me.

I didn't answer. Instead I took deep gasping breaths as if I was trying not to drown. My grip on his shirt gradually relaxed and my hands slipped away from him.

As if I needed further proof that he hadn't done anything, he didn't even bother straightening his clothes. He only took a step *closer*, concern etching his face. "Something just happened. In the lab?"

I nodded. I couldn't speak. My voice was pinched off in my throat, like someone was strangling me.

He cursed under his breath. "They probably saw us drinking in the surveillance cameras and decided to spring something on you. They've woken us all up in the middle of the night before, to make us use the Words while we're half-asleep and disoriented—to prepare us for any situation, they say. I'm so sorry, man, but I didn't know. What happened?"

I hadn't known, either. I hadn't known … but it had still happened. I had still done it.

I staggered, and he caught my arm to try to keep me from falling.

"I … " My voice broke. "I killed someone." I sank to my knees in the hallway, burying my face in my hands. A sob tore out of my throat. More followed, continuing to rip through me, almost like they were physically tearing me apart. The truth poured out like blood, over and over again, as I rocked back and forth against the pain: "I killed someone. I killed someone. *I killed someone.*"

Brehan slid down next to me, his door still open. He didn't say anything, just leaned against the wall nearby, listening to me cry my throat ragged.

fifteen

I wasn't sure when Brehan dragged me to my bed, but he did at some point, just before the sun rose. He even pulled my shoes off and the bedcovers over me, and then he let me sleep.

I tried to sleep forever so I didn't have to wake up and remember, but my stupid body thwarted me. My eyes opened to afternoon sunlight streaming through the windows.

Pie scratched and whined at the closed bedroom door, but I couldn't let her in. My murderer's hands didn't deserve to touch her. I couldn't go to Khaya's garden for comfort either—not the living one or the dead one. The living one no longer existed, and the dead one was too...enabling. It all felt too easy there. None of my refuges could hide me anymore.

And yet, if I didn't float on that river of death lurking in the back of my mind, I would probably drown in it. It was already reaching out, wanting to buoy me—or suck me in—but I kept away from it. But this time, instead of being able to seal it away, I felt more like it was cornering me in my own head.

I couldn't move, either in my twisted inner world or in

the real one. I only stared at the ceiling through the green canopy above my bed. In place of my old mantra, *I'm Tavin,* a new phrase now played in my head on repeat to keep the Words at bay:

I didn't know, I didn't know, I didn't know …

But my silent chant didn't keep the people at bay. Brehan let himself into the apartment at some point—he must have still had my keycard from last night—but I didn't get up. I heard him pouring a bowl of dog food, and then calling out that he and Pie would be next door. Soon after, someone else knocked, shouting they had an important message for me, but I ignored the person.

And then Mørke came by.

The afternoon sun was sinking in the sky outside when I heard the soft tap on my bedroom door, and then her voice. "Tavin, it's me. Can I help with anything?"

I didn't want help becoming a murderer anymore. I wanted to destroy the murderer inside of me, even if that meant destroying myself.

I was tempted to just ignore her like I had everyone else, but I didn't want her to start speaking Words of Darkness through the doorway. And she just might, since she was clearly here to calm me down—whether that meant someone had sent her or she'd come on her own.

"No … thanks," I said, which was about all I could muster. It was muffled, from where the pillow lay half over my face to block the light.

Maybe she hadn't heard me, because she opened my

bedroom door. I wished it had a lock. Then again, a lock hadn't done much good for the outer apartment door.

"I'm not really in the mood for visitors." I spoke without looking at her, my eyes still shielded.

When she didn't answer, I glanced out from underneath the pillow and glimpsed the bottom half of her standing by my bedside. Her nails were now painted a purple so deep they were *nearly* black.

"How'd you get in?" I asked, since she still hadn't said anything.

"Brehan," she said. She'd tolerated his presence enough to have him let her in, apparently.

"So he thinks I need help too? Remind me to get my keycard back from him."

The slight shift of her weight settling on the bed made me yank the pillow the rest of the way off my face and myself into a sitting position.

"I said *no*, Mørke."

Again, she didn't shy away or leap up from where she sat on the edge of the bed or anything sane like that. Her eyes only narrowed for a second, looking fiercer than they probably would have if they weren't lined in so much black. The rays of the dying sun turned her hair into a glowing aura around her face.

Her voice was mildly indignant. "I'm not doing anything." She hesitated. "Though the Word of Darkness *is* more effective than a pillow, you know."

I scrubbed a hand over my face. I couldn't imagine how bad I looked, but I didn't really care. Because I still probably looked a hell of a lot better than the guy I'd just killed. "I don't want help. I don't want... anything."

"Well, then can't I just hang out?"

Such a simple question, and yet I felt like I was leaning over a cliff, staring at where I could end up with just a single step. So simple. So easy.

I took a deep breath, and in my mind I took a step back from the edge. "I told you, now's not the best time."

She looked down, her pale eyelashes glowing now. "Okay." She reached out, resting her hand on the bedcovers somewhere in the vicinity of my knee. "I'll be around if you change your mind." And then she slipped out of the room as quietly as she'd entered, an apparition of contrasting darkness and brightness.

Once she'd gone, I rolled over and stuffed the pillow over my head again.

Luft never came, but then Luft had known what was going to happen last night. That explained the worried look he'd given me. And yet he hadn't tried to warn me. Brehan, and even Luft himself, had admitted Luft was loyal to Carlin above all else, and Carlin... Not only was he involved in what had happened last night, but I had darker suspicions about him. It seemed like Luft had been trying to help me when he'd saved me from Ryse and wrote me that secret note, but then something—or someone—had convinced him to stop. And then he told me not to try to reach Khaya, and to accept being the Word of Death instead.

Which was the exact opposite of what I needed to do.

I had to get to her. She was my last hope, or I would

be finished. I knew this now. I couldn't just let myself slip into the skin of a monster and still live with myself.

So when Drey came, I got up and opened the door. Because of course *he* wasn't coming over to just hang out. I imagined whatever he had to say had to do with the important message someone had been trying to give me earlier—which likely had to do with my new assignment to assassinate someone. Swanson had said I would be debriefed today. He'd also implied that the mission would take me out of Eden City.

It was my last chance to escape.

Drey held a black folder in his hands when I let him in. He didn't say anything, only took it to the dining table and laid it open for me. Inside were quite a few typed documents that didn't hold my attention for long before I saw the glossy photograph inside—a photo of the man I was supposed to kill.

I recognized him.

"He was there in the Alps," I said, picking up the picture. "He was the man who came to meet Tu, to take him to China." Just like in person, the man's smile didn't reach his eyes.

"His name is Jiang Zhijun—Dr. Jiang," Drey said.

Of course the guy would be a doctor, I thought. It seemed like everyone here was, so why not members of other governments? It was a step up from *Mr.*, although still short of *Your Majesty*.

"He's a Chinese diplomat," Drey continued, "who has spent his life studying Eden City's relationship with the rest of the world."

"Didn't like what he saw, huh? Most people don't when they look a little bit closer."

Drey took the photo back, and replaced it in my hand with some documents I was probably supposed to read. "I can't imagine why. Anyway, as you well know, he overstepped the boundaries of diplomacy when he tried to direct Tu to China. He has since claimed that wasn't his intention, and that the whole thing was one big misunderstanding. Apparently he was planning to return all of you to Eden City under the guise of sheltering you."

That certainly hadn't been what it had sounded like. Tu's plan had been to go with Dr. Jiang back to China, but then he learned that Jiang had convinced the Swiss to facilitate it by agreeing to give them Pavati in exchange—which Tu wasn't about to let happen. The Swiss, meanwhile, had made their own deal, arranging to trade me and Khaya back to Eden City in exchange for the City Council giving up Pavati and Tu without a fuss.

It hadn't worked out like that. I hadn't even known that Dr. Jiang had survived our pitched battle out in the snow. With all four of the powerful Tangible Words involved in the fight, not many people had. But at least Khaya, Pavati, and Tu had escaped. I hadn't, of course.

I let the documents fall back onto the table. "So now Eden City wants him dead," I said, tugging out a chair and taking a seat. "Big surprise. I guess it's fitting that I'll be the one to kill him, since I screwed up his little plan in the first place."

Drey tapped the papers back into an orderly stack. "Remember, Dr. Jiang doesn't know you're the Word of

Death. No one does, outside of a select few. So while Jiang likely suspects an assassination attempt will be made, he won't think *you're* there for that purpose. In fact, he has already agreed to meet you."

I blinked. "How? *Why?* He might not know I'm the Word of Death, but if he knows I'm coming from Eden City—"

"He doesn't," Drey said, nodding at the documents with an exasperated look. "At the direction of the City Council, undercover agents have already arranged it, pretending to be you. According to what they've told him, you were separated in the chaos from the Words who've gone rogue, and now you're on the run. You're going to approach him with a deal—a fake deal, of course. We know he's the last person to have been in contact with Tu, and by extension, Khaya. If he agrees to take you to Khaya, you will promise him—and China—the support of the rogue Words."

It was a deal I was damned-near willing to actually make, never mind how I would convince the "rogue" Words to go along with it. Too bad it was fake.

Unless I could actually make it happen.

"So then I just ... kill him?" I asked, waving a hand like it was no big deal.

I didn't know, I didn't know ...

"You'll pretend to give him time to think it over and to contact or locate Tu," Drey said, oblivious to my silent chanting. "But when you shake his hand, use your Word in a way that won't kill him immediately, but slowly, painfully, and inexplicably. You'll have to mix the Words in with a speech, in a way that won't give you away. I've drafted some possible suggestions . . . " He shuffled through the stack and pulled out a few papers.

I only half-looked at them. "Nice—a death speech, sort of like a backwards eulogy. So who will be with me? They couldn't possibly trust me enough to send me alone."

"I'll be with you. More would look suspicious. You're supposed to be a fugitive, after all, with no ties to Eden City. Besides, Jiang only agreed to meet the two of us. We'll have backup, but they'll stay out of sight at a safe distance."

Distant enough for me to lose them, I hoped, after I took care of a few problematic details. That was good news. There was still the slight problem of Drey being with me, but it was a small one in the grand scheme of things. "Will you . . . help me do it, if I can't?"

Drey shook his head. "I can't reveal who you are. If I step in and start godspeaking, the world will know. And then they'll also know Eden City has essentially started a war with China."

Perfect. Drey wouldn't force me. But I couldn't act like that was a good thing, or that anything about this plan was good. I tapped the photo on the table, sounding dubious. "They're going to know something is up if this guy dies."

"They'll have suspicions. Fear. That's different—nothing concrete to rally around."

"So, since Eden City can't invade the rest of the world without Khaya, they're just going to start assassinating anyone who disagrees with them?"

"I can't say. But I can say I'm under strict orders not to assist you in any way, only in the extreme case that your life is at risk. For once this is all you, Tavin. I'm sorry, but a lot is riding on your shoulders." He hesitated, reshuffling the papers. "I'm also worried. I know all of this is happening much faster than either you or I would like. But the City Council wants you to be ready for what's coming. They only want you to succeed, I'm sure."

Which meant he thought they wanted me to fail. Or at least someone wanted me to.

"So you can't disappoint them," he continued. "*We* can't disappoint them. You must complete this mission."

We. The word contained several people's fates: mine, Drey's, and Swanson's. We were surrounded by those who wanted to see us hang ourselves with our own rope—particularly Ryse, and those in the City Council whose support she had gained. But there was a way for me to fail and for Drey and me to survive, at least: our escape. Swanson would just have to fend for himself.

Because if I succeeded in my mission, *I* wouldn't survive. *I didn't know, I didn't know...*

"You once encouraged me to gain people's admiration, not their fear," I murmured aloud, looking up at Drey. "Remember that? What happened to that?"

He met my eyes. "Keeping you alive and sane is what happened."

I gave him a non-smile. "Sometimes I'd rather be dead."

He leaned back from the table, a wince flickering across his face so fast it was almost like it wasn't there. "I'm sorry. I've tried to do the best I can under the circumstances. With any luck, things will settle into a more normal routine for you."

"A routine of killing political figures. Sounds good." I barked a laugh before I hopped up from the chair. "You know, in a sick way, I'm still taking out the Athenaeum's trash."

"Tavin—"

We'd avoided talking about last night so far, and I wanted to keep it that way. "When do we leave?" I interrupted, heading for the bedroom to change my clothes.

"Tonight. We're flying to Beijing just before midnight."

I froze only a few steps from the table, my pulse pounding in my throat and making it hard to breathe. "Wow. Swanson said 'soon,' but I didn't think it would be *this* soon. Not really leaving me much time to prepare, are they?"

Drey shook his head, leaving the obvious unspoken: I was supposed to wimp out and return to the Athenaeum as a failure. Maybe they didn't care if this Dr. Jiang actually lived or died.

"How long will we be gone?" I asked. Never mind that I had no intention of ever coming back.

"Only six hours. Long enough to meet with Jiang and leave. There will be no time for mistakes or second attempts."

"I'm taking Pie," I blurted. "She'll help take my mind off of things, before and . . . after. It'll be easier with her there."

Drey hesitated, and for a moment I was worried that he knew what I was thinking. But then he said, "I'm sure that can be arranged. And there's no need to pack anything else. I have civilian clothes for you."

Right, because I was no longer a civilian.

He retrieved a black backpack from the hallway and unpacked it on the table. Luckily, the clothes inside weren't black. The shirt was long sleeved and dark blue, and there were a pair of denim jeans, white socks, and sturdy brown boots. Drey couldn't easily godspeak through me with this outfit, which meant he was actually telling the truth. He wouldn't use me to kill Jiang once I made my real plan obvious... which didn't involve killing Jiang whatsoever.

When he pulled out the *front*-zipping gray hoodie, I saw that the sleeves had thumb holes—to make sure they stayed down over my monitor bracelets, I realized. I had no idea if Jiang would know what the black bands around both my wrists were, but someone thought he might. And then he'd know there was something very wrong with my story.

If I didn't tell him the real story first.

"We could just take these off, you know," I said, lifting my forearms with their ever-present monitors.

At a glance, they almost looked like black plastic bracelets, but everyone in the Athenaeum, at least, knew them for the highly sophisticated tracking devices they were. There wasn't much chance I could leave here without them, but at least I could try. If it worked, it'd make part of my plan a hell of a lot easier, or at least eliminate an unknown. I was only operating under the hopeful assumption that Jiang would know how to get them off quickly, especially since China had been trying to get their hands on Tu for a while. Tu had removed his monitor on his own, with Pavati's help, but Jiang wouldn't have been expecting that. Which led me to believe that Jiang must have easy, spur-of-the-moment access to something that could do the job. But I didn't know that for sure, and I wouldn't know until I asked him face-to-face.

Drey shook his head. "You know that's not possible. I don't need to remind you that you can't—"

"Can't what, make a joke?"

"Try anything. And no, you can't joke about this."

"*This* wouldn't be a life-or-death situation, would it?" I swept the clothes up off the table. "Don't you think I know? And the bracelets will look pretty damned suspicious if someone notices them."

"Metal detectors won't pick them up."

"And what if the person patting me down finds them? What if they ask me to take them off? Oh right, I'll just ask whoever it is to pardon me while I cut off both my thumbs somehow." I rolled my eyes as if the thought was absurd and then headed for the bedroom again, new clothes in my arms.

Drey sighed. "Let's hope no one notices them. They shouldn't. Cruithear's technology is well-guarded."

I paused with my hand on the doorknob. "*She* made these?"

He nodded.

How ironic. As the Word of Shaping, she was the only one who had a monitor inserted into her brain instead of worn around her wrist, since she could have simply re-shaped the bracelet to get it off. Reshaping her brain would kill her. At least my last resort of losing both thumbs—temporarily, I hoped—was better than that.

I appreciated my thumbs a lot while getting dressed. Last resort or not, it might come down to that, but I'd gladly let Jiang hack them off if it meant I could be free from Eden City. I didn't think Jiang would mind too much, since the only alternative I'd offer would be his speedy demise. Not that I *would* kill him, but he didn't have to know that. All he'd know was that he'd stand to gain the possible support of the rogue Words, including me … and also his life.

And that deal was better than anything the City Council could have me pretend to offer him.

sixteen

The clothes were the first normal things I'd worn in a while, and they fit well. And yet I still felt like an impostor, both in the mirror in my bedroom that evening and getting off the jet in Beijing, China, at four p.m. the next day. It was a private jet, of course, so no one bothered Drey or me within our ring of well-dressed security guards when we disembarked. But I still felt like a handgun hidden in somebody's bag, not like a filthy rich kid from Liechtenstein flying around the world with my filthy rich dad and my purebred greyhound puppy. The ten-hour flight, plus the six-hour time difference, had done nothing to persuade my subconscious otherwise, even though Drey and I had gone over the plan about five hundred times on the plane.

Rich father and son were our pretend roles for now, Drey's and mine, at least as far as the airport went. My shiny new Liechtenstein passport confirmed it for the customs official waiting on the tarmac just for us. I also had a passport with my real name in my backpack, complete with battered edges, dirt stains, and supposedly all of the right stamps in order for me to have trekked all the way from the Swiss Alps to Beijing, if Jiang felt like cross-checking the made-up facts of the *other* pretend story. Apparently, producing all sorts of forgeries on short notice to back up whatever lies they wanted to tell was no problem for the City Council, with the Word of Shaping on hand.

Keeping track of the lies was a different story. But I wasn't planning on bothering for long.

This was only my second time out of Eden City, and most definitely the farthest away from home I'd ever been. As of yet, I couldn't see much but a dusty haze hovering in the distance. But from the jet, the city had appeared endless. We were apparently about a half-hour drive from our hotel in the northeast of the city—close to where Jiang wanted to meet.

The air was crisper and drier here, and smelled…different. Sweet, but it was an artificial sweet. My hopes had better not be the same. I glanced at Drey as we made our way beyond the customs official to the waiting black limo, and I somehow managed to avoid tangling my legs in Pie's leash as she bounded around me in her excitement to be off the plane.

"We won't be cuffed together this time?"

"We might as well be," Drey muttered out of the side of his mouth as the driver got out to open the door for us.

As in, if I escaped, it would be like it was with the cuffs—I'd be cutting off his hand, so to speak, and killing him. Our fates were pretty tied. But if anyone was going to lose any appendages, it would be me losing my thumbs. And I'd be freeing Drey along with myself.

Drey's graying hair was slicked back, and he wore a ridiculous ensemble composed of a pale blue polo shirt, white cardigan, and pale plaid pants with matching visor. The platinum wristwatch probably cost more than every possession I'd ever owned combined. He looked like he was about to go golfing in Monaco, or maybe enjoy a cigar and a tumbler of brandy on his veranda. I wasn't even entirely positive what a veranda was, but, in other words, he was a walking stereotype.

Under normal circumstances, I'd take advantage of this fabulous opportunity to mock him without mercy. But you had to have a sound-enough relationship with someone to mock them, and at the moment Drey and I were anything but sound.

We slipped into the back of the limo after Drey gave the driver the name of our no-doubt-swanky hotel. Behind us, our security guards followed in a black SUV...but they wouldn't be within sight for long, especially not once we went to meet Jiang. And then *I* would be out of sight, once I got the monitors off.

The limo started moving and I got to watch the city rise around us through the tinted black windows. And what a city it was.

In Eden City, the neighborhoods were segregated, but here, the rich and poor were tossed together amid a patchwork of buildings—some that rivaled the best in Eden City, and some that were worse than the worst. People in sleek suits heading for private cars jostled with people in shapeless uniforms waiting for busses. Dirty carts with street food parked on the corners in front of sparkling high-rises.

I loved it. Pie was less interested in the view than she was in the leather upholstery, but Drey kept her from chewing on the seats while I stared out the window in awe.

There was writing everywhere: strung across banners, riding up the sides of buildings, hanging over shops, and even lining the street at some intersections. Tu had the same type of writing as on his back, revealing the Word of Earth inside of him, but now that I'd learned the English alphabet, these characters somehow looked far more incomprehensible than they had before.

"How can they know all of these symbols?" I asked, peering outside as we crawled through bumper-to-bumper traffic that stretched across multiple lanes. I knew I sounded like a dolt, but I didn't care. "How do they remember what they mean?" I hadn't noticed much of a discernible pattern in the complex slashes of script.

Drey shrugged. "It's a difficult language. And yet they have a literacy rate higher than Eden City."

So even the lower classes could decipher these symbols that I couldn't even begin to understand.

I felt a rising desperation at being so close to freedom, but not quite able to touch it. I almost wanted to leap out of the car and make a run for it then and there. But I would have stood out more than a flashing neon sign. The monitors wouldn't even have been necessary in tracking me down; people could've pointed the way to me.

At least that was the case until we made our way into what was clearly a rich section of the city and I saw an embassy flag or two. Foreigners of all shapes and colors began appearing. If I tried to lose myself in this crowd, it wouldn't be as hard.

"Jiang lives near here?" I asked, my breath fogging the window. I practically had my face mashed against the glass.

"Yes, or at least he owns a flat in this neighborhood. He's rich enough to abandon it, most likely, if we're not what we seem. And here's our hotel."

We pulled up to the exact type of building I'd imagined: shiny, sleek, and towering, with what had to be a dozen golden doors facing the street. It would've looked nearly the same a half a world away in Eden City. Maybe all hotels for rich people were this cookie-cutter.

"There's only time for me to change, and then we have to go," Drey reminded me.

"I know," I said, my stomach clenching.

It wasn't dimmer outside only because of the tinted windows. It was nearing dusk when we stepped out of the limo. Drey didn't give me much time to look around before he hustled me into the lobby and checked us in. I saw our room for nearly as short a time as he shrugged out of his clothes in favor of something less dorky, though the gray button-up shirt and black slacks still screamed of wealth. That was the idea, but he didn't want to look like the *exact* same rich person who'd just flown in on a jet. We were supposed to have been hiding here for a couple of weeks, after all.

My clothes weren't deemed remarkable enough to change, and Drey had been the distraction, anyway. He'd argued that the best disguise for me was one that drew no attention to itself.

"Pie needs to stay here," Drey said, buttoning his cuffs. As if he sensed I was about to disagree, he added, "Jiang will wonder how you got her, and besides, she was seen at the airport."

I was satisfied with my minimal preparation, which had involved finger-combing my hair and putting on deodorant, so I sat down on one of the king-sized beds in our suite. "Then I stay too."

He dropped his hands to stare at me incredulously. "You'll risk both of us just to bring her along? Tavin, she'll be here when we get back. And she'd be frightened when you ... you know. I think dogs can sense it. You don't want to put her through that."

I couldn't exactly tell him that I wasn't planning on coming back *or* using the Word of Death ever again, if I could help it. So I just said, "I'll leave her outside. This flat of his is up in a huge building, with a lobby and everything, right? We can leave her down there."

"And I'm sure whoever is watching the lobby will be overjoyed to babysit her." He snatched up his black jacket and whipped it on. "No, she's not coming."

"Please," I said, not needing to fake the desperation in my voice. "Knowing she's there will help. And what if we have to run in a hurry?"

"We won't if you stick to the—"

"Come on!" I damned-near shouted. "You're making me kill someone ... again! It's a pretty small favor to ask in return, to have my dog right there to comfort me afterward, since *you* definitely won't."

"Keep your voice down!" Drey hissed. "Are you trying to risk everything?"

Yes. But I couldn't say that either, so I just stared at him, my jaw clenched together.

"Don't look at me like that," he said. "I'm the only reason you have that dog in the first place."

My voice came out cold. "You're also the only reason I haven't happily been the Word of Death all my life *or* blissfully ignorant as a trash boy. Because, trust me, either one would be preferable to this cosmic joke of a life that you've left me."

Drey looked as if I'd all-out socked him. I felt this bump in my stomach, as if I'd been hit too—or maybe hit bottom.

It was like I'd been trying so desperately not to drown that I hadn't even noticed I'd sunk so low.

"You can take Pie," Drey said. He looked and sounded lost, as if he suddenly wasn't sure where he was or what he was doing anymore... kind of like the junkyard dog I'd gutted. He scrubbed his face, his voice wavering slightly behind his hands. "Gods, you can take Pie."

It was probably the lowest blow I'd ever dealt anyone, never mind Drey—in the figurative sense, of course. But I didn't apologize, because I didn't want him to change his mind.

The cab ride to Jiang's was silent. Even Pie was quiet, sniffing the air tentatively and looking back and forth from me to Drey, each of us staring out separate windows at the nighttime cityscape. It was as if she knew something was wrong—knew something was irreparably broken between us.

Drey already felt so guilty about everything that had happened to me, and I'd thrown it in his face just to manipulate him. But then, he'd been manipulating me into killing people.

Nothing was right with the world anymore. Everything was broken. The Words broke people. Godspeaking broke people. Why had the Gods done this to us? These were their Words, after all. They weren't a gift; they were a curse, and the Gods must have hated us to give them to the world.

I only spoke once, without looking at Drey, as we passed what appeared to be the roof of a lit-up temple with upturned eaves, intricately painted trim, and red pillars—so different from one of Eden City's cathedrals. "Do they believe in the two Nameless Gods here?"

"Not like we do," Drey murmured. "They do think of the Words as aspects of two opposing forces: yin and yang. But they believe each Word originated with an immortal being of legend, and that various things granted these immortals their powers. Elixirs, enlightenment, divine blessings…" He trailed off into silence.

So they had immortals instead of Gods. Other than the number of them, I didn't see much difference. In the eyes of people here, the Words were still seen as good. Which meant they had it as wrong as everyone else.

There, in that dark, quiet car, I realized I hated the Gods. If I could have used their own Word to kill them, I would have. But maybe they were already dead. Instead, I was going to take this Word from the world—take it to my grave. I was going to escape, and *no one* would ever use it again.

seventeen

The cab delivered us to a tall building paneled in polished, shining slate. None of our own security guards were with us, though I had no doubt they were monitoring the situation from a distance—and monitoring me.

The red-and-black marble lobby was as shiny as the outside, I saw, as we passed a pair of Chinese security guards by the front doors. We had to wait by a second pair while they ran the briefcase Drey was carrying through a scanner, and then had to walk through a metal detector ourselves.

After that, we were allowed to follow a black rug up to a large front desk. Drey murmured in English to the man behind the counter and slipped him a small folded stack of Chinese currency. It looked like a lot. Certainly enough to babysit a puppy for half an hour. The man hesitated, but eventually held his hands out. I passed him Pie over the counter. He looked awkward, holding her away from his spotless uniform with gloved hands, but soon he set her down on the floor behind the desk so she was out of sight.

He then gave us a well-practiced smile and said with

barely an accent, "Dr. Jiang has been expecting you. You are free to go up."

We passed several more security guards on the way to the elevators, guys who looked like they meant business. They ignored us for the most part, only pushing the elevator button for us when Drey asked for the top floor. But then two of them got in the elevator with us.

As soon as the doors closed, the men gestured for us to hold our arms out, and then they patted us down, checking for whatever the metal detector might have missed. I held my breath as one of the guard's hands passed over my wrists, but he paid no attention to the monitor bracelets.

Needless to say, the ride up was utterly silent.

The elevator doors reopened on a sleek, dim hallway. At one end was a window that looked out onto the glittering city. In the middle was a pair of black doors that the security guards led us to. One of the guards knocked once, and then turned the golden doorknobs for us.

The front room looked more like an office than a sitting room, with a curving black desk dominating the center of a red carpet. Two chairs faced it. There were more intimate table-and-chair arrangements in the corner, but Jiang was already sitting behind the desk. We definitely would not be getting cozy together.

I supposed that was fair, since I hadn't been very friendly when I'd met him the first time, in the Alps. But now it was time to kiss his ass.

The guards waited until Jiang gave them a nod, and then they left, closing the doors behind us. Jiang likely didn't want them hearing our conversation, but they were no doubt right outside, waiting for a signal to come bursting in. Drey and I took a few more steps into the room, toward the desk.

Jiang wasn't smiling even his fake smile. "Mr. Barnes. What an unusual surprise. I know why you're here, but before you come any farther, I would like to know—who is this older gentleman with you? I recall seeing him on the news last year, dying, and then on a stretcher that arrived with the helicopter that day we met. As I recall, that same helicopter brought several Words who killed quite a few of my people."

I took a deep breath, starting with our fake story to put him at ease in case he decided to stop listening too soon. "This is Mr. Bernstein. He was their prisoner, and the Word of Death was killing him slowly. Khaya healed him, and we both escaped in the chaos." That last part was the only lie, really, and a believable one I hoped. There had been too much darkness and fire for Jiang to have seen what happened. He'd apparently escaped into the trees himself.

"I'm his benefactor," Drey added. "I was the one who convinced Tavin to smuggle Khaya out of the Athenaeum in the first place. I have extreme interest in seeing the Words no longer under Eden City's control."

"And now you wish to join the escaped Words." Jiang's eyes narrowed. "But what if your interests don't coincide with China's?"

"My interests coincided with anyone's but Eden City's," Drey said, with so much conviction I didn't think it was much of a lie. "I'm for...how shall I say...a redistribution of power? If you need an additional incentive to help convince you we're in earnest…" He popped the latch on the briefcase, cracking it halfway open to reveal perfect stacks of crisp Euros inside. About a million of them.

Jiang was smiling now. Still, he asked, "How do you know I will be able to contact the escaped Words? And how do *I* know you will put in a good word with them for China?"

"Mutual trust—" Drey began.

But I cut him off.

"Let me put my trust in you first," I said, unzipping my hoodie. "I'll tell you a little secret, and maybe it'll earn your trust in return."

Jiang looked at me curiously, but Drey's eyes flew wide in alarm.

I rushed ahead before Drey could stop me, yanking up the sleeves of my shirt once I had the hoodie off. "Do you know what these are?" I asked, brandishing my wrists at him. "Tu might have told you about them."

Jiang studied the monitor bracelets for a moment, and then his eyes flew about as wide as Drey's. He knew they were trackers from the Athenaeum. His hand shot under his desk—maybe for an alarm button, or a gun.

"Wait!" I said, turning my back to him. At the same time, I lifted my shirt about halfway up—definitely high enough for him to see. "Do you know what *these* are?"

"What are you doing, Tavin?" Drey asked next to me.

I didn't like the hopeless tone of his voice, but I ignored him, letting Jiang absorb the sight of the inky markings lining every inch of my back.

When I turned back around, he was frozen behind his desk. He hadn't gone for whatever was under it. Yet.

"You…" he stuttered, his composure gone. "You're now a Word. The Word of…"

"Death," I said. "That's right. I was sent here to kill you. That's the other part of the secret. But I won't," I added quickly, before he could move again. "I just want to complete our deal, that's all. And as a Word myself, I'll forever be grateful to you. The others will be too, if you help me escape." I didn't specify *grateful to China*, but I figured this was good enough.

Jiang licked his lips. I could see his thoughts spinning behind his eyes.

"But you have to get these off," I said, shaking my wrists at him. "And then get me out of here. Now."

He hesitated only for another second, then gave a short nod. "We have a tool just for that purpose." His hand now reached for the black phone on his desk.

"I thought you might," I said, practically gasping in relief.

Which meant that everything was perfect.

Until Drey lifted the briefcase and a shot exploded into the room. It was muffled, but still loud enough to make me cover my ears. I should have been shielding my face instead, since blood spattered across it.

And then Jiang was lying face-down in a growing pool of blood on his desk, after rebounding in his chair. It actually took me a second to realize Drey had shot him in the head. With a briefcase.

The security guards outside barely had time to turn

the doorknobs before Drey spun and fired four more shots from the case into the doors. There was a short shout, two thuds, and then nothing. He tossed the briefcase aside. It bounced on the rug, smoking slightly.

"Cruithear designed it," he said. "The gun hidden in the casing is undetectable."

"You just shot three people," I said, completely stunned.

"The security guards were dead anyway, as soon as I shot Jiang."

"Why ... ?" was about all I could manage to say. I had to grab the back of one of the chairs for support.

"I couldn't let you go with him. Now that I've used this gun, an elite team from Eden City will soon storm this building—unofficially, of course. Stealth helicopters will be landing on the roof to take us back to the Athenaeum. Agonya will light this suite on fire behind us ... maybe the whole building."

I stared at Drey in disbelief. "So then you just ... you just ruined everything." And then I was shouting. "Are you even on my side? He could have taken me to Khaya!"

Drey practically exploded, throwing his hands in the air to gesture wildly. "Of course he could have! Because the only person the rogue Words might have trusted enough to reveal themselves to would have been *you*. According to our spies, Jiang didn't know Tu's actual location. So in the City Council's eyes, he was only worth keeping alive if you were willing to go with him." He jerked an arm at the dead man on the desk. "Don't you get it? Half of the City Council *wanted* you to fail in your assassination attempt! And not just to fail, but to escape. But they'd only be letting you go."

When I looked at him blankly, he said, "Come on, Tavin, think! You're smarter than this!"

Perhaps I should have been smarter, but I'd been too desperate. And I still didn't want to understand him.

"How could they be letting me escape?" I demanded. "They couldn't have followed me. I'd have gotten these bracelets off." I glanced at the dead man, then away. "He said he had a tool."

Drey gripped my shoulder and pulled me forward, almost like he was going to hug me, but he only tapped the back of my neck. His expression as he withdrew was ... devastated. "You don't think they have another tracker on you—*in* you?" he said. "The two monitors are there mostly so you wouldn't suspect you have another. When you first got to the hospital, you were in and out of consciousness—"

"They didn't put one in my brain like Cruithear, did they?" I interrupted, horrified. I would have thought I'd notice a scar like that no matter what, but ...

"No, they need Khaya for that, or else the procedure is too risky. But there was nothing to stop them from putting one under your skin where you wouldn't find it, during a time when you wouldn't notice an incision healing. I suspect it's in your neck, though I don't know exactly where. And even if I did, it would be too dangerous for me to try to cut it out in time."

I scrabbled at the back of my neck. I didn't feel anything, but I believed him.

"We have no time, in actuality, so I might as well explain." Drey dragged his hands down his face as he let out a despairing breath. "They *wanted* you to find Khaya. You might have led them right to her. In any case, they would have retrieved *you* and then felt justified in ousting Swanson and treating you however they wanted to afterward. And if they'd found Khaya, they would have just killed you, all of you, to replace you with automatons as soon as possible—because with Khaya back, she could activate Cruithear's childlike automatons that would better adapt to the Words. And then they'd have had their small, all-powerful army of Words, not to mention a much larger automaton army. Cruithear is still building them, day after day, in anticipation of Khaya's return."

I found it harder to breathe. "I thought...I thought the adults were no good as soldiers."

"In many situations they're not, like any that require tactical maneuvers or much thinking. But as a mindless force used to overwhelm a target without regard for casualties taken on either side, they're formidable. Unstoppable, with enough of them."

"Gods," I said. "Why didn't you tell me? About Jiang, about any of it?"

"If I had, I would have been charged with treason and unable to try to steer you away from this. It was bad enough I wasn't encouraging you to find her—though that was my justification for placing you in Khaya's apartment."

It suddenly made sense now, why the City Council had allowed me to have Khaya's things instead of listening to Ryse and cutting me off from my past. They wanted me to remember Khaya, to find her...

Drey squeezed his eyes closed. "The only way for us to have gotten out of this mess was for you to have proved I'd made you a capable Word of Death and rendered Jiang useless at the same time—by killing him. No one thought you would ever knowingly lead the City Council to Khaya, no matter how desperate or even cooperative you became. They hoped you'd side with Jiang and *unknowingly* cooperate by escaping. But if you chose not to, and yet you didn't kill him to demonstrate your progress, either because you refused to or couldn't handle it..."

"Then they'd make me hand the Word over to a prototype automaton, killing me instead."

"As a last resort. Like I said, no one on the Council really wants to chance that process going badly, so they'd probably try harsher training measures on you first, even at the risk of you having a mental breakdown. In any case, they preferred this to go one of two ways: you either killed Jiang, or turned against Eden City and led them to Khaya."

The obvious truth of his words rang hollowly in my stomach. "Luft tried to get me to search for her, but then he changed his mind."

Drey tipped his head back to stare at the ceiling, his hands on his hips. Blood was splattered up there, but I knew he was looking distraught for other reasons. "I imagine he was put up to that by Carlin, but then Carlin changed *his* mind. Anyone who isn't directly connected to the automaton project doesn't know—or doesn't believe—that they're going to be used for the purpose of replacing the Words. Carlin knows, though, as a member of the City Council."

"Then why would he change his mind and stop Luft from encouraging me to find her?"

Drey dropped his head to stare at me. "Why did Swanson break the rules when you were born and let me smuggle you out of the Athenaeum?"

"Because he loved Em, and ... " I stopped and another truth hit me. "Carlin and Luft are together."

"I suspect, but I don't know for sure," Drey said. "Still, the fact is that if the City Council finds Khaya, Luft dies ahead of schedule."

"But ... Luft is barely eighteen! And Carlin ... " I'd only seen the Godspeaker a few times, and I supposed he wasn't hideous, but he had to be in his late thirties. I suddenly remembered the conversation in which Brehan wondered whose "type" Luft's was. Now I knew it was the older, Godspeaker-type.

Drey laughed, a desperation in his voice I'd never heard before. "Do you think now is the time to be judging their relationship?"

He was right, and besides, I was the product of a similarly clandestine work relationship.

I'd failed in every way. Failed to escape, failed to become a functional member of the Words. But Drey shouldn't have had to go down with me so thoroughly.

"Did you have to shoot him?" I asked, sounding as desperate as him. "You could have just dragged me out of here."

"That would have been interfering with the Council's

plan just as much. And Jiang never would have let us leave, not after finding out about you. He might have even tried to kill you instead of letting the Word of Death go back to Eden City. Besides, I told you: I would never ask you to do something I wasn't willing to do myself." He shrugged. "They would have killed him anyway, if you'd gotten cold feet on the assassination but didn't leave with him, either because you'd guessed the City Council's plot or feared what would happen to me if you left." He let out another dark laugh.

Drey had been right, then—we might as well have been handcuffed together. "What actually happens now?"

"The City Council will no longer be able to track you to Khaya, at least." Drey swallowed his sickly smile, looking faint. "I tried, Tavin. I tried so hard to save us. I'm sorry about the things I made you do, but I had to."

Now *this* sounded like a goodbye speech.

My voice rose as I asked again, "What happens to *us* now, Drey?"

"I expect I'll be executed, and you'll … " He couldn't finish. His eyes had filled with tears and he put his hand over his mouth as he looked at me. "I'm so sorry."

I glanced around the office frantically. "Shouldn't we be running, then? You said we don't have much time, but maybe we can—"

He shook his head. "No, Tavin. It's too late."

"Then kill me." I looked at the briefcase lying on the rug, then at him. "Do it. I'm begging you. I can't go back there."

Drey held my eyes, and a tear ran down his cheek. "I can't. You're the only son I'll ever have, Tavin. But it's not just that. You need to do something. Cruithear is the key; I've been trying to prepare you for this all along—"

But he didn't even have time to finish. The doors blew open, cracking apart in several places as if a battering ram had hit them—perhaps Luft's work. Then the entire room went dark in a way that meant Mørke had to be there.

I felt a piercing sting in my chest, and then my mind went dark too.

eighteen

When I next opened my eyes, I couldn't see very well. There was enough light, but nothing seemed right, not in my body or whatever was around me. I blinked and tried to get my surroundings into focus for more than a half-second at a time, but they wouldn't stop bouncing in and out.

I was used to waking up disoriented, but not for a while had I woken up this drugged. My arms felt numb and heavy, and when I tried to move them, nothing happened. Panicking, I tried again, jerking hard enough to practically yank my arm out of its socket. Only a metallic squeak rewarded my efforts as something shifted under me slightly.

I looked down at my body. On my chest, the pale blue of a hospital gown greeted me. There was the white of a sheet a bit beyond that, stretching all the way to my toes though I couldn't quite see that far, and then the silvery shine of low metal bed rails to either side of me. I tried to kick my leg. Only my knee shifted under the sheet, but my foot didn't move.

I knew I must be strapped to the bed. I just couldn't feel the straps because of whatever they'd given me.

Who were *they*? Doctors? Where was I?

Hospital, I thought.

I felt a momentary flare of horror ... but then, wasn't I used to waking up in a hospital? Which hospital was this?

"Drey," I said. Something serious had happened with Drey, but I couldn't quite sort it out. I closed my eyes to try to remember. "Pie." Where was Pie? I needed to go get her. I'd left her with someone ...

"They'll be here soon," a female voice said.

The flare of horror turned into a flash flood. My eyes flew open.

Ryse was standing at my bedside where Drey should have been. And then I remembered why he wasn't here. A lot of it, anyway, if not all: I hadn't killed Jiang. Drey had done it, to keep me from leading the Athenaeum to Khaya, and he said he'd be guilty of treason. He hadn't told me what was going to happen to me ...

Ryse was what was going to happen to me. She was my punishment. Fear hit me so hard it would have flattened me if I hadn't already been on my back.

"No," I said. I screwed my eyes shut and turned my head away from her, willing her to go away and this to not be happening. "You're not here."

I didn't hear anything for a moment, and I wondered if maybe she'd only been a horrible drug-induced hallucination. Gods, I hoped ...

But then I heard a light snap and the most pungent smell imaginable hit my nose. No, it *exploded* in my face and burned down my throat. I gasped and yelled, my entire body jerking, trying to get away from the odor. I still couldn't move. But now I could feel the cuffs biting into my wrists and ankles as I strained against them.

My eyes were open again. The room was suddenly in much better focus—and so was Ryse, leaning over me. My chest was heaving.

"Get away from me!" I cried.

"More alert now?" She leaned back, but only to throw something away. Whatever had smelled so bad, I imagined.

I was definitely more alert. My eyes shot around, recognizing, widening. This wasn't a hospital room.

I was in the lab—the Death Factory, back in the Athenaeum. On a gurney, in almost the exact location as the man I'd killed. I even had an IV tube running from a bag of clear liquid into my vein, just like he'd had. I could see the needle taped to the crook of my arm where I'd knocked the sheet back with my struggling. I tried to reach the tube with my teeth to yank it out, but I couldn't. The effort left me dizzy and my head collapsed back on my pillow.

"Get that out of me now," I said, still breathing hard. "Get me out of here."

Ryse only maneuvered the bed's extendable IV stand farther out of my reach and tugged the sheet tighter over my chest, covering up my arm again with its tube and cuffs.

"What am I doing here?" I demanded. I tried to shake my head to clear it more, without much success.

"You'll see," she said with a slight smile.

With a shout, I started thrashing. I arched my back and twisted, trying to kick off the bed, anything I could manage to free myself. Even if I knocked the gurney over, that would be better than simply waiting. But the metal frame only bounced and swayed a little bit. Still, I kept writhing as long as I could.

By the time I stopped, I was completely exhausted, every bit of my strength gone and every bit as strapped down as before. My one small victory was that the sheet was a mess.

"I hate you," I panted, staring at Ryse through the hair in my eyes. She hadn't moved at all, and neither had her smile. "I hate you, I hate you, I hate you." I was nearly sobbing.

She reached to smooth my hair back. She had a black Necron glove on. Even so, I lashed out, trying to bite her. If I could puncture the glove...

She whipped her hand away in time to miss my gnashing teeth—and then around again, smacking me full-force across the face. My head snapped sideways, and dizziness and stars exploded in my skull. Even so, I lunged right back at her, still hoping to bite her. But I didn't make it two feet off the mattress before the rebound slammed me back down.

I squeezed my eyes closed again, willing the dizziness to go away. That trick hadn't worked on Ryse, though, and it didn't work for this.

"Are you finished?" she asked, if I'd been a five-year-old throwing a tantrum.

The darkness spun and swooped behind my eyelids. *Deep breaths...*

"Answer me."

I didn't want the smelly stuff shoved in my face again, so I opened my eyes to glare hatred at her. If only looks could actually kill. "No. And I won't ever be finished, not as long as you're here. How about you take your glove off and pet me like last time. Come on, flirt with death, you sick bitch, and I'll—"

She smacked me again. My lip split and I tasted copper. As soon as I'd blinked away enough stars to at least see where she was, I spat blood at her. At least that got her to step back in a hurry.

Her dark eyes flashed with fury, probably because I'd managed to gain some ground without being able to move. "This is no good at all. Dr. Bernstein's training has only set you back. We have a lot to make up for."

"I'll kill you," I said, spitting more blood across the front of my blue hospital gown. "I swear I'll kill you."

"Maybe someday...but not yet. Andre had his turn with you, but he failed. Now it's mine. I see you've at least embraced your urge to use the Word of Death."

"Only on you. Where's Drey?"

Ryse's smile grew. "Like I said, he's coming. Once he arrives, we'll give your willpower a test, shall we? Let's call this my assessment of how far you've come."

There was only one thing for me to do: I had to incapacitate myself. It would be hard to touch someone to kill them if I couldn't lift my arms, and I'd already nearly dislocated one shoulder. I twisted again, this time wrenching all of my force against that joint. Something tore inside, and I screamed.

"What are you doing?" Ryse's voice came out higher pitched. She hadn't expected this.

I ignored her and tried to pull against my other arm, but twisting onto my injured shoulder was agony. No matter how hard I tried, my body held back and I couldn't get enough force.

"For the Gods' sake," she snapped, crossing her arms, "stop being so disobedient."

It was the first time I'd heard her truly frustrated, and it brought a grin to my face even through the tears. "Then for the Gods' sake, crawl into a dark hole somewhere and die."

She looked like she wanted to hit me again, but I beat her to it, slamming my head down onto the bed. It was padded, of course, but I was pretty sure I could give myself a concussion and maybe some brain bleeding or something if I bounced it hard enough. I slammed it down again and again.

I heard Ryse yell for me to stop, but I wasn't paying attention to her. I only had to focus through the explosions in my brain enough to keep going...

Warmth in my arm told me that wasn't going to happen. In my peripheral vision, Ryse was squeezing something into the injection port of my IV tube. The warmth spread, leaving heaviness in its wake. Suddenly, no matter how hard I tried, I could barely lift my head, let alone bang it anymore.

Ryse yanked the syringe out of my tube, shaking her head in anger. "You annoying little bastard," she hissed under her breath through gritted teeth.

"Not a bastard," I gasped. "Have a father."

She set the syringe on a tray and then peeled back each of my eyelids, shining a small flashlight in my eyes. I wasn't sure if she was checking for head trauma or the effect of whatever she'd given me. In any case, I couldn't turn away.

"I want you to be fully present for this," she said. "You

will be, for the most part, but a drop more muscle relaxant seems necessary."

So that was what she'd given me. I glanced at the syringe. She hadn't used all of it, and the tray held two other syringes. I wondered what was in those, and if I would have the chance to stab them into Ryse.

She followed my gaze. "Just in case," she said.

I'd been trying to say something earlier. "Swanson...where's Swanson?" I tried to roll my head to look at the windows, but had to be satisfied with rolling my eyes.

"Ah yes, the father you call by his last name only, a last name you don't even share. I'm sure he would love to be here—*I* would love for him to be here—but he's only been arrested and suspended for now, not sentenced to be executed." She shrugged. "Can't say the same for Andre."

I stared at her, panting. "Why...do you hate me?" I hated *her*, of course, but my reasons were pretty obvious.

She bent down, putting herself on my level. "I don't hate you, Tavin. Not at all. In fact, I feel a kindred spirit inside of you."

I tried to shake my head, which meant it just twitched. "Not me. The Word."

"Yes, and the Word is inside of you." She leaned closer. "And I love *it*. It speaks to me. It's a part of you, but I want it for myself."

"So you want...to break me down...make it all yours." My tongue was clumsy in my mouth, but I met her eyes and actually held them, something I was usually too repulsed to do. I tried to see something in *her* that I recognized. If Tavin and not just the Word of Death could speak to her, maybe she wouldn't do this to me. "Why...are you like this?"

"I think all Godspeakers are like this to some extent. We're each just drawn to different Words, called by them. And death, *pain*, is what calls to me."

I tossed my head as much as I could. "I already knew...you were sadistic. But *why?*"

"You think you can psychoanalyze me in the minute or two you have before our guests arrive, hmm?" She flipped her short black hair over her shoulder with a slight smile. "Perhaps you want to understand *why* I'm doing this to you?" She waited until I nodded weakly, and then leaned back. "Nice try. But not knowing is another form of torment, I feel. Helplessness and fear in the face of the unknown puts you on a mortal plane with the rest of us, doesn't it, even though you have a bit of a God inside of you?"

So she wanted to torment the Gods, or as near to it as she could, by torturing one of their Words. And not just any Word, but the one most often used to torture humankind.

Too bad I was the innocent bystander, because I *almost* couldn't blame her. Not that I could tell her that. She either wouldn't believe me or else she'd just want to encourage that side of me. And "almost" wasn't quite enough in a lot of situations, I'd discovered—I could definitely blame her. Because even if she hated the Gods, she also had some crazy God-complex going on herself.

"You must've had...a tough childhood," I said. I hoped the sarcasm was coming through well enough.

Ryse's eyes narrowed and she straightened all the way. "Shall we begin, then?"

She turned away from my gurney, heading for the door out of the Death Factory. I remembered what was about to happen. The room tipped disconcertingly around me, but I still tried to lift my head to talk to her.

"No," I said, speaking as fast as I could with my drug-heavy tongue. "Gods, no. Please... Ryse. Dr. Winters, whatever. I'm begging you. I'll do whatever you want. You won't even have to make me. I'll do whatever you ask... just not this."

She shot me a considering look over her shoulder. But then her chilly smile returned. "What if this is what I want?"

"Then I'll fight you with every last breath in my body." The words sounded more desperate than threatening.

Her smile stayed. "It's more fun for both of us that way, I think. And besides, you also carry the breath of one of the Gods, and it doesn't want to fight me."

"No!" I cried as she moved again for the door. I tried to struggle, but all it amounted to was me shifting weakly on the bed in my restraints.

The door to the Death Factory slid open after she swiped her card. "Bring them in here," she said.

Security guards wheeled three chairs into the room, not just one. Strapped to the wheelchairs were Jacques, Chantelle, and Drey, followed by Pie—who was dragged bodily inside by the neck, on her purple leash, when she planted her paws and tried not to enter the lab.

Everyone who had ever mattered to me.

nineteen

Pie, Drey, Chantelle, Jacques—all of them were now in the Death Factory, ready and waiting ... for me.

I'd told Ryse about Chantelle and Jacques, I realized, when I was trying to remind Drey of the people who were important to us. Drey had been right to keep everything hidden and act as though no one really mattered to him. Because once people knew, they did this to you.

It wasn't only the Gods who were cruel.

Chantelle was sobbing as a security guard wheeled her to a stop near my gurney and set the brake. Her hair was a wreck and remnants of eye makeup streaked black down her cheeks. Her slightly creased face looked older.

"Tavin!" she cried when she saw me. "Honey, what's going on? I'm so scared!" She saw the cuffs on my arms and shook her head in confusion, sobbing even harder. "What's happening?"

The security guards left in a hurry. No doubt they would wait right outside, but no one wanted to be in here other than Ryse. The one holding Pie secured the end of her leash to a metal handrail along the edge of a counter near Drey and left. The door slid closed behind him. Ryse walked up to it, her black Necron boots clicking over the white tiles, and punched a code into the door's keypad. The bolt clunked home, locking us all in.

"No one to interfere, I'm afraid," she said.

Jacques's chiseled face was steely and grave. He probably guessed some of what was going to happen, since he'd knowingly helped Khaya and me escape on his trash barge. Chantelle hadn't even known what she was doing when she sheltered us under the bridge, in the break room she and the other ladies used. It was all my fault she was here.

Drey's eyes were dry. He was calm. He looked at me from his wheelchair and said, "I love you, Tavin. Know that. Whatever happens, I love you."

Tears of helplessness ran down my cheeks. I couldn't look at them anymore.

"Ryse, I can't do this," I said, my voice cracking apart. "I'll be broken inside. I won't be able to be the Word of Death after this."

"I think you need a little breaking to *be* the Word of Death," she said calmly, walking back over to me. "Others agree. So you're going to break for me today. And once everything from your past life is gone, you'll be able to focus on the future. Besides, all three of these individuals have been charged with treason and sentenced to immediate execution. The law must be upheld."

At the mention of execution, Chantelle started wailing.

"I will have no future!" I shouted over her. "If you make

216

me kill them, I swear to the Gods, I will kill myself! There will be no Word of Death!"

Then I realized that I could do that *before* I killed anyone else—if the Word could work on me. It was probably a long shot, but I folded my fingers up to the edge of my wrist, just where the cuff began, and threw everything I had at it.

"Cut, sever, gash, gape…" It wasn't working, so I went deeper, practically screaming at my internal organs. "Falter, fail, hemorrhage, explode, eviscerate…die, die, die!"

The Words dissolved into my own gasping. I might have just been speaking normally for all the effect I had. When I turned the Word against myself, it just slipped away, like a knife turned away by armor.

Chantelle was moaning. Drey was shaking his head and shouting for me to stop. Jacques looked scared for once, and Pie was whining and backing against her leash so hard the skin of her neck was bunched up around her head.

Both of Ryse's eyebrows had shot up, but her expression smoothed when I stopped speaking. "We'll just have to take precautions against any self-destructive tendencies, won't we? I think restraints will be necessary at all times." She stepped toward me. "Unless, of course, I'm godspeaking."

"I won't cooperate," I said. "I'll do everything I can to be the worst Word of Death. They'll take me away from you, make me pass the Word to an automaton that you won't be able to torture…"

This was the first thing I'd said that truly seemed to make her pause.

But then she only said, "I won't give you the chance to

be anything but the best Word of Death, after this." She looked at the others and tapped her lips with a black-gloved hand. "Perhaps we should ease into this. Start with the one who matters least to you and then work our way up from there. What do you think? Jacques first, then Pie, Chantelle, and Drey? Or would it be Jacques, Chantelle, Pie, and then Drey?" She sounded genuinely intrigued by the question. She glanced at Jacques and Chantelle. "It must sting to realize you matter less than a dog."

I yelled wordlessly, as loud as I could, since I could do nothing else. Ryse only winced at my volume and picked up the controller hooked to the gurney. She used it to sit me up higher on the bed—so she could get at my back. I tried to press myself flat into the mattress, but once I was in a sitting position, her death-proofed hands shoved my head forward with hardly a protest from my muscles. My hospital gown was already open in back, so she didn't even need to move the fabric aside before her voice was inside of me.

Death, she crooned. *Death, my friend. Relax.* Maybe she was saying it aloud too, but I heard her in my mind, my body.

And then I didn't protest at all. My arms relaxed entirely.

I was Death. *We* were Death.

Ryse unbuckled my straps and unclipped the IV tube from the junction near the crook of my elbow, leaving only a handy injection port dangling from the needle still in my arm—in case she wanted to give me something else, no doubt. As she did, she moved slowly around the bed, keeping in constant control with her voice and in constant eye-contact with the Words on my skin. At her direction, I even helped her with the straps on my ankles and then slid off the gurney. My legs were wobbly, but I could stand. The blood-spattered hospital gown slid off to pool at my feet. It was a small consolation that I was wearing blue hospital shorts underneath.

She put a hand on my bare shoulder to help direct me, and I noticed that she'd taken off her Necron glove. She was toying with death again, like one would do with flame. Not that I could do anything about it, even though part of me wanted to. I tried—oh, that part of me tried, screaming in a soundless, solitary confinement in my own brain—but my body didn't listen.

She walked me over to Jacques first. *This will be simple. We're easing into this, remember? I am not without mercy.*

I leaned forward, placing my arm, the uninjured one, on his shoulder. I stared him right in the face. His eyes were wide at first, but then they relaxed. He even nodded at me.

"Rupture," Ryse said behind me—through me—to a few of the arteries in Jacques's brain, right behind his left eye. The pressure must have been a little excessive, because his eye flooded red. He jerked once and then sagged against the straps of the wheelchair, unblinking.

I distantly expected Chantelle to scream, but her eyes were squeezed shut and she was murmuring under her breath. Maybe praying to the Gods.

Pie was the one who screamed, or near enough, yipping and howling at an ear-piercing pitch. She whipped back and forth, thrashing against her leash like I'd been thrashing on the gurney.

I felt Ryse's grimace through her words: *Pie dies next, then.*

I straightened from Jacques, turning away from Chantelle, and moved in the direction of Drey ... and my puppy. She was tugging so hard on the collar that some of her shrieking noises were coming out in rasps.

Let's make this silent. I can't stand any more noise.

I bent forward, leaning toward her on the ground where she struggled. I could see the whites of her frantic eyes. My good arm reached for her.

"Asphyxiate ... " Ryse began.

Just before my fingers grazed Pie's fur, Drey and his entire wheelchair came crashing down. He must have thrown all his weight toward me, tipping the chair. He crushed my arm to the ground underneath him, dragging me to my knees ... and away from Ryse.

"Gods damn you," she snapped, turning her attention to Drey for a brief second.

Which was long enough for me to turn on her. I ripped my arm out from underneath Drey, ignoring the wrenching pain, and threw myself at Ryse. Both of us went careening into a counter. Neither of my arms was working right, fumbling uselessly at her Necron sleeves, unable to find her ungloved hand or her neck. And so I pressed my cheek against hers as she tried to push me off.

"Break for me." I was nearly kissing her as I breathed the Words. "Slowly."

Her head snapped back at the sound of the first crunch in her arm. And then she screamed.

Before I shoved myself away from her, I found her bare hand and squeezed it. "Silently."

Her scream choked off into a hissing gurgle. She slid to the floor, her mouth working and her face twisted with pain, but she couldn't make a noise.

My legs buckled and I had to crawl the rest of the way to Drey. Pie was fine, whimpering, huddled in the corner between the wall and the counter, watching me warily.

Drey was not fine. On his side still in the wheelchair, his face was turning from red to blue. I'd touched him when he'd fallen on me. When Ryse had said "asphyxiate" to Pie.

"Gods, no! Drey!" I ripped at the buckles holding him down, eventually spilling him out of the wheelchair. I rolled him on his back on the tiles. His hands were already at his throat, shaking, clawing. His eyes were wide with panic.

My own eyes shot around at the lab, as if there was something that could help me in here. But there was no cure for the Word of Death. There was nothing I could do to stop this.

His hands suddenly seized my face, dragging my eyes level with his. He gave my head a jerk, and then hit himself in the chest.

There was one thing I could do to stop this. Drey knew it, and he wanted it.

"Drey, no," I gasped.

He thumped his chest harder, his eyes flying wider. His face was turning a darker purple.

He couldn't get much clearer than that.

I cupped his head, bringing my forehead against his. "I love you too," I said, my tears dripping on his cheeks. "It'll be all right. You can stop now."

He stopped. His arms fell to his side.

My mind was still. No justifications, no mantra, could ever save me now.

The room was oddly quiet too. There was pounding on the door from outside, but it was muffled. The guards hadn't decided to blast it open yet, I guessed. Inside, Pie was only trying to hide, Chantelle's eyes were still closed with tears glossing her cheeks, Jacques was silent in death, and Ryse...

Ryse was *crunching* more than anything else, which was a sound no human being should have made. She was on the floor, her back arched in agony, but she wasn't screaming. What skin I could see was swelling, blossoming with bruises. Her face was almost unrecognizable.

I wanted to watch it through to the end. I wanted to make it *worse*. Slower, even more painful. I wanted to tear her apart, piece by piece.

But Drey was still looking at me. Part of me wanted to slide his eyelids closed, but then another part of me knew that I would torture Ryse for as long as possible if I thought Drey could no longer see me.

So I dragged myself away from Drey's side, and he seemed to watch me as I went. I hauled myself across the tiles over to Ryse, pulled myself into a kneeling position next to her, and put two fingers against her temple. Her eyes were swollen shut, so she couldn't look at me.

"*I am not without mercy,*" I grated in her ear, leaning over her. "Now, go away—forever. Disappear."

She dissolved, rather, turning into a weird sticky pile of

mush on the floor. Some of her ran into the drain indented in the tiles. Her Necron suit stayed, still whole but deflated.

I just sat there for a few seconds, hunched on the floor, staring... and I knew: this was hell. The Word of Death had brought me here. It had been Herio, at first, and then it had been me.

The pounding at the door had stopped, but I knew they'd be here soon. They would knock me out, and then this hell would continue—at least long enough for them to pass the Word on to an automaton, if they finally decided the risk was worth it. And then everyone else would be at risk. Unless I actually decided to do something about it— something I should have done from the beginning.

I closed Drey's eyes in preparation for what I was going to do next. Ignoring Chantelle and Pie, for the most part, I did a cursory check of the lab, looking for a scalpel or a razor or something sharp. But the cupboards and doors were locked. I was too weak to hurt myself without any tools, so I stumbled back over to the gurney, near where the three syringes were still on the tray.

Might as well try, I thought. If they got to me in time, then I'd only be doing them a favor and knocking myself out for them. But if I died, so much the better. I lined the syringes up and pulled the plastic caps off the end of the needles with my teeth. I'd have to do it fast, get through them all before they took effect.

With the first syringe in hand, I noticed how little liquid was in each one, even in the two that Ryse hadn't tapped into yet, and remembered that air in your bloodstream could supposedly kill you. So then I went through them all, pulling the plungers all the way back so that each barrel was filled with air, not just drugs. The syringes were small, but I hoped it would be enough.

I sat on the edge of the gurney and positioned my arm with the IV needle in it over my lap. I didn't wait. I jabbed the first syringe into the injection port, depressing it as quickly as possible. The air and liquid hurt, straining my vein, but the pain was microscopic compared to how much everything else hurt.

I made it to the third syringe, at least. I managed to find the injection port with the tip of the needle, swaying as I tried to stay upright, and was depressing the plunger when I lost consciousness.

twenty

I wasn't upset when I woke up ... *because* I woke up, rather. I wasn't happy either. Nor was I surprised, or intrigued, or whatever people feel when they realize they're not dead.

I was nothing.

I sat up, and wasn't even surprised to find I wasn't cuffed to the bed. It was a hospital-style bed, but with no metal rails, and the room looked a lot like a hospital room, except the walls and floor were padded.

So it was *that* type of hospital room. Even the two doors didn't have knobs; they were merely flat, equally padded rectangles in the walls. One had a small observation port, but other than that there was only a single window, set high out of reach and letting in dusky light. Or maybe it was dawn. I had no idea.

I was wearing only the hospital shorts. My shoulder was bandaged, and my arm too, folded and wrapped against my chest like a mummy's. That had been the arm with the IV in it, so I couldn't see what damage I'd done. There was a new IV needle taped in my other arm, but I wasn't hooked up to anything. That didn't mean I hadn't been given anything.

I was awake and alert, no doubt, and I remembered everything. I'd killed Jacques, Drey, and Ryse. Jacques's death had been against my will, but then I'd very willingly killed Ryse. Drey's death had involved a bit of both.

But I felt … nothing.

They had definitely given me something. They'd done things to numb my body before, but this time my body was fully functional, short of my shoulder. No, they'd screwed with my mind, completely suppressing my emotions.

I would have been pissed if I could have felt pissed. I even tried to muster something, *any* feeling at all, and I just couldn't.

What I felt was the need to *piss*. I couldn't remember the last time I'd gone. As I stood up, I considered pulling out the IV needle, but then I shrugged and left it. If I removed it, they would only have to put another one in. Besides, I would have had to do it with my teeth, and that would have been a pain.

A minor inconvenience, rather. But my damned bladder was another story. With my good arm, I knocked on the door with the observation port. I knew the drill.

"Hey," I called. "I need to go to the bathroom."

Ten seconds later, a buzz and a click came from the second door. Inside was a toilet. Even the seat was padded.

When I was finished and back out in the room, I heard the bathroom door re-lock behind me. I rolled my eyes. Another minor inconvenience.

"You don't have to do that," I said. "I'm not going to bash my head on the toilet rim or try to drown myself in the bowl or something unsanitary like that. In fact, I don't even want to kill myself anymore."

Or at least I felt neutral about it.

"And hey, I don't really care about anything anymore, so if you want me to pass the Word on to someone else, or have me kill a few more people, I'm fine with that."

I wasn't sure why they hadn't just done this to me from the beginning, honestly. Then again, I figured it must have been because neither Ryse nor Drey would allow it, for drastically different reasons: Drey wanted me to keep my conscience, and Ryse wanted me to feel as much pain and misery as possible. And since they'd both been my God-speakers, they'd gotten their way.

Now I didn't have a Godspeaker. Nor did I have a conscience.

Really, it was freeing. I mean, I still cared about certain things or certain people in an abstract way. I cared about Pie. I wouldn't have minded seeing her. I cared about Khaya, and I wouldn't have minded seeing her as well. I appreciated that Chantelle was still alive. I would have preferred Jacques and especially Drey to still be alive, but I wasn't broken up about it.

Break for me, Ryse had said, before making me kill them. But I hadn't. And then I'd said the same thing to her, and *she* had broken. So it had all worked out in the end.

I had a hunch that I might actually be broken and I just didn't know it yet, but at least this was how the mathematics of my non-emotions seemed to be working at the moment. I sat on the edge of the bed, my chin in my good hand.

Then again, maybe I should fix things in case I was

broken—make everything as right as possible before I finally fell apart. I'd told Drey things would be all right, after all.

And Drey had told me something, back in Jiang's flat in Beijing: Cruithear was the key. He'd been preparing me for something to do with the Word of Shaping. At the rec-ollection, a thought took *shape* in my mind:

What else could he have been preparing me to do? There was only one thing I could think of. And why not?

If I pulled this off, it would realistically be the last thing I ever did. I was fine with that. But to get close enough to her in the first place, I'd have to do a few other things first.

And honestly, I was fine with that too.

When I banged on the door, I didn't ask to see Cruit-hear or anything obvious like that. I asked to see Swanson.

He came. I was surprised they even let him, since he was supposedly suspended and under arrest. But then when I saw him enter my padded room without death-proof cloth-ing, his normally immaculate hair and suit disheveled, I real-ized it was at his own risk. And that no one would really care much if he died.

I certainly wouldn't. But I didn't really care enough to kill him, either. I didn't even get up from where I sat cross-legged on the bed.

Before he could open his mouth, I said, "You people really need to decide what you want to do with me. I'm will-ing to either hand over the Word of Death to an automaton, or, if that route has too many risks, I'm also willing to be the Word of Death and kill whomever you want, whenever you want, however you want, but with a few conditions."

Swanson blinked, then sighed. "Tavin, you can't mean that. You nearly killed yourself. They had to pump you with so much oxygen ... " He grimaced as if remembering. "No one would trust you enough to let you—"

"Then I'll earn their trust. I'll stay locked up, drugged. Hell, I like the drugs. Bring me the people I need to kill at the start. I don't even have to leave the Athenaeum ever again, as far as I care, though I would be happy to do that too once they trust me enough."

He folded his arms. "Are you serious?"

"As death." I smiled, and he stepped back. "And I'll start proving it immediately. Or ... let me hand the Word over to an automaton right now. I'm bored, and *something* needs to happen."

"Boredom can be a side effect of the drugs you're on."

I scratched my shoulder, trying to get at an itch under the bandages. "Well, whatever. Make up your minds."

"Do you ... " He hesitated. "Do you still want to die? Is this some kind of death wish?"

I scoffed and dropped my hand. "No, it's impatience with all the dithering. But I see the City Council's dilemma: an adult automaton might turn into a death machine if I give it the Word, and, more importantly, it can't lead them to Khaya. Meanwhile, I'm too unstable and might take the Word of Death into oblivion with me, given the chance. Or, at least, I *was* unstable. But I'm not now. So what I'm suggesting is they take a risk either way, and either kill me *or* let me kill people who aren't myself."

Swanson frowned, mulling over what I'd said and looking

doubtful. "I'll...bring your suggestion to the Council. They might not listen to me at all, but I'll deliver the message."

He turned for the door. He was clearly uncomfortable being around me like this. He no doubt didn't recognize anything that had been his son. That was too bad...for him.

"Then tell them this too," I added. "Tell them I can give them the best of both worlds. I'll be a model Word of Death, almost as good as an automaton, until I can pass it off to an actual one...one designed for the Words."

He had frozen. "Are you suggesting..."

"Yep. I'll help them find Khaya. Voluntarily." I felt nothing when I said it. "And then she can bring all the child automatons to life, for the Words. That seems to be the best solution, doesn't it?"

Swanson turned back to stare at me in disbelief. "Why would you do that?"

I shrugged. "Drey always said the Words didn't belong to people...only to the Gods. I think they're too much of a burden, frankly. I mean, look at what I've had to go through, and now I'm only fine with it because I can't feel anything. I might as well be an automaton. If the Words were with automatons in the first place, no one human would have to bear this. And you people would no longer have to mold kids into tools...or monsters. Automatons are already tools."

Swanson was gaping at me, almost in awe. "I..." he stuttered. "That's been my goal all along."

He meant it. All this time, he hadn't just been cruelly using children. It had been eating him up inside, in spite of the fact that he, like everyone else, couldn't witness power like the Words' without trying to take it and use it. Maybe, at one point, he'd had a soul like I'd had.

But neither of us had one anymore.

"Now we share the same goal," I said.

Swanson practically hammered on the door in his eagerness. "This could change everything."

"Oh, I hope so," I said as he hustled out.

It didn't take long. I didn't think it would. My suggestion got the City Council's attention, and fast. Swanson returned with Carlin, Angelina, and five other people in tow who were vaguely familiar, all men and women in suits with gray or graying hair. Council members, I imagined, and other God-speakers I hadn't yet met.

But only Swanson came into the room. The others had to huddle around the observation port or just listen, which almost made me smile. I knew they could hear me through a hidden intercom, which would pipe their own voices inside if they wanted to talk.

"First," Swanson said, after the door was re-bolted behind him, "the Council wants to know what your conditions are."

I had them all ready to go. Still sitting on the bed, I leaned back on my good hand, heedless of the fact that I was wearing nothing but hospital shorts.

I started with the one that would be hardest for them to swallow. "One: You can't make me kill anyone I don't want to." Before they could object, I added, "But my standards are pretty relaxed right now. Basically, I don't want to kill Chantelle or Pie"—I glanced at Swanson, considering—"or, hell, maybe not him either, since he's technically my dad. Or any children, but you shouldn't want to kill children anyway, because that's just mean. Anyone else is fair game."

Swanson had looked frightened, then relieved, and then dubious. He glanced at the faces crowded in the observation port, which were whispering back and forth. "Your willingness will need...demonstration, of course," he said carefully.

"Fine by me." I went on before their whispers could get any louder. "Two: No one touches me. Ever again. Except to take restraints on or off, which I understand will be a necessity at first, until you trust me. But I'll give myself my own drugs. Feel free to watch me to make sure I take them. Just don't ever touch me or godspeak through me, or I will kill you. I can't imagine anyone would be too eager to touch me anyway, since both my Godspeakers are dead."

There was some louder murmuring at that, but I spoke over them again. "Three: Chantelle goes free. She gets a nice house in the city somewhere and a decent monthly stipend. I don't even want to see her again. And no one else will lay a finger on her or bother her *ever*... including after I'm dead, since I'll probably die before her." The murmuring tapered off and my eyes narrowed slightly. "She's not already dead, right?"

"No, no," Swanson assured me quickly. "Just...incarcerated and quite distraught. But I'm sure we can take care of her."

"Good," I said. "Of course, I'll want proof that you haven't just shot her, such as a legally binding contract signed by all of you, promising to provide for her for the remainder of her life no matter what happens to me, etcetera, and some photos of her in her new house or something. Also, I want you to apologize to her."

After another glance outside the room, Swanson said, "I think that can be arranged."

I went on without waiting. "Four: Similar to the last condition. I'm pretty sure Jacques had a wife, and maybe kids. Give them a lot—and I mean *a lot*—of money. And if he did have kids, they go to school and learn how to read. Again, I want proof."

Swanson only nodded this time. It was just as easy for them to make someone fantastically wealthy as it was to kill them, I imagined. "Understood."

"Five: I want Pie back. She stays with me, wherever you decide to put me, and if you won't let me walk her then someone else has to. Also, we'll need some dog food." I paused. "And that's it."

Swanson blinked. "That's it? Those are your conditions?"

"Yep." It was just as I'd planned—after the first two conditions, the others were practically a relief they were so easy. But I didn't want it to seem *too* easy, so I added, "Wait. Six: Once you trust me, I want to get out of Eden City, like go to an island and see the beach . . . and not because I have to kill someone on that beach. I can have as much surveillance and as many armed guards as you like, but I want to travel. Again, only once you trust me."

It didn't matter if they thought I was hoping to escape through such a ploy. In any case, they'd now think I was waiting for a treat, like a good attack dog, and would be more inclined to obey in the meantime.

An older female council member spoke up from outside, peering through the observation port. "And in return you'll perform as the Word of Death, doing whatever we wish outside of your conditions, including finding the Word of Life? You will allow us to take her and the others back into custody, with the eventual intention of transferring the Words to more appropriate vessels?"

"Agreed," I said. "That is, if you agree to my conditions. Otherwise, no."

"We'll need to discuss this amongst ourselves before we give you an answer, of cou—"

"Okay, wait," I interrupted, sitting up straight. "I guess that's a seventh condition: you can't take forever to decide. In fact, I'd prefer you decide today."

"Just like you need proof," another Council member said, though I couldn't see him, "we'll need proof."

I nodded. "I understand. Like I said, outside of my conditions, I'll do whatever you want. I'll even stay strapped down, drugged, locked up for as long as you need to feel comfortable."

"But we also have to know you're ... capable," the voice continued. "You killed Dr. Winters in anger, and you were either forced or cajoled with all the others."

This would be like the chimpanzee all over again. They'd want me to kill, probably slowly and horrifically, just so they knew I could follow orders. So they knew I belonged to them.

I shrugged from my seat on the bed. "I repeat: I'll do whatever you want."

And I meant it.

———

My first trial came relatively quickly. After observing me for a week to make sure I was taking my drugs and no longer suicidal, Swanson took me to a locked room in the depths of the Athenaeum that was filled with people. Their hands were cuffed behind their backs. They were prisoners, enemies of the state, the unjustly accused—whoever they were, it didn't matter. They'd been rounded up for this purpose, and he'd told me what needed to be done.

The people didn't look so scared when I was wheeled into the room strapped to the chair—my only mode of transportation these days. But when Swanson, who'd somehow been nominated as the person to get me in and out of restraints, unbuckled me and I stood up to look at them all...they looked afraid, then. With good reason.

I killed every single one of them. I deadened their pain receptors, like I had with the chimp, but the resulting picture was just as gruesome as if I hadn't. No one would have been able to tell otherwise. It was a bloodbath—literally. I looked like I'd showered in blood, afterward.

I didn't mind it, other than the physical discomfort of being so sticky and needing a real shower. The blood, the people—they didn't really matter in the long run.

I'd been so selfish, thinking only about seeing Khaya again, or about her rescuing me, that I hadn't even considered the one thing that could keep *her* and even the world safe forever. But Drey had pointed me in the right direction: Khaya would be far less useful to the City Council, and therefore less of a danger to the world in general, if Cruithear—the other Word necessary for their plans—was dead.

And if there was one thing I could do now, it was kill.

twenty-one

I waited another few weeks, after several more "demonstra-tions" of my abilities and proof that Chantelle, and Jacques's family, were safe and secure, before I brought up Cruithear. I'd already been moved to a room without padding the week before, though they still kept me locked deep in the hos-pital, away from many, if any, passersby. Even to use the hospital gym, I had to go at night when everyone else was gone. Swanson would wheel me down the empty hallways in restraints and bring me inside while security locked the place down. Only then was he allowed to turn me loose. All that fuss to just lift some weights or jog on the treadmill. And I thought I'd been isolated before.

As an odd side-effect, I was spending a lot more time with my biological father. After Swanson got used to my lack of emotion, he actually seemed not to mind being around me. Not that he had much of a choice, since the City Coun-cil had basically demoted him from the head Godspeaker to my babysitter. It was better than prison, I supposed. Then again, our routine wasn't much different from a prison's, and hanging around with me was probably more dangerous.

Swanson was the one I decided to tell about the Word of Shaping, since he would no doubt be a better messenger to the City Council than I would be. He'd just brought me back from the gym to my room for the night, handed me my evening dose of pills, and was waiting around in the center of my small room to make sure I took them. Pills had been an upgrade from injections, since they flattened my mood just the same minus the needles, but no one trusted me with a bottle's worth yet.

"So here's something interesting," I said, tossing the pills in my mouth. I took the plastic cup of water from him and swallowed before continuing. "Drey's last words—well, not quite his last, but from when we were in Beijing—might give us a lead on Khaya."

I didn't miss the wince that flickered across Swanson's face even though he tried to mask it. Drey had been his friend, or at least someone he'd once placed a lot of trust in, and so he was getting over my surrogate father's death far more slowly than I was. Rather, I'd gotten over it almost instantly with the help of the drugs, and Swanson didn't like discussing it at all, especially not casually.

"How so?" he asked.

Ignoring his reaction, I chucked my empty cup into the trash and sat down on my bed to yank off my gym sneakers. Pie took a break from her chew-toy in the corner to come try to scale the side of the bed. I lifted her up with me.

"When he killed Jiang," I went on, "I was pissed because I thought my one chance to find Khaya was gone.

But Drey said Cruithear knew a way to get a message to her, since Cruithear was in on Khaya's escape plan."

Swanson looked genuinely surprised. "She was? We questioned her, and she claimed to have no knowledge of it beforehand."

I used my good arm—my other shoulder was better, but still healing—to play-fight with Pie as I spoke. "Of course she would tell *you* that. You people put a monitor in her brain, so I don't blame her for not wanting to share much with you. Anyway, in Beijing, Drey said she could tell me how to contact Khaya, if the opportunity ever arose for me to talk to her or escape—actually escape. Don't ask me how he knew this, because I don't know. But he was obviously assuming I wouldn't tell you, which is why I think it might be true." I shrugged. "Then again, he was also probably assuming that the opportunity *wouldn't* ever arise. He might have just been trying to make me feel better."

A lie often sounded more believable seasoned with a little doubt, somehow.

Swanson's expression turned considering ... and then uneasy. "A conversation like this would require you to be alone with Cruithear."

I nodded as if this were no big deal and scratched Pie's tummy when she rolled over. It certainly didn't feel like a big deal to me. "And it would require *proof* that no one can hear us, along with a convincing cover story, because she probably won't tell me anything about Khaya if she thinks I'm going to turn around and get her captured."

Swanson was pinching his bottom lip between his thumb

and forefinger—a habit I'd noticed he had when he was lost in thought. "You realize the City Council will suspect you of wanting to kill Cruithear, which would not only destroy decades of crucial planning, but also the last Word of Power."

It would definitely be a huge loss. With Movement, Naming, and Time gone, the Words of Power were nigh extinct. Only the Tangible and Intangible Words would be left—still too many in the hands of the Godspeakers, in my opinion.

I rolled my eyes, and Pie yapped as if backing me up. "That's why you would take all necessary precautions so I couldn't get at her: restraints, a full Necron suit and gloves I can't get off, etcetera."

"And what would your cover story be, to present to Cruithear as a valid reason for being in her presence before you 'betray' us? As you say, she needs to think we didn't send you."

"I could say this was one of my conditions before I started cooperating with you guys—to be able to ask her for something of personal significance to me, like a sculpture of Drey or stories about Khaya's childhood, whatever." I waved my hand in dismissal and Pie leapt up from the blankets to try to tackle it. I caught her shoulders and tackled her instead. For a few seconds, I used both hands to tickle her, and then turned back to Swanson. "The point is, I supposedly don't want to tell the City Council *what* it is, because I want privacy when I ask. I'll tell her that's what I told you, anyway. And then when we have some sort of proof that we're not being listened to, I'll ask her how to contact Khaya."

In actuality, my fake lie was the truth. I would be asking Cruithear something I didn't want the City Council to know about. There was no telling if she would grant my request, and I had no foreseeable way of taking it by force, but it was the only chance I had. She had to see reason.

She had to die.

Swanson rubbed his forehead. "I think I have a way to keep you two from being overheard, one that Cruithear will trust. I'll let you know ahead of time once it's finalized. But as far as everything else, I don't know. In the past I would have been able to arrange this myself, but now my influence is limited. My role in the automaton project has downgraded from ... well, leading it, to indefinite suspension."

"You trust me, right ... Eli?" I said hesitantly. "Can I call you Eli?"

He nodded. "Of course you can." The touched expression looked foreign on his face.

I smiled. "Hell, Luft does, so I figure I can. Anyway, Eli, I only want things to get better for you. And if we can find Khaya ... well, some of our past mistakes might be forgiven, right?"

I didn't feel the slightest bit bad about manipulating him emotionally, mostly because I was incapable of feeling much remorse. Besides, after everything he'd done to me, this was nothing.

He took a deep breath and squared his shoulders. "I'll do my best to convince the City Council."

"Thanks," I said, then rolled back on the bed to full-body wrestle with Pie. She was already pouncing on my chest and licking my face half off before the door closed and re-bolted behind Swanson.

––––––––––

He definitely did his best to get the Council's attention, because he brought word from them before noon the next day.

They would let me see her. But I'd have to go to her work area, because she didn't often leave. She wasn't allowed to, rather, and her rooms deep under the hospital were equipped to emit some kind of electrical impulse that would trigger the monitor in her brain and knock her out if she tried. It was the only reliable way to hold her.

For me, they went beyond restraints and a Necron suit, giving me a death-proof straitjacket and a stiff face mask so I couldn't even resort to biting, like I'd tried with Ryse. There was literally no part of my skin that was exposed once Swanson helped me get it all on. And before he did, he gave me an injection of a mild sedative, which joined the mood-flattening drugs swimming in my system.

"It'll make you a lot weaker, and tired, but still coherent enough to speak," he said. "It's just a precaution."

I was only wearing a black undershirt and Necron pants at this point, but I held out my arm and let him stick me anyway. I no longer had the IV needle installed and would probably miss my vein if I tried to do it on my own. Once I was all dressed, he had to help me into the straps of the wheelchair, since my arms were securely wrapped around my back and I was a little dizzy.

"I'm going to get so hot in this," I muttered through the mask as he tightened the belts of the chair around my chest, waist, and ankles. "And I look like a serial killer. I mean, I guess I am, but Cruithear is supposed to want to trust me."

Pie was watching me warily from the bed. Not even she wanted to get near me in this outfit.

"This was the only way the *Council* would trust you," Swanson said, straightening. "And they were more important to win over, since without them you wouldn't even have the chance to talk to her."

"Fine, but please tell me you have a way for Cruithear and me to speak privately that they approve of. She has to trust that we're not being overheard." So did I, but I didn't add that.

Swanson moved behind my wheelchair and backed me toward the door. He knocked for it to be opened. "Remember when I first spoke to you at the lake about … about being your father?" He sounded as if he still wasn't quite used to saying it out loud.

"Ah," I said, remembering. "Luft's trick. He made some sort of sound barrier."

The bolt slid open and the door opened. Sure enough, Luft and Carlin were out in the hallway, along with a whole team of security guards.

"Hey," I said to Luft through the mask, completely unconcerned about how I looked. "And while you're here, you can also suffocate me if I get any funny ideas."

Luft's blue eyes were sharp as he stared down at me over folded arms. He was shirtless, while I was covered from head to foot. "How are you doing?" he practically demanded. "I've been worried about you, and so has Brehan. They wouldn't let us see you."

"That's probably for the best," I said, nodding down at myself.

"Tavin, I'm so sorry about Drey—"

"Don't worry about it," I interrupted. "I'm not."

His eyes narrowed. "What are they giving you?"

I shrugged, or at least I tried to. "Not sure. I don't mind, though."

"Of course you wouldn't." He let out an exasperated breath. "I think that's sort of the point."

Carlin put a hand on his shoulder, and I noticed the slight squeeze and the emotion in his eyes as he exchanged a glance with Luft. Luft looked angry, but he stepped back and shut his mouth. So that was all his Godspeaker had to do to get him back in line.

Illicit relationships with the Words seemed more effective than the standard kind. Maybe the City Council should have lifted the ban on them long ago. I almost said that out loud before I remembered I was supposed to be on my best behavior.

Swanson began pushing my wheelchair down the hallway and our entourage followed. Some of the security guards moved up to flank us as an escort.

Cruithear's quarters were actually a lot closer than I thought they'd be. Since I was back in the hospital and stuffed down in some dark corner of its basement, we were practically neighbors in what was, essentially, an underground fortress beneath the Athenaeum's medical center.

As Swanson pushed me through the white hallways and down one floor in an elevator, I pondered whether I hated hospitals. I was pretty sure I did. I didn't *feel* the hatred, precisely, but I figured it was lurking around inside me somewhere.

The floor below mine was built out of solid concrete, without the white walls as even a pretense. It looked like we'd entered a military base. Cruithear's quarters were sealed off behind steel doors that made the Death Factory's look tame. The guards positioned themselves in the hallway around the doors while Luft and Carlin stood behind me and Swanson.

"After you take him in, I'll make the sound barrier," Luft told Swanson.

Swanson nodded, swiped a keycard, and the doors opened. As he wheeled me into the white-tiled space, he said, "Cruithear, please don't move beyond the center of the room or toward Tavin at all. If you do, we'll have to interfere." He rightly assumed I couldn't move an inch.

A girl I'd never seen before stood looking at me curiously from across a long steel table in the center of the room. It was similar to the table in the Death Factory but full of all sorts of things, from raw chunks of plastics, metals, and clay to complex gadgets and sculptures. Eerily, there were several human bodies in miniature that almost looked real rather than like dolls. They hadn't bothered restraining her, since no restraints could hold her—other than the room, I supposed.

"As you know, Tavin wishes to speak with you—privately," Swanson emphasized. "You're safe, and we'll be right outside in any case." He set the brake on my chair and headed out the door. It sealed closed behind him.

Before long, I felt the odd change in air pressure, which made my ears pop. I focused on Cruithear then.

She had red hair, long and curly, but woven together in the most intricate pattern I'd ever seen in hair. She must have shaped it. Incredibly green eyes peered out at me from a pale face, so pale it was like she'd never seen the sunlight. And maybe she hadn't, locked up down here. At some other time, maybe, that would have made me sad. She was a girl Khaya's age, who'd worked closely with her, and she was as innocent as Khaya was.

But I was here to kill her.

"Cruithear," I said from behind my mask, "I'm not sure where to begin. But I'm Tavin ... Death ... and I need to talk to you about something incredibly important."

She only looked at me.

"They can't hear us, I can promise you that. Here, let's test. You think I'm here for some stupid personal request, but that's not true. I'm actually supposed to ask you how to contact Khaya, and report what I learn to the Council. That isn't going to happen either. I'm pretending to lie to them so I can supposedly lie to you, but I'm actually lying to them—anyway, long story short, I have no intention of lying to you *or* asking where Khaya is. I'm sure you don't even know, and what I want is for her to be left alone anyway."

I waited, looking at the door through the eye-holes of my mask. No one came bursting through.

"See?" I said. "I'm pretty sure they'd have had me out of here in no time if they'd heard that."

Cruithear gazed at me as if I were a mildly difficult puzzle she was piecing together. Her voice was quiet when she finally spoke. "You could have just asked me if Luft's sound barrier is secure. It is. I can feel the shape of it."

"Oh." I tried to shift to a more comfortable position in the chair and failed. "Right."

"If you're not here for any of that," she said, cocking her head, "why are you here?"

I didn't hesitate or stumble. "You need to let me kill you."

Her green eyes widened. To her credit, she didn't start waving her arms at the cameras for help.

"I can't reach you myself," I continued, "or else, I'm sorry, I would just kill you. You have to stop this, Cruithear. Your creations—these bodies you shape—are going to devastate the world once they carry the Words. You can't let that happen."

Her eyes wandered off to the side, as if she were looking at something next to me that wasn't there. "The bodies I shape," she murmured. "I follow the chain. Molecules to cells, cells to organs, organs to bodies, bodies to death, to fly apart, to bleed, to cry ... "

"Cruithear," I said, trying to get her attention.

She blinked and looked back at me. "Sometimes I shape my memories, so it all runs together and I don't

246

remember how long I've been doing this. But it's only a superficial change. Part of me still knows."

She closed her eyes, and part of me wished I could feel bad for her, like the part of her that still remembered underneath all of her memory modification.

"But what can I do to stop it?" she finished quietly.

"You have to let me kill you. That's the only way. If it was me in your place, I would happily die, but I'm not the important one." I nodded at her to the extent that I could. "It's *you*. These Words shouldn't be with us anymore. We don't...*people* don't know how to use them. So the only thing we can do is take them away. Mørke, Brehan, and the rest could eventually escape from those who would use us, but you can't, and you'll doom everyone else if you don't let me do this."

She held my eyes for a long time. The green of them bore into me, and somehow I saw endless gardens taking shape inside of them. Not growing and dying, just...interweaving, forever.

I had no idea what she saw in my eyes, which was about all of me she could really see through this black mask. Probably only death. And who would want to agree to that?

But then she said, "I believe you."

I felt lightheaded. Not happy, or nervous, or terrified that this was finally happening; only the physical effect.

I exhaled. "Good. You have to reach me somehow. If they see you, they'll try to stop you, but we can think of something."

"It hurts to shape a body. So many cells stuck together, blood vessels, nerves..."

"I know. I'm sure it's terrible to be down here, doing this…" I tried to improvise some sympathy.

Her voice was less soft, like she knew I was full of shit. "No, I mean to reshape *my* body."

"Oh…can you?" I asked with what was nearly hope—and then doubt. "You can reach me from *there*?" She was a good fifteen feet away, on the other side of the table.

"I can only reshape small or superficial areas or I'll go into shock…and they'll know." She nodded upward, as if at the ceiling. But she probably meant to indicate the monitor in her brain.

"You'll try, though, right?" I held her eyes so she wouldn't lose her focus. "You'll let me do this?"

She squinted at me, more like through me, and I worried she was going to drift off again anyway. "I can feel the shape. To rebuild, the end must be the beginning. Death was last, and now it's first."

"I'm…not sure what you mean," I said, as patiently as I could manage. "I'm sorry, but we need to hurry."

She put her hands on the table and stared straight ahead. "A God spoke the Word of Naming to create the universe and everything else to come into it thereafter, naming himself Day and naming the God of Night as a balance."

Gods, she was quoting *scripture* at me?

"Now really isn't the time…" I began. Or maybe it was. Since I was about to kill her, it was the least I could allow. I shut my mouth, trying not to squirm in my straitjacket in impatience.

"The God of Night spoke and gave the universe Darkness first," she went on...and on. "Then Day brought Light to brighten it. Night called forth Time next, so that Light and Darkness could take turns without strife, and then Day gave Movement so they would be able to dance to the beat of Time. Next, Night made the Earth, dark and rich, and Day set a bright crown of Air over her head. Night dressed Earth in a gown of shimmering Water and Day bejeweled her in glowing Fire."

"Yeah, I know—" I said, trying to interject.

"Do you?" she asked, looking at me so intensely now it was like she was seeing inside of me. And then she just continued. "Night then gave the power of Shaping, and Day gave the gift of Life, so Earth could become the Mother of All. Finally, because Day named Night for balance from the very beginning, Night spoke last, and the Word of Death came to be." She paused meaningfully. "And Death came to the Gods first, because the two of them had given all to the universe with their Words, including themselves. They disappeared, becoming Nameless, never to be seen again. Only heard in their Words."

"So..." I said. "Death came last." I hesitated. "I actually didn't know that. Or that the Gods were called Day and Night. Now that I think about it, I don't think I've ever heard this version of the story before."

"Because no one has," Cruithear said with certainty— certainty that bordered on serenity. "Only the Gods. And now me, because I saw it—the shape." She nodded at me. "Death was last, now it's first."

I hoped that meant she would let me kill her now. "Sounds good to me."

"Tell me you understand." Her soft voice took on a stubborn edge. "Tell me how it works."

I tried to think, to remember her story, since this was the stupid game she wanted to play right now, of all times. "If Death was last and now it's first, that means you're going backward, so ... Life is next?" I really hoped that wasn't what she was going for. Life was *not* what we needed right now, as much as I wanted to see Khaya again.

I would never see her again, after this.

Cruithear shook her head, sounding nearly as impatient as I felt. "No, Life belongs to Day."

"Right," I said. "Right. So, counting back, the next one that belonged to Night is ... " I grimaced behind my mask. "I'm sorry, I really can't remember."

She sighed. "Shaping."

"Got it. So ... so you're next." Now we were on the right track. "Death to Shaping." It sounded terrible, saying it like that, but it was what needed to happen. There was no use sugarcoating it.

She nodded, her eyes intense from across the room.

I breathed a sigh of relief. "Now can you reach me, somehow?"

She nodded again, except her eyes dropped this time as she began muttering Words in Scots-Gaelic. Seeing what she was doing was difficult from my vantage, but it looked like the tip of her shoe, more of a slipper really, cracked a hairsbreadth. From out of that crack came what looked like a string no thicker than a hair. I could barely see it. The security cameras definitely wouldn't be able to, especially since her feet were under the steel table.

"Is that ...?" I couldn't help grimacing slightly.

"My skin?" She winced as it grew longer, shooting across the floor toward me. "Yes." And then she continued muttering Words.

It reached the bottom of my wheelchair and touched the tip of my black Necron boot. The material might have been death-proof, but it certainly wasn't shaping-proof, because it split just like her slipper.

Just before she touched me, she said, "You have to get out of here right after this, as fast as you can."

"Huh?" I looked up in surprise, the Word of Death ready on my tongue. The plan wasn't for me to go anywhere after this.

"I can't leave this room, but you'll be able to. The field won't work on you." She must have meant the invisible barrier that interacted with her monitor and knocked her out if she tried to leave the area. Of course it wouldn't work on me, but ...

"The straitjacket sort of does, though," I said.

She smiled at me. It was a sweet, sly smile. Like she was sharing an amazing secret with me. And I suddenly realized she was not just a girl, but an incredibly beautiful one. *Fine time to think of that,* I told myself, *right before you kill her.*

"Not for long," she said. And then she touched me.

Before I could speak the Word of Death, she spoke.

She spoke a ton of Words in that rolling language, her

voice loud and assured. Something shot into me like an electric current, seizing my muscles almost like Ryse's stun gun. It felt like the deepest massage imaginable, crossing the line into painful, but not painful enough for me to scream. I only hissed and shuddered in my restraints.

And then I felt it in more than my muscles. My mind was suddenly grappling with it—another presence. I heard myself gasp, though I was no longer focusing on what was happening in the room. The Word of Death roiled, twisting, mixing with this new presence in my head. And suddenly the Word of Death wasn't only that, anymore.

It was something else. I looked up at Cruithear in blank bewilderment, but she'd slumped forward onto the table, scattering her creations. She slid off and fell to the floor. Her red hair spread in a tangled fan around her on the white tiles, no longer held in its intricate shape. She wasn't moving. She wasn't breathing, either. Her green eyes stared at the ceiling.

That was when blaring alarms went off and the door burst open ... and when I remembered Cruithear had told me to run. More than a half-dozen security guards began to pour through the door, circling around me in my wheelchair but keeping a safe distance. On impulse, I strained against my straitjacket.

"Get off!" I said. And then for no apparent reason, I added, "Pieces!"

And then something insane happened. The straitjacket fell away from me.

I ripped the mask from my head and stared at the shreds of the straitjacket and at my freed hands. And then I looked down at the wheelchair. "Pieces," I said again, shoving away from it. Its straps and buckles flew apart as I stood up, and even the chair itself collapsed under me.

I laughed and glanced up in time to see about eight tranquilizer guns aimed at me.

"Dull, they're dull!" I yelled, just before the guards fired.

The darts bounced off my undershirt, newly rounded metal tips stinging like mad, but they didn't break skin. For a second, the guards and I exchanged looks from across the room. They were surprised.

I nearly was too.

Then one of them hollered, "Grab him!" and they all charged me.

TWENTY-TWO

The guards' boots squeaked over the tile floor of Cruithear's lab as they came at me all at once. They all had Necron gloves and suits on, so maybe they were hoping they could pin me to the ground before I could touch them.

That wasn't happening. I didn't know how; I only knew that it wasn't. I raised my hand.

"Stop!" I cried.

Somewhere in there was a Word. More than one. Because what looked like focused beams of black light suddenly spiderwebbed out from my fingertips, catching the guards at the neckline. In unison, they collapsed around my feet in matching black heaps.

They were dead, as dead as Cruithear on the floor. I stared at my hand.

The Word of Death couldn't do that, *or* the Word of Shaping. This was something else entirely. This was Death's physical form. It had shape. Not only that, *I* could shape it.

"Gods," I said. I should have been feeling amazement, shock, horror... but nothing was forthcoming. In any case, there wasn't time for anything, because white gas started pouring from vents into the room.

They sure had built this place with locking it down in mind.

"Air—only air—in a bubble around me," I said, and it happened. A clear space formed around me in a sphere about ten feet across. I could shape air too. *How handy.*

The white smoke billowed against the edges of my bubble, making it hard to see beyond. Perhaps it was tear gas, or maybe something stronger to induce unconsciousness. If they knocked me out now, I definitely wouldn't wake up until they'd built an even stronger room than this one around me, and then chained my brain to it at the same time. I could see more guards peering through the haze in the doorway, trying to get a line of sight on me. And then I saw a more familiar, blond-haired figure step into view.

Like me, Luft was keeping the gas away from himself and everyone else out in the hallway. He said another Word in German, and the hazy air between us billowed, clearing enough for him to meet my eyes.

He was looking at me in disbelief. "Did Cruithear just give you the Word of Shaping?" He must have known the answer already, because he said, "How could you let her do that?"

My voice was calm, even if my words sounded like they should be angry. "I love how people just keep *assuming* I ask for this shit. For your information, I was trying to kill her, not steal her Word. I didn't even think it was possible to have two."

Luft glanced behind him at the people out in the hall.

No doubt Swanson and Carlin were back there, and maybe a gathering army of security guards waiting to storm the room once I collapsed.

"Neither did anyone else," he said. He looked back in the room, at Cruithear on the floor. "Well, she's dead, so you succeeded after a fashion. What the hell are you doing, Tavin?"

I shrugged. "You saved me once. Consider the favor returned."

"What does that mean?"

"Ask Carlin. Or better yet, come with me and I'll explain on the way out of here."

He didn't move. Of course, he'd have to leave Carlin if he came with me.

"Good luck then," I said. "And for the record, I forgive you for screwing with me about contacting Khaya." I paused. "I think, anyway. I'll get back to you on that."

He didn't take his eyes off me this time. "How about I just ask you what the hell you're talking about once this situation is under control?" He said a Word next, one that started collapsing my bubble of fresh air.

"Harden," I said. What looked like white dust flew at me, and suddenly the edge of my now-small bubble, only a foot or so in radius around me, was like hard plastic. It must have taken shape from whatever material was in the room. No doubt Luft could puncture it if he tried, but he wasn't trying. Not yet. He was still gaping at what I had done.

I had to get out of here, if only before my air ran out—though that was probably the least of my concerns. I spun to the wall.

"Hole, big hole. Bigger!" I wasn't being careful or subtle, and a giant tunnel ripped through the solid concrete—all three feet of it.

I told my bubble to lose its shape and jumped through with my breath held. On the other side I commanded the concrete to become a wall again behind me. It did so with a grating crunch, and then I couldn't even hear the shouting I'd left behind on the other side. Losing my balance after my leap, I fell back against the wall and had to take steadying breaths. Adrenaline was helping me power through the sedative, but the latter was still going strong.

I looked around and found myself in an expansive cold space, stretching like a low-ceilinged warehouse to a distant opposite wall. Large, coffin-sized tanks filled the giant room. From what I could see, they held bodies suspended in ice.

The bodies weren't exactly coming at me, so they could wait. First things first—I looked at the monitor bracelets on my wrists.

"Pieces," I said.

The black bands fell to the floor in chunks.

The next one would be less easy. I touched the back of my neck, closing my eyes and focusing. And then, I could feel it—the shape of what was hidden there—but not with my fingers.

"Tiny, *tiny* hole," I told my skin. "Let's start with a pinhole."

Pain and blood blossomed at the back of my neck, and then even more when I shaped my flesh to push the microchip out. My work wasn't as precise as I would have preferred, but it was fast. I plucked the thing out with my bloody fingers and flicked it to the floor. It was so small I didn't hear it hit. But it was out of me.

My neck was swelling and bleeding, but it was nowhere near fatal. I was too wary of reshaping it closed anyway. Even if I smoothed the skin, I'd probably just keep bleeding on the inside. So I left it, and I looked around again.

So many tanks, and all of them with occupants. They had to be the automatons Cruithear was—had been—making. The ones Khaya was supposed to bring to life. They weren't exactly alive, so I couldn't kill them. But...

I brushed the cool glass of one of the tanks with a fingertip. "Pieces. *Shards*," I added, trying to get more creative. I wanted tinier pieces anyway, so no one could ever put them back together.

The tank burst apart, raining glass, ice, and what looked like frozen shredded meat to the floor. I backed away from the mess and looked up at the entire massive space... at *all* of the tanks. I repeated the Words.

The power swelled inside of me, and I wondered for a second if I would rip myself apart. But then the pressure vanished and every tank in the room exploded. Sparkling flecks of ice and glass filled the air like snow. Even if there was some red in there, it still was almost beautiful.

I heard someone cry out. A man in black—a security guard—had entered the room about half of its length down from me. He was covering his face and yelling. Glass must have sprayed him in the eyes. But even if *he* couldn't see anymore, the others following him would.

I looked at the ground. "Tunnel," I said.

A tunnel dove downward, right through tile, insulation, and concrete, until it hit rocks and packed dirt. I let it level out there. Tu had shown me how to "earthworm," what felt like ages ago, and, like with air, I could shape earth. I could shape it all. Even the Word of Death, apparently.

Jumping into the tunnel, I discovered I'd made it a little too steep and slid half of the way down it on my ass. I'd also busted a pipe, or five, somewhere, which were spraying water and hopefully nothing else. A sewage pipe would be unfortunate, but I'd really have to watch out for gas or electrical lines since those could actually kill me.

I closed the hole above me so no one could follow, then cursed when I realized it was pitch black. After poking smaller holes back up through the floor, I hesitated while my eyes adjusted to the limited light.

I figured the smart thing to do would probably be to just get out of here right now, *under* and out of the Athenaeum. But I couldn't leave Pie. And I would tear this hospital to pieces to get to her if I had to. Fortunately, Swanson had only taken me down a couple of hallways and one floor to get to Cruithear's quarters. I was still relatively close to my room.

I opened more of the tunnel and moved along it until I had to be out from under the tank room—probably underneath the room across the hall from it. I made a crude step ladder out of dirt to poke my head up through another tiled floor, the alarm screaming into my ears with renewed vigor.

"Holy Gods." I was in another tank-filled room, almost identical to the first. How many of these automatons did they have? It took me two tries to lift myself out of the floor, but only one attempt with the Words to make another patchwork ladder up to the ceiling. Before I climbed up into a storage closet on the floor above, I shattered every tank in that room too.

When I poked my head out into the upstairs hallway—after reshaping the closet's doorknob so I was no longer locked in—everything was still, except for flashing red lights illuminating the white walls. The only sound was the blaring alarm.

I recognized this hallway. It was adjacent to the one with my room. I tried to dart out of the door in a run, but instead stumbled out and had to lurch along, using the wall as support, while my legs took their sweet time. I soon grew impatient and cut across the floor, shaping a rough path through two unoccupied surgical rooms to get to my hallway. This deep under the hospital the rooms weren't being used for anything good, so I wasn't careful about how I did it. Although I probably wouldn't have been careful anyway.

When I reached my door, I peered through the observation port to make sure Pie was on the bed—she often was, when I was gone—and then I enlarged the port into more of a portal.

I should have closed it behind me, but I was too focused on scooping Pie up off the blankets. She showered my face with puppy licks and I murmured into her fur, "We're getting out of here."

"Tavin."

I spun to find Swanson outside the doorway, his hands raised, breathing hard. He'd obviously run the entire way.

Several security guards had followed him, and their tranquilizer guns were trained on me.

"I thought you'd come back for her. You—you can't leave," he stammered. "You can't do this to me."

"I can't?" I said, tightening my grip on Pie.

He put a hand on his chest. "The City Council will think I was involved. I'll be accused of treason."

I pursed my lips. "That would be a shame."

"And this ... this is unprecedented—impossible! Tavin, what has happened to you should be studied. Two Words in one body! The world needs you. *I* need you." He reached out to me through the hole in the door. As if I would take his hand and submit myself, just like that.

"Do you realize how messed up you are?" I asked, and he flinched. "You don't need me. You don't need the Words. And you definitely don't need any automatons—most of which I just destroyed, by the way." I raised an eyebrow at him, his face disbelieving. "But if the *world* needs me so much, don't you think you should share?"

And then I muttered a Word and dropped through a hole that opened right under my feet. On the floor below, I narrowly missed a counter in what looked like another lab— one filled with white gas. Pie yelped as I landed straight on floor tiles, probably because I pulled her fur to keep hold of her. I almost yelped too as the impact jarred my feet and buckled my weak legs. But I kept my mouth closed and the breath in my lungs.

There were masked security guards in the hazy room, and yet they hadn't been expecting me. Before they could raise their guns, a black spiderweb of death caught them. I only regretted it because it used up the first bit of my held breath.

Something metal grazed the back of my neck—a dart fired from my own stupid hole that I'd left open in the ceiling. I ducked, tucking and rolling farther away, opening my mouth again to say, "Tunnel!" Another bit of breath was gone. I didn't have much left.

A tunnel widened in the floor, and I dropped down with Pie, landing on dirt this time. I was under the hospital again, but only gas had come with me, no fresh air. I blocked the hole overhead, plunging us into darkness, and blindly expanded the tunnel as far as I could with just about the last of my breath. And then I ran.

By the time I ripped another air hole open overhead with a final croak from my struggling throat, my lungs were about to implode with the desire to breathe. My vision sparkled in the darkness, and Pie was limp in my hands. It was dark up above—an empty room of some kind—and thank the Gods there was no more gas. I inhaled just enough mixed air to close the tunnel behind us, sealing in the gas, but even that blacked me out for a second, bringing me to my knees.

The stuff was strong. Definitely knockout gas. I kept my head down, gasping and blinking, trying to stay conscious. Then I listened at Pie's chest for her fast heartbeat and quick, shallow breaths. She was alive.

I waited only long enough to be sure I could stand, and then I closed the hole overhead except for an air vent no bigger than my fist. One hand against the wall, one holding Pie to my chest, I continued to move sightlessly in the darkness down a tunnel I kept having to shape in front of me—in the opposite direction from where I'd come, of course. Not that I knew anything more about where I was headed than that. Tu had some sort of built-in GPS as the Word of Earth, but I definitely didn't.

Since I was under the hospital's deep multilevel basement, I didn't hit anything but dirt as I moved forward. Or at least I couldn't feel anything but dirt with my extended hand. That was convenient, but going higher would probably be worth the risk of bumping into something else. The air was already feeling stretched down here, and it would be useful to see where I was going.

Besides, I was pretty sure I needed a car.

twenty-three

When I resurfaced, I came up through a building's foundation and then into a dim basement. Heading up from there, I found myself half in a brick wall and half in what smelled like an elderly woman's closet, though it was too dark to tell. I reshaped the brick wall into enough of a hole to make sure someone's living room wasn't on the other side, blinked in the blinding light, and then I widened it the rest of the way. I stepped out into an alley. It was a nice alley, as these things went, outside of the Athenaeum but still in the wealthy sector of Eden City. I closed the wall behind me.

It was afternoon, sunny. Early spring. Traffic hummed in the warm air beyond the alley. The rest of the world was carrying on like nothing had happened, oblivious to the chaos in the Athenaeum's hospital.

Pie hadn't yet woken up, but she was still breathing.

Without having any idea how I was doing it, I rearranged something—maybe the molecules—in my black undershirt, turning it red. I also turned my Necron pants into something resembling denim. I made my hair straight and blond instead of wavy and brown—likely looking like an idiot, but I didn't care—and borrowed enough plastic and scrap metal from a nearby trash can to shape myself a decent pair of sunglasses, though I had no idea if the lenses were actually UV resistant. I also took an extra bit of metal with me when I strolled out onto the sidewalk, whistling.

It didn't take me long to find a suitable car. Choosing one was like being back in Brehan's apartment playing his video game: a red Porsche, a black Aston Martin, or a green Lamborghini? I settled for something a little less flashy and strode up to the driver's side of an older silver Mercedes-Benz convertible, one that still had a keyhole instead of a keypad.

It only took closing my eyes and focusing for a second to feel the shape of the lock, and another second, plus a Word, to shape the key. The car alarm went off as I slipped inside, but starting the car cut it off immediately.

After laying Pie on the passenger seat, I dropped the top on the convertible to get us some air and sun. Then I pulled out into traffic. No doubt I was driving under the influence of a whole cocktail of drugs, including a sedative and a partial dose of knockout gas, but I was pleased to note I didn't even swerve in my lane. As pleased as I could be, anyway.

I briefly considered trying to go back for Brehan, but for the moment it made more sense to get out of Eden City. Not only to get the Word of Shaping as far away as possible, but there was something else nagging at the back of my mind.

I no longer had any drugs. I would have taken some with me if I could have—the mood-flattening kind, not the sedatives. But they'd never given me a supply. I'd only taken my morning dose today, which meant I had until this evening before they started to wear off.

As I flowed through traffic with the wind in my hair, the sunlight glinting off the silver hood, nothing much could have made me feel afraid. And yet the thought of facing what was hidden deep inside of me came as close to scaring me as possible. I knew that by the time I came down off of the drugs—or erupted out of them—I had to be far away from everyone.

When I flew to pieces, a lot of things might come with me.

I drove to the airport. I wasn't planning on flying anywhere, but it was as near to the outskirts of the city as one could get without having to go through a checkpoint to leave. After parking in one of the long-term outdoor lots, I searched inside the glove box and found a sleek little flashlight with plenty of battery power. I picked up Pie and ditched the car, walking only far enough away to duck between two tall SUVs before I dropped into another tunnel in the ground.

I walked under the border of Eden City, carrying Pie and the flashlight. I knew it was only a few miles to a small French town on the other side. There, I closed my tunnel behind me and stole another car, this one with French plates.

Trading cars every few towns, I worked my way southeast into the French countryside, climbing higher into the hilly terrain beneath the Alps. The air grew cooler out of the city, but it was still spring and the snow was melting on the mountains, the fields turning green. This was the exact territory that Khaya and I had crossed at night during my first escape from

Eden City, in the fall, and I remembered stumbling across a few vacant-looking country houses with her.

Pie woke up in the early evening as I drove in search of a place like one of those. I pulled over to pet her and talk to her, but she only looked at me and then curled up, going back to sleep.

Watching her, something in my chest twinged almost painfully. That wasn't normal. With another vague feeling, which I recognized as worry, my eyes shot back to the road drenched in the red light of sunset. I stepped on the gas. I needed to hurry.

I turned down smaller, residential dirt roads as the sunlight faded, searching for a house that was isolated enough and, of course, empty. I had a couple of near misses: a hidden car parked at the end of a long driveway, a dog barking from inside a dark house, lights turning on after I pulled up. By the time I found a silent, shadowy two-story house next to a field, the moon was rising and I was feeling borderline frantic. I focused on the sensation, nearly letting it overwhelm me in an attempt to let nothing else in. I snatched Pie off the seat, leapt out of the car, and ran up to the porch.

Gods, I could run again, which meant the sedative was nearly gone. I would have even settled for another sedative. Anything to dull what was coming.

I pounded on the front door and nobody answered. I didn't bother shaping a key. I shaped the lock instead, blowing it open. Kicking inside, I scanned the front room. No dogs or people or strange noises. Everything was dark and smelled a little musty.

I laid Pie on the floral-patterned couch and rushed into the kitchen, throwing open white cupboards until I found a can of cat food. It would do well enough. I started looking for a can opener until I remembered I could reshape the damned can. I made it into a bowl, softening any sharp edges, and snatched a real china bowl out of the cupboard to fill with water. After setting both in front of Pie, who was now awake and looking around at the unfamiliar surroundings in sleepy confusion, I wasted no time in getting the hell outside.

I was hyperventilating as I stood on the porch. The stars were beginning to twinkle in the sky. My fingers couldn't stay still; I kept flexing them at my sides and making fists.

Farther. I needed to be farther from the house.

My throat was tight and pressurized, like I was going to puke. But I forced air into my lungs and vaulted off the porch. Running for the field, I could feel it coming, swelling inside of me like a dam about to overflow and sweep me off my feet. I made it a decent way into the grass before I collapsed.

On my hands and knees, I didn't puke.

I screamed. The sound tore through the quiet night, echoing across the field.

I screamed, and I screamed. I sat back on my heels and gripped my head in my hands as if I could shove the feelings back inside, along with the memories those feelings were dragging out of me … and I screamed again.

I'd killed people. So many people, in so many ways. There were so many screams, echoing mine. So much blood.

I opened my eyes enough to see my red T-shirt and remembered being drenched in blood.

I ripped the shirt from my back, literally tearing it off and hurling it away from me. And then I threw up. But since I hadn't eaten much recently, it was mostly dry-heaving, so powerful I thought my ribs would split.

Just as I was spitting into the dirt, thinking the worst was over, I remembered Drey: him telling me he loved me. The way he'd looked at me when he'd asked me with his eyes to kill him. His face turning purple. The way he'd simply *stopped*, ceased to be, after I told him to.

The screaming began again.

The memories never paused: Jacques, as his eye burst red. Ryse, as she disintegrated. Cruithear, as she collapsed. I hadn't used the Word of Death on her, but I'd asked her to die just the same.

I'd *convinced* a girl to die. She'd been a prisoner as much as I'd been, and for far longer. And then she'd died for me, while I'd gone free.

I was a monster. A monster through and through.

My screams seemed to shake the trees, vibrate in the ground. Some part of me realized they actually *were*, because I was shouting Words without realizing it and punching the ground at the same time. My fists left deep indentations in the earth and sent black webs of death crackling out around me. The grass was dying across the entire field. What good spring had done for it was completely undone. Beyond undone. I was turning the field into a wasteland as dead as Khaya's garden.

I would have punched it again, but then I heard something. Looking up, I spotted a small black and white shape running toward me from the house, barking.

I'd probably ruined the front door's ability to stay closed, blasting it open like that.

"No, Pie, stay!" I cried. My throat was so wrecked the words were barely understandable, but I'd never taught her to stay anyway. So I fell over on my side, curling my body around my hands. The dead grass stabbed into my bare skin, but I didn't care. I had to protect her. From me.

But the memories were too strong, wracking my body. Too sharp, flaying me until I felt like I had to be dripping with as much blood as they were. The Words were in my mouth, on the tip of my tongue, wanting to come out with more screams.

A desperate thought came to me: they were too strong. Too sharp. But maybe I could change them. Cruithear had said she'd reshaped her memories.

I spoke Words, but they weren't the ones that had been pressing against my lips. And I didn't shout them at the field. I whispered them to the darkness, to the deaths, to the blood. "Shrink. Dull."

And the memories quieted. The screams were still there, but they were distant; muffled. The red of the blood was less vivid.

At some point I heard, and then felt, a nose snuffling around my head. And then a puppy's tongue, licking the tears off my cheeks. Her breath smelled like cat food.

For whatever reason, it was that stupid detail that

brought me back to myself. I lifted my head enough to look at Pie, her black-and-white splotched face coming into focus. She whimpered, and then bounced on her front paws, letting out a little yip.

And then I was sitting up, hugging her to my chest. She licked my face like mad, as if trying to wipe away the tears as fast as they were coming.

"Oh Gods, Pie, oh Gods," I said over and over again. My throat mangled my words along with my voice, but the sound was better than the screaming. Better than the Words.

When I felt like I could stand, I carried her back to the house, my legs shaking underneath me. The front door was definitely hanging open, so I wedged it closed with one of my boots. I figured I shouldn't collapse right there on the couch in case someone came bursting in, like the owners of the house or worse, so I went upstairs. I found a linen closet where there was room enough for me to stretch out underneath the bottom shelf. I crawled in, pulled Pie inside with me, dragged some sheets and towels over us, and nudged the folding doors closed.

I slept, somehow. But the nightmares reached me, slipping around the foggy pane of glass I'd put up between myself and my memories. And they were even worse than the original, unfiltered version of reality.

In my dreams, I opened Chantelle's wrists with the Word of Death while she cried and begged me to stop. I strangled Cruithear with my bare hands, her red hair falling over my wrists, and when she tried to breathe I reached into her mouth and tore out her tongue. Ryse smiled at me as her eyes dribbled out of her sockets like tears. Drey came at me with his purple face, trying to stab me with a scalpel, but I always ended up killing him as I tried to fight him off. And so many others … I killed. I was drowning in blood at one point, choking on it.

Several times I woke up screaming. But Pie was always there, sniffing at me, chewing on my fingers, licking my face, and reminding me that maybe, just maybe, I wasn't a monster … until I eventually fell back to sleep.

When I awoke, hoarse and puffy-eyed, to predawn light glowing through the cracks of the closet doors, I knew what I needed to do.

I needed someone else to remind me that I wasn't a monster. Another human, who could recognize what was left of the human in me. And if anyone could do it, Khaya could.

I needed to find her.

The fact that my plan might turn the rest of the world against Eden City was just a bonus.

Twenty-four

Swanson had given me the idea, really.

The house had a computer that was set up for video calls, which meant it had a camera and a microphone. I booted it up and went to find a shirt. From the upstairs bedroom closet, I borrowed a white tee and blue long-sleeved plaid shirt that were made for someone shorter and pudgier than me, but a little shaping fixed that. I also fixed my ridiculous straight blond hair in the bathroom mirror, changing it back to normal.

Next on my short mental list was a suitable prop. Outside, sitting on the ground next to the porch stairs, I discovered a flowerpot filled with some newly sprouting grass. I lifted the pot and carried it inside. Plunking it on the desk, I sat down in the computer chair, opened a recording program, and clicked the record button.

"Hi," I said. My voice was pretty rough. Maybe I should have found a throat lozenge too. "My name is Tavin Barnes. I'm the Word of Death and, what do you know, I'm also the Word of Shaping."

Demonstration time. I looked at the potted grass and told it to die, with my hand a good two feet away from it. Blackness shot across the open space and did the job in a half a second.

"Need more proof?" I asked the camera. "Well, take a good look, because this is the last time anyone is going to see." I pivoted in the chair and bared my back to my shoulders. I counted to five and then yanked my shirt down. Spinning back around, I scooted up to the desk again. "See that? Yeah, I couldn't make sense of it either. I might not be the world's best reader, but I think it's too mixed and moving for even a Godspeaker to make much out of."

I'd made that interesting discovery in the bathroom mirror—the Words running together like bleeding ink, Words of both Death and Shaping. I wasn't sure, but I guessed it would take a team of Godspeakers years of studying me to figure out how to use me. An opportunity I had no intention of giving them.

I shrugged at the camera. "If you didn't think this was possible, well…neither did I. Nor did Eden City, for that matter. And so I'm not there anymore. I got out, because they can't control me anymore. But they tried for a long time, and took almost everything that mattered from me."

I closed my eyes for a second, until I could continue. "They do whatever they want with the Words, just like they do whatever they want with the rest of the world. The Godspeakers hold the real power. We're prisoners there." I leaned back in the chair and folded my fingers together on the desk. "And it's time for it to end."

My voice hardened as I imagined addressing the City Council. "It's time for you, Eden City, to stop pushing everyone around with strength that doesn't belong to you. Four of us Words have escaped now... five, if you count me twice. You're losing your power. No one has to listen to you anymore. And the remaining four Words should be free if they want to be. Give them the choice, or else face consequences like this—like me."

If my voice had been hard before, it was nothing to what it sounded like now.

"And if you think for *one second* you can come after me, think again. I'm beyond your reach. You can't use me anymore. If you try, I swear to the Gods I will tear a hole in the Athenaeum so large that the rest of the world will see you for the parasites you really are, and then I will *rain* death and destruction down on your heads."

It probably wasn't everyday that someone got to say that, and even less often that someone could actually deliver on the threat.

I could, and I would. If they decided to test me, I would turn the entire Athenaeum into a Death Factory.

But I didn't want to. I really only wanted one thing. I took a deep breath, cleared my throat, and forced calm into my tone.

"Mostly, I just want to see someone again. I have a message for the Word of Life: Khaya." Saying her name when she could actually be listening took any remaining anger out of my voice. Her name tasted sweet on my tongue, so I said it again. "Khaya, tell the person who only wanted a sofa, a good book, and a cup of tea to go to a place similar to where you and I first kissed—really kissed—but bigger. Remember, you taught me its name. And then you'll know where to find me...if you want to."

I clicked the stop button.

From there, it wasn't difficult to surf the web until I got the emails of the top news stations in every major European city. I added Beijing and Washington, D.C. to the list too, just for kicks. Under my name, Tavin Barnes, I made an email account—deathandshaping@roguewords.web—thankful that I could at least type now. Then I attached the video clip and hit send.

It might take someone a few days to notice it, and a couple more to verify that it wasn't a hoax. But then it would be absolutely everywhere. Tu, at least, was probably monitoring the news, so it was my best chance of reaching Khaya.

This was how Swanson had gotten a message to me when Khaya and I were on the run—a news broadcast. Of course, it would also mean that everyone would be on the lookout for me, like they'd been before. And, of course, someone would be able to pinpoint the location that the video was sent from. I was sure I had some time, days, but I didn't want to take any chances. Besides, I had a rendezvous to make.

I stood up and maneuvered around Pie, who'd been trying—mostly successfully—to eat my shoelaces while the video was recording. I went into the kitchen and stuffed some cans of food—for both cats and humans—into a pillowcase, along with a jug of water and a couple of bowls. And then I got into the car with Pie and drove away.

The midnight blue Audi was nice, but I traded it in the next town for a more subtle car of French make. And then I drove to the southern shore of Lake Eden. Or Lac Léman, as the rest of the world called it.

Khaya had first told me that name, and we'd first kissed under another lake. Pavati—who'd told me all she wanted out of life was a sofa, a good book, and a cup of tea—also happened to be the Word of Water, so she was about the only person who could walk around under a lake to find a message.

Aside from me. But I was the one who'd be leaving the message.

I slipped into the lake from a chilly, empty stretch of the shore, shaping a discreet tunnel into the water. I had to shape the ground into something firmer and less muddy, but it was manageable.

It didn't take long for the lake to get deep where I was. That was why I'd brought the flashlight. Soon it looked like I was walking through a tunnel of black glass. I trekked only a few miles out along the lake-bottom, shaped a note, set it on the ground, and pinned it down with a rock. From there, I shaped a series of underwater tunnels spiraling outward from that spot like a twirling starfish. Pavati couldn't miss it. If she came across even one of the tunnels, she'd be able to follow it to the center. I shaped a quick shaft skyward through the water, only a foot in diameter, for air. Then I followed my first tunnel back to shore and closed it.

While I waited for the news to break, I located a cabin in the mountains that looked like it hadn't been used in years, all the while stealing a new car every day. Drey would have given me shit for that, but I always returned them. Rather, I left them in a different spot, for the owner to eventually find. I also "borrowed" some younger guy's wallet in a cafe, but only long enough to duplicate the ID, with my face instead of his.

I also might have left the guy short a few euros, since one of my activities to kill time soon had become shaping more of them. A sculptor needed a model, after all. I went through a stack of old newspapers, using the paper, and, after trial and error, ended up with a pretty nice stack of money in its place. I was sure someone, somewhere, would be able to identify them as forgeries, but I sure couldn't tell the difference. They had a watermark and holographic stripe and everything.

I needed money because, even if I could shape a sandwich or a cup of coffee, it still weirded me out. I wasn't *quite* sure what was actually in it, and besides, no amount of shaping could make it hot. I went grocery shopping in the nearest town the second day, stocking up on dog food for Pie, human food for me, water, propane for the cabin stove, and clothes. As far as clothes went, I didn't even look at what I was buying since I could easily change the color and shape on my own without worrying about having to eat them after.

I actually didn't mind shaping my own clothes. There was no black or red. Nothing that zipped in the back. I made everything comfortable and loose enough to breathe, unlike those stupid Necron suits.

In spite of the changes, I still woke up screaming every night.

On the third day, I was sitting in a cafe sipping a cappuccino when I saw my face on the TV. It didn't look exactly like I looked now, since I was currently sporting short auburn hair, a trim beard, a blue blazer, and nice Italian brown leather shoes—well, the Tavin-made rip-offs. In the video I looked pretty haggard, with regard to both my face and that blue flannel shirt I'd already reshaped into something else. But the point was, the news was out.

My video clip repeated all day long on almost every news station. It was weird to see myself everywhere, sometimes talking, sometimes frozen in still-shots with people attempting to analyze what the hell I'd done to the pot of grass or what was on my back.

More importantly, you had to be living under a rock not to see it. Khaya might indeed be living under one, thanks to Tu, but it would be hard for even them to miss this. So once I was satisfied with what I'd seen, I hopped into the most recent car I'd acquired, picked up Pie from the cabin, and drove to a town closer to the lake. I booked a hotel for a few nights, since I figured it could take a while.

It didn't. It was only the next day that a tall, dark-skinned girl strode into yet another coffee shop with giant sunglasses, a black leather jacket, and a magnificent smile on her face. She'd already spotted me, even with my auburn hair and beard— probably because under my tan jacket, I was sporting a hot pink shirt with a white skull-and-crossbones.

She strolled up to my table, her smile threatening to split her face in half.

Bad image, I thought when the Word of Death began suggesting ways to make good on that. I silenced the whisperings as best I could.

She reined her grin in only a little to clear her throat and say, "Why hello ... *Sven*. It's been so long. Just so you know, your shirt really clashes with your hair."

I stood, grinning nearly as widely. "*Ester*. You, my friend, are a sight for sore eyes."

She spared enough time to grimace over the name I'd chosen for her, and then we seized each other in a rib-creaking embrace. Pavati gave as good as she got when it came to that.

When she finally released me, she said, "Found your rather damp message to meet here." She sat next to me, pulling her sunglasses down enough to glance around. "Quaint."

"They have tea," I said, sipping my coffee.

She grinned again, but what she said afterward was more serious. "I'm not sure I want to get too comfortable. Certain individuals, namely my boyfriend"—I raised my eyebrows at that—"think that I'm going to run off with you and never return." She laughed. "Or, worse yet, that you'll get your other lovely lady friend in on it."

Tu *would* think this could be a trap set by the Athenaeum ... and for pretty good reason, I had to admit.

"He should trust me," I said, holding her eyes, trying to communicate more than our limited innuendo could. "I've had plenty of opportunity for that already. What can I say, I'm a changed man, breaking out of the mold."

She sputtered a laugh. "You're telling me. Want to get the hell out of here?"

"Yes," I said gratefully.

She stood and practically pulled me out of my seat, then linked arms with me as we left the cafe. I steered her toward my car, but she already seemed to know the way.

"We were watching the place before you went in," she said under her breath.

"Ah. So will a *certain individual* crush me with a boulder if I try to take you for a ride?" I muttered out of the side of my mouth.

"Nope, because he's already in the car, lying in wait behind the driver's seat." She rolled her eyes behind her sunglasses. "You left the door unlocked, genius."

I shrugged. "Locks aren't much of a concern for me anymore." I opened the passenger door of my pewter gray BMW for Pavati, and then moved around to the driver's side. I slid in, closed the door, and said, "Hello, Tu."

"Drive," his voice said behind me. "Now. And if you don't go exactly where I tell you, we'll end up in a ditch even if I have to gouge one into the road. And hi," he added. "It's cool to see you, man, but it would be a whole lot cooler if we don't all end up back in the Athenaeum."

I couldn't help smiling as I started the car and pulled out onto the street. "For some crazy reason, it's cool to see you too … maybe because even your face is better than seeing Swanson's all day." My attempt to make light of it sounded only a bit forced. "And, like I already told Pavati, I have no intention of ever going back to the Athenaeum. Nor do I intend for you guys to either," I quickly added.

"So you expect me to believe that you just walked out of there?" he demanded, still too low in the back seat for me to actually see in the rear-view mirror. "Turn right."

I turned. Luckily, we were headed in a direction I needed to go. "When you can walk through walls, it's less difficult to believe," I told him. I couldn't help sounding a bit smug. But then I thought of Cruithear and felt awful.

"Yeah, and there's that, too. I saw what you did in the video, and it was a nice act, but there's no way you can be the Word of Shaping *and* Death. That's imposs…"

My eyes still on the road, I reached over the center armrest to slide Pavati's sunglasses off her face. She only had time to blink before I said, "Miniature pyramid, like the Athenaeum," and her sunglasses morphed into exactly that, sitting in the palm of my hand.

"Hey, I liked those!" Pavati cried, and then laughed. "Although this is kind of cooler." She plucked the model pyramid from my hand and grinned at me. "Can I stomp on it?"

"They're your sunglasses," I said.

Tu sat up in the back seat in a rush. "Man—turn right again—that is so insane! How the hell did this happen?"

Tu's long black hair was in a high bun on the top of his head, a style I was nearly positive only he could pull off, and his biceps were as huge as ever as he leaned forward between the front seats, practically wedging himself between me and Pavati. As always, he looked way too confident to be insecure, and yet he was anxious all the same when it came to Pavati. At least some people hadn't changed.

I wasn't quite prepared to recount the ways I'd changed, yet.

"Uh, it's a long story. And one sec—I have to make a stop." I pulled over and leapt out onto a sidewalk that just so happened to run right in front of the hotel I'd been staying in. Fortunately, I only caught the first part of Tu's storm of swearing before I shut the door.

When I returned to the car with a little something tucked under my jacket, he looked about ready to tear my head off…until I turned around and plopped Pie into his lap. I'd never seen Tu's jaw drop quite so far as when Pie started waggling and sniffing him, her thin tail whipping back and forth.

"You have a *puppy*?" Pavati cried in delight. It was the closest she'd ever come to squealing, at least since I'd known her.

"Her name is Pie," I said as I started driving again. "Where to?"

"Left up ahead." In the rear-view mirror Tu didn't look as grumpy as he sounded, ruffling Pie's ears for a few seconds. But then he set her aside and shoved himself back between the front seats with his jaw set in a determined clench. "Okay, now I have to hear your story. Spit it out."

"Can I tell it later over a beer or something? Or never?" I suggested as I merged onto a highway.

"How about immediately?" Tu said, but then Pavati's elbow slammed into his arm. "Or at least I'll take a beer immediately."

"There's some in the trunk."

Tu grinned for the first time. "I just got a lot happier to see you."

Pavati threw her head back against her seat and released a sigh that was more of a growl of frustration. "So you decide to trust Tavin not because of anything he's said, but—get this— because of *beer*. I think this well illustrates some of our issues as a couple."

Tu's hands immediately found her shoulders and started rubbing. "Hey, the puppy also helped, not just the beer.

Besides, you trust him, and I trust *you*. I think that proves we're an awesome couple."

"Nice one," I faux-whispered.

Tu chuckled. "Thanks, I thought so."

A grudging smile appeared on Pavati's face. "I find your massage more convincing than anything." She closed her eyes and let out a groan.

I was suddenly uncomfortable to be in the car with the two of them. "So..." I said. "Where are we going?" I wanted to ask when I could see Khaya, but I held the question in. Part of me was afraid of when I might see her, because of what she might say to me when I did.

And what if she didn't even want to see me in the first place? I assumed she wasn't here because Pavati and Tu wanted to determine it was safe beforehand, but what if she hadn't even wanted to come?

"To a location of our choice," Tu said, infuriatingly vague.

"And what happens when we get there?" I asked, trying not to sound impatient.

"We strip search you for tracking devices."

Pavati's eyes flew open. "Tu! He's kidding," she told me, glancing over.

Tu snickered while I grimaced.

"I'm afraid you'd have to skin me, with what they're doing these days." I reached up to tap the back of my neck. "See the half-healed hole back there?"

They both recoiled from me in horror.

"Yeah, that was pleasant," I said in answer to their expressions. "But I got it out. I'm positive there aren't any more in me, because I'd feel it now. I'm clean." I hesitated. "In a manner of speaking."

Something in my tone made the two of them fall quiet. To my immense surprise, Tu was the one who asked first.

"Are you okay, man? It was probably rough in there with, you know, everything they wanted you to do."

"I'm okay," I said, in a way that sounded like I was anything but, in spite of what I'd intended.

"Did you ... kill anyone?"

"*Tu*!" Pavati practically screamed, and Pie yelped.

I winced at the volume as much as anything and swerved a little on the highway. "Gods. Yes, Tu, I killed a lot of people, including both of my Godspeakers—one who was a sadistic psychopath and one who was the closest thing I've ever had to a father. Plus, I'd say, roughly a hundred other people." My own voice rose as I snapped, "Do you want to know *how*?"

Pavati was covering her eyes. "Tu, don't answer that— whatever you're planning on saying. In fact, just shut up entirely."

"Sheesh, sorry," he muttered, sinking into the back-seat. "I was just asking."

"Next time, shove your big fat foot in your mouth first."

"Gods, fine."

She rounded on him. "And we're going to the clearing. No *buts*," she said when he opened his mouth, probably to object.

"What's in the clearing?" I asked, my heart suddenly trying to fly out of my chest, ahead of the speeding car.

Pavati smiled a mysterious smile. And then, as vague as Tu, she answered, "You'll see."

Twenty-Five

We drove for a couple of hours into the foothills of the Alps. We had to have been nearing the Swiss border as we curved up climbing roads. Eventually Tu directed me to turn off on a dirt road that grew more and more potholed, bouncing us around to the point that I wished I'd stolen an SUV instead. I'd feel bad for the owner if I destroyed the underside of the BMW.

The road finally dead-ended at a sunny clearing. The day was stunning, and the air warm enough for me to take off my jacket even at this elevation. Noticing my hot-pink skull-and-crossbones shirt again, I self-consciously changed it to solid blue, my hair back to its usual messy brown, and my face back to beardless.

"Good," Tu said, getting out of the car to stretch. "You were weirding me out before."

I shielded my eyes with a hand. "So now what? A strip search?"

Pavati smiled and pointed. "Just walk into that field there. We'll be over here."

"Drinking beer," Tu added, moving around to the trunk.

I tossed him my makeshift key, bemused. I was also hopeful, nervous, and flat-out scared of what might be waiting for me in the clearing. I took a deep breath and wandered away from the car, leaving Tu and Pavati peering into the trunk. Tu was holding Pie, maybe to keep her from going after me, and maybe because once you picked her up you didn't really want to put her down.

"Dude, you have so much food ... and cash!" Tu cried as I moved out into the field. I eventually lost sight of the car behind a stand of trees.

It was an ocean of green out here. Bushes, trees, and snow-peaked mountains ringed the clearing, all of it radiant in the sunlight. I didn't think the view could get much more beautiful until I saw someone step out of the shadows at the other end of the field.

I couldn't help it. My breath caught in my throat at the sight of her, and I suddenly had to swallow and blink a lot.

Khaya's eyes were huge in her face, as if she couldn't believe she was seeing *me*. She wore a yellow tank top and jeans, her rich brown hair wild and free around her face. She looked so warm, shining brighter than anything else out here.

My voice was locked in my throat.

"Tav—" Khaya began. She was the girl who hardly ever cried, and yet her voice broke and her face crumpled. And then she was running toward me through the grass.

But my feet were rooted.

I stopped her just before she reached me, holding up my hands to keep her from hugging me. Gods, she was so achingly beautiful, even with tears—and hurt—streaking her face.

"I've killed people," I said as soon as possible, so she would know why I was stopping her. "*A lot* of people. I won't hurt you—I would never hurt you—but you should know what I've done before I let you hug me like everything is still the same … like I'm still the same."

She wiped her eyes almost angrily. "I don't care. I mean, I do, but it's not your fault. I knew they would make you." She stared at me, taking me in, and then her lip quivered again. "I'm so sorry I left you. I never should have. And I'm so sorry I couldn't come get you out of there. That was exactly what the City Council wanted me to try to do. I knew that, but every day, Pavati and Tu still had to talk me out of trying to help you escape—"

My heart was twisting in my chest in a way I didn't think was possible, not anymore. "You did help me escape," I said, my voice tight. "Every day. I just … pictured your face."

Khaya threw her arms around me before I could try to stop her again. Her skin was so warm and fragrant. She smelled like spices and spring.

"I know I'm Death," I said, suddenly babbling into her hair, holding her as hard as I could without crushing her. "And that you hate Death, but I'm Shaping too, and maybe I can make something else out of myself that you won't hate … "

"Tavin, you idiot," she gasped. "I *love* you. I love *you*. The Words aren't you; they're only passengers. And honestly, I would rather you only carried the Word of Death." I almost wanted to smile over her analytical side kicking in, if not about what she was saying. "If it were just that one, maybe they'd let you go in peace. But now that you're Shaping too..." She shook her head against my chest and then pulled away to look at me. "They'll never let you just walk away."

"I'll die before I go back." My breath came faster. "I'll wipe Eden City off the map before I go back, not just the Athenaeum. I'll—"

"Shh, Tavin, it's okay." She touched her fingertips to my lips.

I wanted to kiss her fingers. But then I wanted to punch myself in the face, because I wasn't sure how I could think about kissing her after I'd thought about destroying an entire city.

She stared into my eyes, grounding me, bringing me back to her in the here and now. She gave her head a tiny shake. "I won't let them have you."

Somehow it was the sweetest thing she could have possibly said.

I remembered her using the Word of Life as a weapon, once, to keep me from going for a gun; it felt like a lifetime ago. But it was no longer about having a gun, or even being a gun in someone else's hand. I was—and held—the key to an entire arsenal. And the frightening thing was, I was ready to use it. How far could Khaya follow me and still see me as someone worth saving?

What would people feel when they looked at me now? I heard Drey's words echoing in my mind: *Admiration or fear?*

I looked at Khaya. Neither was in her brown eyes,

which were so deep I wanted to fall into them. Or else maybe the love in them was overpowering everything else.

Before I knew it, my fingers were interwoven in her hair and I was kissing with a desperation I had never felt before. Her lips and mouth were sweet and hot, like sun-filled honey, and my head was buzzing like a hive of bees on a summer day. Gods, she tasted like nectar, ambrosia, everything divine and wonderful that humans weren't supposed to have. My knees suddenly felt so weak her kiss should have knocked me over. But instead it kept drawing me in, lips and tongue moving in a beckoning dance against mine. I kissed her like my life depended on it.

It did depend on it, in a sense. Because my humanity did. If I could still feel the good in this—and it was so, *so* good—maybe I could feel it in the world. And in myself.

I didn't notice the tears on my face until Khaya felt them and pulled away to blink up at me in surprise. Letting go of her, I half-turned away to wipe my eyes.

"Sorry," I said.

She seized my ears to pull my head down and laid a solid, almost chastising kiss on my cheek. "Never, ever apologize for showing me how you really feel."

I grimaced. "You might want to retract those words soon … especially if you ever have to sleep next to me."

"*Have* to? I *want* to. And what do you mean?"

Before I let myself get excited about what she'd said, I clarified, to the extent that I could. "What I'm feeling inside tends to show itself more when I'm asleep. Let's just say that I hope you like screaming."

She put her fingers over her mouth when she realized I meant *my* screaming.

"Sorry," I said again, without quite knowing why. And then my hands were involuntarily covering my face and I sat down hard in the grass. "Gods, Khaya, I'm so sorry. I'm so sorry."

She was quiet for a few moments as I shuddered and tried to breathe. Then I heard her footsteps rustling in the grass and I felt her sit down behind me. She leaned against my back, her warm arms threading around my waist.

"You don't need me to forgive you," she murmured, her cheek pressed against my shirt. "You need to forgive yourself."

"I … I can't." I shook my head and dropped my hands. And then I told her. I told her everything I'd done in one long grisly list, leaving out none of the gory details. Facing away was easier, so I didn't have to look at her expression while I did.

Afterward, I expected silence, for her to stand up and walk out of this sunny clearing … and maybe out of my life forever.

Instead, she waited only long enough to make sure I was done talking, and then said, "None of that was you. You were always acting under the influence of someone, or something, else: Drey, Swanson, Ryse, those drugs they pumped into you. Maybe you killed Ryse, but she pushed you so far, and honestly, I think I would have done the same in your position. If she wasn't already dead, *I* would want to kill her, and I haven't even experienced the things you have." She sounded like she meant it. "Look how hard you tried to fight it, Tavin! *That* was you."

These were the words I'd wanted so desperately to hear her say, but now that she was saying them, I found them hard to believe. Maybe because I'd wanted it so badly, and I wasn't used to getting what I wanted.

"But I lost," I said. "They broke me. I did everything they wanted and more...and there's some part of me that might be willing to do it all again." I tried to laugh, but it came out as more of a gasp. "Can you heal a broken mind?"

She pulled on me suddenly, and I lost my seated balance and toppled back onto the grass with her. She slid onto her side and propped her head up on her elbow, looking down at me. With the sunlight in her hair, she was definitely the most beautiful thing I'd ever seen.

"You're not broken, Tavin," she said. She ran her hand down my chest, and I was pretty sure every cell in my body lit up at her touch. Like the sunlight was now inside of me. But she was brighter than the sun, her brown eyes molten.

I covered my face again. "I can't even look at you."

"Why?" To her credit, she didn't sound hurt, even though what I'd said probably sounded rude.

"You're too...good. You're too good for me."

She gently took my hands and pulled them down. "Now for *that*," she said with a smile, "I want an apology. Of my choosing," she added, before I could open my mouth.

Her hand toyed with the hem of my shirt, and then slid up underneath it and rested on my stomach. I was suddenly dizzy. There definitely wasn't enough oxygen in the atmosphere anymore.

"Khaya, you don't have to ... " I cleared my throat as my voice came out strained.

Her eyes narrowed and her hand went higher up my shirt, skimming over my bare chest. "Oh, you think I'm doing this because I feel sorry for you?" She swung her leg over my waist, and then she was sitting on top of me, straddling me, with *both* of her hands up under my shirt, the wide blue sky haloing her. "What if *I* missed you?"

With her weight on my hips and her warm hands wandering over my skin, my entire body grew so bright and humming it threatened to dissolve right there into the sunshine.

Dissolve. Like I'd dissolved Ryse's body, making it run away into the drain set into the floor of the Death Factory ...

Suddenly, I was holding Khaya's wrists to keep them from going any farther. The panic and darkness in the back of my mind threatened to swallow me.

Khaya pulled her hands away from mine, long enough to cup my cheeks. "Tavin. Tavin, look at me."

I glanced at her, breathing too hard. The last time I'd been this close to someone, it had been Drey, *his* hands on my face, and he'd been silently begging me to kill him. "I can't, I'm sorry, I'm—"

"Look at me," she interrupted, leaning over me so I was forced to stare right into her eyes. "I know how you can apologize to me. Kiss me, right now. I want you to kiss me. I mean, if you want to ... "

Her eyes swallowed me instead of the darkness.

I wanted to.

I kissed her, and with the flood of warmth and goodness, the memories stopped. Rational thought threatened to cease all together when Khaya eventually sat up and pulled her shirt off over her head. Her dark wavy hair tumbled down around her bare shoulders. Her chest was bare save for a lacy cream bra that was mostly see-through anyway.

My hands hovered over the curve of her hips. I wanted to kiss her there. And maybe everywhere else. But something was holding me back.

"Touch me," she said.

I glanced up at her. "If I do, I don't think I'll want to stop."

She wore a nearly wicked grin. "That's the idea."

I wondered if I could pass out from lack of blood in the brain while already lying down. I tried to focus. "I don't know about this."

"Why not?" She didn't sound impatient, sitting on top of me in her bra. She sounded assured that I would soon quit being an idiot.

"We're ... uh ... in a field?"

She leaned over me again, planting her hands on either side of me, and said a few Words. Twigs and leaves rose around us, braiding together, until we had our own little bower shading us. Soft, pillowy flowers bloomed underneath my back.

"And?" she whispered, her lips grazing my earlobe. Her breasts were brushing against my chest.

I couldn't use the fact that I wasn't carrying protection

as an excuse, since, as the Word of Death, I was nearly positive I could neutralize my "genetic material" pretty easily. It took me longer to think of another reason, but I managed. "Pavati and Tu could still come knocking. They probably don't think we'd do this during my first meeting with you after, oh, I don't know, months of—"

She kissed my nose, cutting me off. "I told them to stay away. And?"

I trusted her. Which meant I'd run out of excuses, leaving only the real reason for my hesitation. "I just don't see how you could possibly want to do this with m—"

This time, her lips cut me off. That was all I needed. I surged into her, sitting up with her legs still straddling my waist. I wasn't sure whose hands went for my shirt faster: mine or hers. In any case, it practically flew off of my back. And then my hands couldn't get enough of her. They skimmed her shoulders, her rib cage, her hips. Her skin was as silky smooth as warm water. Between feeling her with my hands and feeling her everywhere else—against my lips, my tongue, my chest—she was liquid light, enfolding me.

Her own hands skated over my collar bones and down my sides to my waist. They paused only long enough to unbuckle my belt before dancing over my back.

I froze for a second, my fingers now on the clasp of her bra, my lips on hers, as I remembered a flash of someone unwelcome touching my back to get at the Words. But in a blink, the memory was gone. I hadn't even pictured a face. And luckily Khaya must have only thought I was having trouble with the clasp, because her hands joined mine and her bra parted.

Rationality ceased, then. And it ceased for some time.

Another coherent thought didn't enter my brain until we were lying side by side, still naked. My arm was around Khaya, under her head, and she was tracing the skin over my ribs where the Words were just visible, beginning to curve around my back.

"Can I see?" she asked softly.

I tensed when I realized she meant the Words. Somehow I felt more exposed in showing her my back than ... well, everything in front. But I remembered being in another leafy shelter with her, where we were hiding from the Athenaeum's forces trying to hunt us down. I'd accidentally used her to godspeak, and yet she let me hug her afterward, never mind stay in the same tent with her, in spite of how vulnerable she probably felt. It was my turn to feel as vulnerable—and still let her in.

I slid my arm out from under her neck and rolled over. I closed my eyes, as if that would somehow help me feel more covered.

I felt her finger touch my back ... and then it just continued its tracing motions. It felt so good that I kind of forgot about being freaked out. I even started to doze until her voice brought me back.

"They're beautiful, the Words," Khaya said.

I blinked. "That's ... not possible."

"They are. I can hardly tell what they say. This is amazing, Tavin. It's like they're not two separate Words anymore, but blended together. I don't know how anyone would even use you to godspeak." She rolled me back over, as if she knew talking about godspeaking was best done face-to-face rather than while staring at my back. "Is this … do you think this is why Andre—Drey—wanted you to go to Cruithear?"

I shrugged against the soft ground. "I assumed he wanted me to kill her."

Khaya bit her lip in thought, which was pretty sexy. The fact that she was naked and leaning on my chest didn't hurt. "I wonder. This is so huge … it feels like there's more going on here."

I didn't quite know what she meant, and I didn't have time to ask. A sudden gust rattled our leafy bower. Then a shout cut across the clearing, high and scared.

My first thought was that it was a helicopter or something because of the wind, but I couldn't hear anything like that. Only the shouting.

Khaya and I were up and moving in the time that it took to exchange a look. We threw on our clothes as fast as possible, and then Khaya unraveled our shelter around our feet.

The sky outside was like nothing I had ever seen before. Darkness was bleeding over the blue, like black clouds blowing in on a storm. Just as we started watching, the darkness hit the sun and devoured it.

TWENTY-SIX

The world grew drastically darker.

Pavati and Tu were running across the field toward us, yelling, Pie barking at their heels. Khaya and I met them at a run.

"What the hell is happening?" I cried, gesturing at the sky.

Pavati was wild-eyed. "We don't know … but come on, we're picking up all kinds of chatter on the radio!"

We all dashed back to the car, me scooping up Pie as I went. I was barefoot, I realized. I'd left my shoes in the field. But it didn't matter. This … this mattered. The sky was the most frightening thing I'd ever seen. I glanced up to see the darkness continuing to seep across the blue.

It looked like the end of the world.

When we reached the car, Tu threw himself into the driver's seat and cranked up the volume. The radio stations were practically screaming:

"—*encore rien de neuf à propos de ce qui cause ce phénomène*—"

"—assure people that this is not caused by nuclear winter. I repeat, there are no reports of any nuclear detonations anywhere—"

"—*rien à voir avec le temps*—"

"—nothing man-made, and yet representatives of Eden City's government remain unresponsive—"

Even where we were, at the edge of an abandoned field in the mountains, I could feel the panic rising around us like an apocalyptic flood. Fitting, since the sky looked about ready to deliver one. I didn't need the speculation to tell me who was behind this.

This was Eden City's doing. This was...

"Mørke," Pavati breathed. "But this is impossible. There's no way she would do this. There's no way she's *powerful* enough to do this, not even with Angelina controlling her. I've seen everything she can do, and this isn't..."

"No." I shook my head, but not in denial, numb to a creeping realization that was stealing over me even as I voiced the thought. "This isn't her. They probably killed her, made her transfer the Word of Darkness to an automaton."

"*Mørke.*" Khaya's hand was over her mouth, tears in her eyes. She let out a gasp. "What are they doing?"

I closed my own eyes, and behind my lids I saw Mørke's black lace skirt swishing around her legs as she walked away from me down a long hallway. Gone. Perhaps forever.

My eyes snapped open and the numbness vanished with her image. In its place was rage like I'd felt only once before—once when I'd wanted to make the world bleed. This time, there was no Mørke here to calm me down.

I wasn't sure what their purpose was, but if the Athenaeum wanted a flood, I would give them one. I would open the veins of everyone in Eden City and drown them in a red ocean. The Words rose in a torrent in my head.

Tu looked up at me as he continued scrolling through stations. "I'd say *somebody* really pissed them off."

Pavati's wide eyes turned ferocious as she looked from me to Tu. "Don't you dare blame this on him!"

"I'm not mad at him! But why else would this be happening? He breaks out of the Athenaeum, stealing two Words while he's at it, and embarrasses Eden City in front of the world, and then the sky just coincidentally starts turning black?" He glanced up through the windshield, where nearly the last bit of blue was gone. "Correction, *turns* black," he added. "Why else would they be desperate enough to use a prototype, and risk losing the Word of Darkness in the process?"

Numbness that had turned to rage now turned to a sinking, choking feeling like I'd been swallowed by my own flood. Was this entirely my fault? "No." I shook my head. "They couldn't do all of this just because of me."

A new radio voice crackled into focus. "—a radical preacher in the United States is already predicting that this is the retribution of the Gods, saying, and I quote, 'The Gods created the world, and now they are destroying it.' Meanwhile, political analysts feel more of a mortal hand in this drastic development, citing Eden City's recent upheaval over the defection of Tavin Barnes, a young man thought to be both the Word of Death and the Word of Shaping—"

My breath crashed in my chest, blood pounding like cymbals against my eardrums. I put Pie into the back seat of the car and then spun away, not wanting to hear anymore. My hands pressed against either side of my head, as if I could force out what was happening, while my bare feet carried me a short ways into the field. But that didn't help me escape from it, especially with this view. The darkness fell like a sweeping curtain behind the rugged mountains. If the world was a stage, it looked like the show was over.

Fingers grazed my back. I spun on Khaya, my hands flying away from my head. She flinched but she didn't step back.

"Do they ... do they *want* me to kill them all?" I gasped. "Because I'm going to, Khaya, I swear to the Gods, I'm going to kill every last one of them. I told them what I'd do if they came after me—"

"Tavin, listen to me." She gathered my flailing hands in hers, speaking in her most soothing voice. "You're not going to do anything like that. There's another way; there will always be another way. We just have to find it first."

I squeezed my eyes closed so I didn't have to see either her pleading, frightened face, at odds with her tone, or the darkness. "They're not leaving me many other options."

"We don't even know for sure what they want yet."

My eyes flew open. "Whatever they want, what else can I do to stop this? I *kill*, Khaya, I'm a killer, a mass murderer, and that's all I'm good at—"

"If you start thinking like that, then you're letting them win."

"Then maybe they've won—!"

A voice interrupted my tirade, hitting all of us like a bucket of ice water in the face. It carried from the car radio, strong, cold, and functional—a wake-up call. My feet carried me back over in a daze as it spoke.

"As you can see, this is not a game. The darkness will continue to spread until our sole demand is met. First, after all major sources of food begin to perish, will come panic. Then chaos, and then complete devolution of the world as we know it. You have only a short time before the darkness begins to cause irreparable damage. The world is our hostage, and only one person can free it. Will you, Tavin Barnes, let the world die simply because you can't do your duty to your country?"

The bottom seemed to fall out of my stomach. I dropped into a crouch, my face in my hands. The gravel biting into the soles of my feet somehow no longer seemed real. This was unreal. This wasn't happening...

"Tavin—" Khaya began.

"Shh!" Tu said.

The voice continued. "All we ask is for your surrender. One life against the world. And we're not even asking you to give up your life—only give it in service to your nation. All we're asking is for you to come home."

It was a broadcast—a challenge—to answer mine.

Tu punched the steering wheel so hard that a honk ripped through the surreal twilight. It wasn't real light anymore. Everything was as dark a gray as the pewter of the car—silvery, colorless.

"Bastards! You bastards. First Mørke... and now the *world*?" he shouted, gesturing, as if the person on the other end of the broadcast could hear or see. "You're threatening to *end the world* just to get your way? Just to get *him* back?"

Tu had often tried to make me sound unimportant, like a nobody, but I knew he didn't mean it quite like that anymore. Besides, I would have given anything to be insignificant. To simply vanish.

"Gods damn them all," I said, glancing up at Khaya.

I tried to get one last look at her, framed against the darkness above. It was like she was standing in for the sun in her yellow tank top. But she wasn't enough, not for the rest of the world, even if she was for me. She tried to hold on to my arm as I stood, to pull me toward her, but I stepped away from her, closer to the car.

"I'm such an idiot," I said. "I should have gotten the others out when I had the chance. Luft wouldn't leave with me, and Agonya probably wouldn't have either, but Mørke…maybe. And Brehan would have. I know he would have. He's my friend, and I just left him. I thought I'd go back for him later, but now he'll be locked down tighter than Cruithear was."

I'd been drugged and wound up like a ticking time bomb when I'd made the decision to leave without him, but it didn't matter. Now the entire world was the ticking time bomb, and it was my fault.

Time—I had no time. Every second I wasted, the world died a little bit more.

I shook my head as if I could deny the truth. "Brehan could have stopped this. But now…"

Only I could.

For a second, I folded over, as if my back couldn't bear the weight of it. Just when I thought I'd gotten at least a little bit of what I wanted, a breath of fresh air, a ray of sunlight ... they stole it from me. My hands were in my hair again, squeezing my skull, trying to keep the sting from my eyes or my mind from breaking.

Either I'd break them or they'd break me. No matter what, they'd won. But they'd given me another way to fix this that didn't involve mass murder; a way to keep Khaya from hating me. And a way to save the world. Because if I tried to destroy Eden City to save the world—and myself—I might just destroy everything. They could kill Brehan to try to stop me, or *I* could accidentally kill him ... and then the world would be lost.

There was only one sure way. Only one person had to lose everything.

Me.

I straightened. After all, if the choice was between me or the world, that wasn't much of a choice. There was no way I could be that selfish or that afraid, never mind that I was more scared than I'd ever been. Because my own life didn't weigh much against the lives of everyone else.

Not that I had any doubt they would make me hurt people again in horrible ways, but that was in the long-run, and probably wouldn't involve the *entire* world. In the short-term—which was all we had right now—it would only be me dying. Maybe not actually dying, now that I had two Words that they might not know how to untangle and force me to pass on ... and that was almost worse. Because, as I'd learned very, very well in the past few months, there was more than one way to die.

I'd have preferred the usual way.

"You were right," I said to Khaya, meeting her terrified eyes. She looked nearly as scared as I felt. "I'll never be free of them. I'll never be free."

"No, Tavin, you're not—"

I interrupted her and held out my hand. "Tu, get out of the car and give me the key."

He looked at me in suspicion from the driver's seat. "Why?"

I laughed, and the sound was blacker than the sky. "Because I'm going back to the Athenaeum."

Acknowledgments

As always, many thanks to my mother, Deanna, my husband, Lukas, and my good friends Chelsea Pitcher and Michael Miller for being guinea pigs (who hopefully weren't as tortured with my rough drafts as poor Tavin's guinea pig). Thanks also to Bob Birdsall for being my books' champion, and to Pam and Dan Strickland for tolerating my presence in their beautiful space while I was being an antisocial workaholic—and for happily reading the results!

And again, thanks to the awesome team at Flux, among them Brian Farrey-Latz, Sandy Sullivan, Mallory Hayes, and Katie Kane, without whom book two would still be a pile of digital code on my computer.

Also deserving of all the love are the wonderful booksellers who deliver what Flux gives them into the hands of readers—most especially David Cheezem at my favorite small, independent bookstore in Palmer, AK: Fireside Books.

Last but not least, thanks to the people who weren't involved directly with the project but kept me sane throughout. One Fours, my dearest debut group, I don't know what I would have done without you. Thanks for the shoulders to cry on, the deep belly laughs, and all the virtual wine and chocolate I could have hoped for. You have all the virtual hugs in return—especially my fellow Flux One Fours: Helene Dunbar, Kathryn Rose, Lisa Maxwell, and Kate Bassett.

And if I borrowed my brother Daniel's personality for book one, I channeled my other brother Eirin's morbid sense of humor for book two. Thank you, Eir, for that and so much else. I'll miss you more than words can say.

© Lukas Strickland

About the Author

AdriAnne Strickland was a bibliophile who wanted to be an author before she knew what either of those words meant. An avid traveler, she spent two cumulative years living abroad in Africa, Asia, and Europe and now shares a home base in Alaska with her husband. While writing occupies most of her time, she commercial fishes every summer in Bristol Bay, because she can't seem to stop. Visit AdriAnne online at http://www.adriannestrickland.com.